BROKEN

R V BIGGS

Originally published 2021
Copyright © 2021
Author R V Biggs
All rights reserved.

ISBN 9798712235643

Broken

DEDICATION

For Julie.

'Everybody's got someone they call home.'

From the Roger Waters album

Radio K·A·O·S

.

ACKNOWLEDGMENTS

To everyone who enjoyed Song of the Robin and Reunion and hence gave me the encouragement to continue writing.

My thanks to Stephen Donaldson for inspiration taken from a single line within The Chronicles of Thomas Covenant.

And to my neighbour and her daughter who unwittingly gave me a central theme.

'Each person comes into this world with a specific destiny – they have something to fulfil, some message has to be delivered, some work has to be completed.
You are not here accidentally – you are here meaningfully. There is a purpose behind you. The whole intends to do something through you.'

Osho

Prologue

John wandered alone in a darkness so all-encompassing he thought he must be asleep. But if that was true, what strange sensation caressed his face? Like midges on a warm summer's eve, though less irritating. Instead, more of a comforting touch – soft and gentle. But the gloom weighed heavy upon his soul and a silence that was tangible cloaked him, pressing on his senses, robbing him of motivation.

He felt warm and at peace, and it seemed good to give in to the harmony of his thoughts and drift away. But then three tiny points of light appeared within his twilight world, three centres of need.

The points of light spoke to him, though not with words. Soundless they were, but the urgency emanating from them demanded his attention. The call they sent forth awakened his spiritual energy and that awakening aroused more earthly senses. Pain blossomed at the back of his head and in his chest, pain that was both physical and emotional.

Recent memories flooded back, recalling words of madness and fury, and with the memory anger arose in his heart, a black cloud of rage that overwhelmed his other senses, dulling the pain. The words he'd heard were full of conviction and finality – the end of everything he cherished – the end of all things.

Within moments his vision returned and the reason for the soft caress upon his face became clear. A steady drizzle descended, soaking through his clothes and onto his skin. Wiping the rain from his eyes, John Macintyre caught sight of a dark shadow receding from where he lay, a shadow that to his spiritual sense conveyed an aura of evil, one to be wary of but one he must confront.

Responding to the three lights, and driven by sudden urgency, John lifted his sturdy six-foot frame from the ground and rose to his full height. Heedless of the pain, he wrapped his fingers around the handle of the thin blade that was buried in his upper chest. Gritting his teeth against the agony that flared from his ruptured flesh, he withdrew the blade and raised his hand, the razor-sharp edge aimed towards the shadow. As he moved forward on silent feet, other shadows arose ahead that for a moment puzzled him, but then he ignored them, even the vivid coloured shade that wafted back and forth a short distance from the others. Dismissing them as a manifestation of his struggling consciousness, he crept onwards.

As he approached the shadow, John lifted his arm still higher, his mind bent on one act, an act driven by his own fury, the intensity of which drowned all other thought. Time

Broken

and movement slowed as he readied himself for a single violent, downward thrust – the last movement he felt sure he would ever make. But within his mind's eye, the three pinpoints of brilliance became one and blossomed forth into a huge spinning wheel of light that screamed at his very soul not to do what he intended – but to no avail. Sure of the need for his act and his sacrifice, a sacrifice based on protecting all he held dear, his arm began its downward plunge and as his thrust met resistance, the rising shadows engulfed him and he knew no more.

One

'Three weeks?' Peter asked.

'Three weeks,' John confirmed.

'But three weeks?'

'Yes, three weeks. Is there an echo around here?' he said without humour.

'No, I mean three weeks and you've not mentioned it to Sarah.'

John shook his head and lifted a bottle of pale ale to his lips. It was late afternoon and the end of a long and productive Saturday in late September. The two friends relaxed on wooden chairs under the covered terrace John had erected along the full length of the southwest side of the cottage. A walkway and roof extended from the terrace across to the nearby converted barn, and afforded sheltered passage between the two buildings for clients, John and the rest of the family. From where they sat, and to one side of the kitchen door, a long table stood which they used often for meals or drinks. Further along the deck towards the ruined cottage, named by Sarah as Memorial cottage, a few comfortable chairs were kept for their own use or close friends. While John and Peter sat on these chairs gazing out across the countryside, the light faded and the shadows lengthened under the tall trees of Scots Pine and Mountain Ash that stood to the rear of, and sheltered the ruined croft.

John had spent most of the day tending the garden beyond the rear of the main house, though the space was more than just the average back lawn or herbaceous border. Closest to the cottage lay a well-established kitchen garden containing the hardiest of herbs, with pots carrying more tender varieties. These would overwinter indoors or in the greenhouse and were kept for their own use. Extending out from the cottage garden were two large raised beds that John planted out for commercial use, and this carried on into a half acre space for vegetables they sold to local wholesalers. Further out was a so far unused area left to run wild but with a view to expand into if they thought manageable. A fenced paddock stretched to the edge of the property where they planned to keep a few pigs when time and funding allowed. With a henhouse near Memorial cottage housing a dozen chickens, they also kept four geese on the advice of an old friend of Hamish, John's Grandfather, as these were excellent for security, an early warning of marauding foxes.

During that busy day, John brought tender plants into one of the greenhouses, taking cuttings where needed and digging up late potatoes and onions for laying down or selling. They would never be self-sufficient from the sale of produce, but it ensured that crops would not go to waste and their earnings covered part of their living costs. The rest of their income came from the business they had resurrected and expanded after moving into the cottage over a year ago.

Since the summer of 2008 when they had settled in Scotland, the lives of Sarah, John and Claire had been transformed. The change began with John's acceptance of his own spiritual gift and the discovery that he and Sarah were descended through diverged ancestral lines from the same family. John's open acceptance of his spiritual awareness and Sarah's realisation of that acceptance appeared to increase the skills they each possessed in ways that neither fully understood. Sarah's analogy to the conundrum was, she explained, the same as bringing together missing pieces from a jigsaw – pieces that created a complete picture enabling a presentation of the entire image. It brought a deeper meaning to the whole, she argued.

The next major event occurred on the twenty-first of September, the autumn equinox, with the birth of their son Robert. Sarah was unsure if the date were mere coincidence or had a hidden meaning considering their family history, their Pagan roots. But she let John choose a name for their new son and he had pondered for several days before suggesting Robert, Graham, David Macintyre.

'Robert was Papa's middle name,' he said. 'Then Graham after your dad, and Dave after … well, you know.'

During his time working with the West Midlands Police force, John's closest friend and colleague David had died at the hands of a young man caught thieving while under the influence of drugs. The crime was not premeditated, but David's action on that day had saved John from harm or even death but led to his own fatal injury.

John struggled with such intense loss following the tragedy that it triggered a desire for a different life for himself and his family. And unbeknown to John at the time, the event awakened an inherent though long dormant spiritual awareness.

Sarah possessed her own gifts of seeing and healing. She could sense at a deep level of awareness the emotional and spiritual turmoil affecting people she came into contact with, though she also sensed the opposite – joy and peace. In many ways, she had the power to relieve the negative sufferings without conscious effort, if asked for help. She knew not to interfere, though. She'd learnt that lesson over a year ago, when the outcome of her inexperienced and uninvited intentions was the tragic death of a close friend. Not long afterwards, Sarah discovered a method of shielding herself from spiritual energy. Without this weapon, she realised, the intensity of spiritual chatter could be overwhelming.

John's gifts were less potent or maybe underdeveloped compared to Sarah's, but his strengths lay elsewhere. He possessed great enthusiasm and ability with flora and fungi, knowing how to nurture and cherish the growing things around him. With intrinsic intuition, he understood the whys and wherefores about plants, and hence always had success maintaining a steady supply of fruit and vegetables. However, John still possessed the ability to perceive spiritual energies when he wished to do so, which was rare. Learning from Sarah's experience, he used his wife's auric colour to shield himself from the outside world – a pure and brilliant white that drowned any energy around him if he remained focussed. Only when concerned for someone dear to him did he let the shield drop. And Sarah learnt to recognise when this happened. The dramatic change in John's mood was easy to perceive, and he often complained of feeling nauseous afterwards. Hence he was wary of his gift and preferred to use those strengths he excelled in for the benefit of his wife and family.

Claire, as children often did, accepted the changes affecting herself without question. Unsure of the range and strength of her gifts, her parents were, however, aware of her spiritual activity. They had little knowledge of what she could do or perceive and they didn't question her about it, judging that if needed she would talk to them or ask for help.

Not long after young Robert arrived, Sarah and John discussed what they wanted to do with their lives. Time was not important as they had no debts against either the Cottage or Hamish's house which John inherited when Hamish had passed away. With initial reluctance they accepted a rental agreement on the house from their closest friends Peter and Rachel who followed them to Scotland with Peter's daughter Sophie and their new baby boy John. Little John was conceived on Christmas day, the same day fate led Sarah and John to a secret place buried deep within the Ayrshire woods. A place that lay near their new home, and described as a sanctuary to Sarah by Beryl, Sarah's long hidden Great Grandmother.

While settling in to Manseburn they discovered from their solicitor and the accountant Beryl had used before she became ill, that a well-established alternate therapy business existed at Manseburn. Beryl offered weekend retreats in a peaceful setting for people who needed a break from everyday pressures, or for those who were so damaged, spiritually, they required an intensive spell of help. Beryl also offered shorter treatments ranging from half hour to a full hour. Sarah and John agreed to rebuild this business, offering the same range of treatments and weekend packages, but bringing in elements of land management or horticulture as occupational therapy. John suggested this since, he argued, most people enjoyed being outside with a fresh breeze and the sun on their face. So, with money coming in from the rent of Hamish's house, Sarah enrolled in formal training for a variety of alternate energy therapies. John attended agricultural college to learn the practical basics in horticulture in order to choose what would grow well in their environment and how to manage the land as a small holder.

Within a few weeks of re-instating the business, Sarah had more clients than she could manage and raised the question of work with Rachel who had become restless.

'I've been wondering,' she said. 'It's getting quite busy here at Manseburn. We've not talked about what, if anything, you wanted to do once baby John was getting on ok.'

'Funny you should mention it,' replied Rachel. 'Was talking to Pete about it recently but didn't come up with anything.'

'Well, why don't you come and work here with me?' Sarah suggested.

'What, at Manseburn? Doing what? I'm no gardener.'

'You have different skills than that. You have a nurturing soul, loving and caring. I think you'd be able to offer other services and leave the horticulture to John. You could train in massage or reflexology, those sort of treatments. Whatever you feel most comfortable with. And, bringing little John with you would not be a problem.'

Rachel needed no convincing, just confirmed her plans with Peter. Needless to say, it wasn't long before Rachel herself had qualified and achieved her dream job – working once more with her dearest friend.

For everyone, life was good at Manseburn. The business Beryl had created was thriving once more and with the addition of a small market garden offering produce to local residents, income was not an issue. And though Peter faced a commute to the University Hospital in Glasgow, the journey was manageable compared to the Midlands, and coming home was never a chore.

And so for the past six months they enjoyed living mostly off the land, had reinstated a local client base and, with the help of Sarah's brother David, increased their reach with a website offering weekend retreats bookable online.

Everything was ticking along just fine until John's dreams began.

'So why haven't you said anything to Sarah?' asked Peter.

'Because I'm not sure of its meaning,' replied John.

'Meaning? Does it have to mean anything to share, and how many times have you had it over the last three weeks?'

'Every night.'

'Every night! That's a lot of times for the same dream. As a neurosurgeon I understand how complex the brain is, how intriguing and unanswerable the purpose of dreams are. And recurring dreams are common. I used to have one myself that came time and time again, though not every night. I used to dream I was trapped in the house and that Jenny, my first wife, was out in the garden. I could see her as clear as day, but couldn't get to her because if I took my eyes off her she'd disappear. All this while she was ill and I had the dream many times, but like I said never night after night. You need to tell Sarah, at least. That's if she hasn't already guessed.'

'Guessed? Guessed what? That I'm having dreams.'

'No of course not, but if I understand anything about you two, she's probably guessed something's amiss, however hard you try to hide it.'

'Yeah, of course. You may be right.'

John fell silent again and sipped his beer. The dream disturbed and worried him. If he'd had such a dream a couple of years ago, he'd have put it down to a scary film or bad curry. But given the change that Sarah and he had gone through, he wondered if it was more of a premonition than a dream, and if a premonition then it was doubly unnerving.

'So what's the dream about?' Peter continued.

'I kill someone.'

'What? You kill someone? Do you know who? Or why?'

'Not a clue, though …'

A voice from the front door stopped John in mid-sentence. Both men glanced along the porch to where Rachel had stepped out. She wore a pinafore around her waist and clutched a tall wine glass in one hand. 'Are you two coming inside for dinner? It's too cold out here tonight.'

'Yes!' called Peter. 'Just coming.'

John turned back and smiled at his friend as both men rose to their feet.

'You jumped up quickly. Do you always respond so fast?'

'Maybe, especially when she says "are you coming to bed". Anyway, I don't see you lingering.'

'No, but I'm hungry,' and both men laughed.

John and Peter made their way along the deck and only then realised the temperature had indeed fallen. September days were often this way in Ayrshire, as John and Sarah had discovered over years of holidaying. A pleasant and barmy late summer or autumn day could descend without warning into a chilly evening, if the wind turned and blew from the North. However, a thick jumper or a cosy fire was all that was needed to keep out the cold.

'Hang on,' said John and pulled his friend up short. 'What did you say? Especially when she says 'are you coming to bed'? What's happened to you. You're a changed man. I think Rachel's appetite has rubbed off, or more likely rubbed all over you if you take my meaning.'

Peter laughed, a deep quiet laugh. 'I'm sure I don't know what you mean.'

'C'mon you two!' called Rachel, and the two men hurried indoors as a gust of wind escaped the tall trees that sheltered Memorial cottage.

The evening meal, prepared by Sarah, Rachel and the two girls Claire and Sophie, comprised good wholesome fayre, a warming cottage pie with plenty of home-grown vegetables. A crumble made from locally picked soft fruit, foraged by Claire and Sophie from around the local hedgerows, completed the feast. Leaving the dishes to soak until morning, they headed for the living room, a large space typical of stone cottages with comfy sofas set around two of the walls and a substantial log burner as the focal point. John had set a match to the fire just before they settled down to dinner and throwing more logs inside, soon had a roaring blaze going. They could hear the freshening breeze rattle the wind chimes hanging around the property, and John closed the living room door shielding them against a cool evening.

Rachel, Sophie and Claire shot across the room and threw themselves into the corner sofa, battling for prime position in the comfiest seats.

'Now, now children,' laughed Sarah. 'Will you ever stop doing that?'

'No,' said Rachel.

'Mom?' said Claire.

'Yes, sweetie.'

'Can Sophie have a sleepover?'

Sarah looked at John with a smirk. 'Well, that's up to Peter and Rachel. But I've got a feeling they'll be having a sleep over too.'

'I agree,' answered John. 'Since they've both had a drink without discussing who would drive home. What do you think, Sarah? Did they plan this?'

'Yes, I think they did. It's just as well I made up the spare bed.'

Peter and Rachel looked at each other and then at Sarah and John. Peter looked embarrassed.

'Sorry … ' he began.

'Pete,' Rachel said. 'It's already arranged. Sarah asked me hours ago when you were helping John out back. They're only winding you up.'

'Oh!' and he took another slurp from his glass.

While the grownups engaged in banter, Claire and Sophie spotted a film on television. It was almost seven thirty and the two young girls were in pyjamas sitting comfortably. Having played the game, Rachel relinquished her position and settled next to Peter.

'What's the film?' asked John.

'It's a comedy,' answered Claire. 'It's called Sister Act. It's very old, I …' Claire stopped and turned to stare at her mother.

Sarah glanced across at John and they smiled at a memory. Sister Act was the film Sarah asked John to take her to see on their first date. In many ways it seemed a lifetime ago, or maybe a memory that belonged to a different life.

'Sister Act. I remember that,' John said. 'But it's not that old – nineties, I think.'

With a whispered voice, distant and barely attentive, Claire answered automatically. 'That's ancient, but it might be funny.'

'Claire, sweetheart? You ok?' asked Sarah.

But the young girl never had a chance to answer as a short news bulletin appeared on the TV screen. A female voice spoke with sincerity and concern.

"…. looking for any information leading to the whereabouts of ten-year-old Graham Campbell, who has not been seen since early evening of yesterday. The parents of Graham, Susan and Michael Campbell, are pleading for anyone who has seen Graham or has any information at all, to contact the Police on the number shown on your screen. Graham is around four feet eleven inches, is slim of build and has bright red hair. He was last seen after school yesterday wearing his school uniform with a dark blue jacket. He is described as a quiet boy who enjoys fishing and being outdoors. Since this morning, along with friends and family, Police have been searching all of Graham's known local haunts but have yet to find evidence of any sighting. Once again if anyone has any knowledge of where Graham Campbell may be or if anyone saw him yesterday between three thirty and five o'clock, they are asked to contact the local Police."

Broken

Everyone listened in silence to the report, but both Sarah and John sensed a disturbing energy radiating from Claire, an interference that spoke to them of fear and worry. A few moments after the broadcast finished, Claire spoke. 'I know Graham. I sit next to him in class. He's quiet, but he's really nice. We help each other at school.'

'I'm sorry, sweetie. Where does he live?' Sarah asked.

'Somewhere near Kirkmichael I think,' Claire sat upright on the edge of the sofa and began to fidget.

'Not far then,' John remarked. 'Don't worry sweetheart, he'll be ok I'm sure. Sometimes children wander off if they've had a row or something. He won't have gone far.'

But Claire was unconvinced. 'You don't know that. What if he's been taken, or something horrible,' Claire's voice was shrill and the change in her manner so profound, Sarah became quite concerned.

'Ok angel. Let's not try to worry too much just yet. What daddy says is often true.'

'But not always,' interrupted Claire. 'Not always and I think he's hurt. Oh mom, I'm going to be sick!'

Tears glistened in Claire's eyes as she shot up and ran out of the room. Rushing to the downstairs toilet, Sarah and John were only a short step behind, leaving a shocked Peter, Rachel and Sophie in the living room.

Claire managed to get to the toilet before she emptied the contents of her stomach.

'Ok … it's ok,' said Sarah. 'Just let it go. John? Can you fetch a glass of water, please?' John knew the signs and closed the door, giving his wife and daughter a little privacy.

'Sweetheart,' Sarah focussed on Claire. 'What is it? What scared you so much? Did you sense anything?'

'No. I just felt horrible, like something bad had happened. Mommy? He's going to be ok, isn't he ... really?

'I won't lie to you, sweetie, but I hope so. Sometimes bad things *do* happen. But I really, really hope he's just hiding.' Sarah paused a moment, staring into her daughter's eyes. 'Claire? You never say anything to us about your gift, and we've never asked. Is there anything you want to share with me at all, or ask me? I won't talk to anyone else if you don't want me to.'

Responding to a light tap from behind, Sarah opened the door, reached for the tumbler John had left on the floor and handed it to Claire before closing the door once more. Claire took a sip and then gulped the rest.

'Sometimes I feel things,' Claire began, a little calmer. 'Y'know in my chest.'

Sarah nodded.

'It started one day when you were in hospital. I could feel Daddy at the hospital when I was at home with Auntie Rachel. I could feel how unhappy he was, but I couldn't see his face or anything like that. I knew he was unhappy because I was too. And you were ...' Claire struggled for the right words. 'You were missing. That's how it felt. You weren't there and we couldn't find you because you were stuck somewhere and couldn't get back and you didn't know who we were.'

Sarah was shocked at how her daughter described Sarah's coma, how she interpreted what had occurred in Sarah's dream world. It was too easy, Sarah realised, to dismiss or not fully understand what went on in a child's thoughts when faced with problems or immense stress. It was too easy to talk about the resilience of children and not realise there was so much going on underneath that a child wasn't always capable of vocalising.

Claire had begun talking again. 'When I stayed at Auntie Rachel's, I could feel your unhappiness and daddy's as if I was in the room with you, like I was feeling it all myself.' Claire frowned with the effort of trying to describe her thoughts. 'And I was unhappy, but I could feel your unhappiness as well as my own. It was horrible and made me feel sick.'

Claire was still kneeling in front of the toilet and Sarah settled next to her, pulling her daughter close. With huge eyes, Claire stared straight at her mother, but it was clear her focus was outside of the room.

'Mommy. I can feel people all around me … whether they're unhappy or not. I could feel it when we still lived in England, at school or when I was out playing. I didn't know what to do because I didn't want to see that stuff all the time.'

'Oh sweetheart, you should have said something.'

'I didn't want to worry you and Daddy because of everything with Beryl and Steve and David and Auntie Rachel.'

'Claire, you brave girl. I'm sorry if we were all wrapped up in problems last year. I'm sorry if we didn't pay enough attention.'

'No mommy. It's ok … really. You were busy and I understand that you can't always pay enough attention to me.'

Sarah took a deep breath, and her heart filled with love and pride for this ten-year-old sitting on a cold stone floor sharing her thoughts. How did she get all grown up, Sarah thought, and felt humbled by the notion.

'Claire, I love you so much, but sweetheart, you and

little Robbie are the most important things in me and your daddy's life. If you need to talk in the future, just interrupt whatever we're doing and I promise I won't let you down.'

'You didn't let me down mommy, neither you or daddy, but I listened to you.'

'Listened to me … us?'

'Yes. I heard you both talking about protecting yourselves against all of the … the bad things. About a shield?'

'Yes that's right, a shield. Do you want to tell me what you use? Does it work?'

'Yes mommy it does work except when something really bad happens. Then I don't seem to be able to stop those things.'

Huh! Sarah pondered. *Yes, I can identify with that.* In the early days after Sarah met Beryl, she'd suffered overwhelming dread and nausea as the most powerful spiritual attacks from distressed souls invaded her wellbeing. People with severe illness or whose own spirit was troubled. Sarah had by pure chance found what John referred to as a talisman, an everyday item she could focus on and use as a spiritual shield. Almost at once it worked for her. John had found his own shield, which was Sarah herself. But she'd not stopped to ponder if Claire needed such a device and was annoyed with herself for being inattentive.

'Do you want to know what my shield is, Mommy?' Claire asked, and Sarah sensed a new struggle within her daughter, regret or loss perhaps.

'Only if you want to, sweetheart.'

Claire drew in a deep breath. 'It's nanny Rose. She helps me.'

Sarah's mother.

Broken

Claire once said that Rose spoke to her while Sarah was in hospital, talked to her about several crystals that Sarah had taken from her Mother's house after she'd died. The notion shocked Sarah when Claire told her, but this was before Sarah understood her full family history, before any of their new life began.

Sarah leaned forward and with tenderness kissed her daughter on the forehead. Claire folded into Sarah's arms. With a smile in her voice, Sarah spoke.

'My angel, I can imagine no better way to protect yourself than nanny. And I'm so happy that she's with you. Were you worried about telling me?'

Claire nodded her head but did not speak.

'Y'know, I'm not sad at losing nanny Rose any more sweetie,' Sarah continued. 'So you can talk as much about her as you like.'

Claire remained silent.

'Sweetie?' Sarah said. 'What did you feel when we heard the news about Graham?'

The answer came in a whisper, and so quiet, Sarah struggled to hear the words.

'Very cold.' A few seconds passed before Claire spoke for the last time. 'I think he's hurt,' she sighed.

A gentle tap on the door indicated that John had given them enough time to talk.

'Can I come in?' John asked.

'Yes, of course. She's fallen asleep,' whispered Sarah. 'Can you help put her to bed?'

'Yes. Here, let me. It's a bit cramped in here.'

John reached in and lifted his daughter, cradling her like a baby as he carried her upstairs. He laid her on the bed, slid off her slippers and covered her up, leaving her to sleep within the comforting glow of a night light.

Back downstairs, Sarah was chatting to Peter and Rachel in the hall.

'Is she ok? Perhaps we should go,' Peter suggested.

'No need,' Sarah said. 'She'll be ok in the morning. She's sensitive to psychic disturbance and this boy going missing has obviously worried her.'

Rachel spoke. 'She's definitely sensitive, but that's what I'd expect from your daughter.'

Sarah led them back into the living room.

'Here, let me top up your glasses. Try to relax a bit.'

It was gone half-past eight when Sophie yawned. Rachel held a hand out to her. 'C'mon sweetie. You look ready for bed. Shall I come and tuck you in?'

'Yes please,' Sophie stood up and wrapped her arms around Rachel.

By the time they all turned in for the night, it was near eleven o'clock and the day's efforts had taken their toll. John spoke to Sarah as they settled under the covers.

'That was a bit disturbing … Claire's response. I've never seen her change so quick.'

'No, nor me. But remember, she's ten, she's reached puberty and her hormones will be playing havoc, not helped by the effect of her spiritual gifts. But she's still sleeping, so the respite will be good for her.'

They both fell silent and Sarah pondered the past twelve months and how they, as a family, had embraced their gifts, how those things had become the norm. Peter and Rachel were their closest friends and accepted them for what they were, even though sometimes it was hard for them to understand. But then Sarah had in effect saved Rachel's life in every way imaginable and in turn Peter's, bringing him a new purpose following the loss of his first wife. Occasionally Sarah questioned her own gifts, wondered why they had arisen, and why *they* as a family had been chosen, why they were different. But then a brief spiritual connection to Beryl comforted her, as if Beryl, or what remained of Beryl, sensed Sarah's temporary struggle and a gentle hand on her forehead convinced her of the truth and validity of all they were. After all, she reminded herself, amazing things did happen to normal people.

Two

Sarah was aware of the voice, though she did not comprehend its scale or power. Voice, however, was not a satisfactory description of the phenomenon, because there was no sense of sound, no vocalisation – she did not 'hear' the voice with earthly senses. Sarah once tried to describe to Rachel what she perceived and had struggled to make her friend understand. The first time she became aware of it, she'd explained, was the evening John's grandfather Hamish passed away while Sarah and John walked along the beach. Hamish had fallen asleep as the sun melted into the horizon. A powerful energy had passed through Sarah and she'd heard the voice, or what she described to John at the time as Hamish's 'song'.

At the time, the sensation brought great comfort, even amidst her grief, but she didn't sense it again until she visited the maternity unit before and during the birth of little Robert. There she perceived many songs, most of which flowed through her soul, creating a tranquillity that brought a smile to her lips. On one occasion, the song was different and conveyed a sense of loss, of pain, though she did not feel it in a physical or emotional sense. Rather, it touched her soul in a way she could only describe as poignant, that emotional reaction that creates a mix of sadness and joy – essentially very moving.

It didn't take Sarah long to realise that in the same way she felt the spiritual essence of Hamish moving on, she also perceived the beginnings of life at the Maternity unit, and the songs she experienced were associated with spiritual transition. The essence of harmony, these songs spoke of perfect synchronisation, of beauty and purity, whether the spirit was entering or leaving a body. In fact, she then understood that everyone had their own song which, as the strength and range of her gift grew, she sensed with ease when she lowered her shield and opened her heart. With increasing skill, she learnt to 'feel' the varying spiritual chatter of her immediate family and close friends, and to sense when a powerful energy flowed through them, or to use the emotional description, if they were angry, sad, joyous or worried. And she could sense these effects from afar.

Trying to explain this to Rachel and convey its meaning proved to be difficult. Everyone, Sarah said, had their own song, as unique as a fingerprint or DNA. As an atheist, Rachel had difficulty accepting the links to spirituality, souls moving back and forth, but she understood that her friend was blessed with abilities far beyond her own and so recognised the simple fact of Sarah's belief. As John once said to Sarah herself, trying to explain the power within a dream to someone who hadn't experienced it was impossible, since the listener felt none of the emotional or spiritual effects.

'Y'know,' Sarah said, 'When you get a client in for a treatment, how some of them leave you edgy or unsettled?'

'Oh yes. There are a few of those. They project their emotional state onto you.'

'Exactly, but is it because they are miserable and you respond emotionally to it, or is it because their dis-eased state of mind is affecting their spirit and your own spiritual energy reacts the same way?'

'Maybe. Is that why we take to some people and behave in a calm way around them whereas others we would avoid if possible? Isn't that what love's all about, responding to a specific person with ease?'

Sarah nodded. 'I think so. Makes sense to me … projection of feeling or a heartfelt connection. But here's the difference between us. For those clients we have who appear disturbed or distressed, it affects you when you meet them and spend an hour with them in the treatment room. But I sense them as they come through the gate or up the drive. Unless I'm concentrating or blocking.'

Sarah paused and sighed. 'Rachel, I don't know if any of this is right or wrong. I don't have anyone to ask. I have tons of journals written by Beryl, but I've only scratched the surface. All I know is what I sense and believe. Song is the best way I can describe it, because it seems like the purest harmony.'

The truth of the matter was that Sarah's gifts were developing at an increasing rate as Beryl suggested, growing in range and strength. So strong was the connection to John and Claire, she decided she needed to shield herself from them because it felt to her as if she were prying. Everyone needed privacy, and perhaps this was even more important when living in a close relationship. Since moving to Manseburn, Sarah had become quite adept at tuning in and out of psychic energy in order to respect privacy and protect herself. Not that she could read minds – that was impossible. But she was able to sense a person's mood and this foresight could alter her behaviour to that person, which with her clients may not always be appropriate. In the line of work she had chosen, this was important to ensure impartiality. Only when they shared their difficulties, opened up, would she consider probing their psyche.

The bond with her family's spiritual heart meant Sarah was aware of them on a deep ethereal level, detected any disease that distorted the harmony of each person's own song. She may choose to maintain a protective shield, but experience had shown her that a hidden channel lay permanently open, and if any great stress affected her loved ones, a warning signal, impossible to ignore, would surge through without restriction.

And this proved to be true. For deep within the darkness of that Saturday night, while everyone relaxed in well-earned slumber, and Claire wandered in and out of a disturbing dream, two such signals reached into Sarah's soul, reached in and with sudden violence nudged her awake.

Three

Sarah opened her eyes and in one swift movement rolled over and swung herself into a seated position. Her heart pounded in her chest as she tried to work out why she had awakened. With a glance over her right shoulder, she expected to see John's head, but the pillow lay empty. Peering over her left shoulder she spotted John, a mirror image of herself, sitting upright on the edge of the bed, head bowed. With her sight unblocked, she perceived his aura, but it wafted pale and tortuous as if disturbed. Then she noticed the movement of his chest, the fast expansion and collapse, a sign of rapid breathing. She reached across and touched his shoulder.

'John? Are you ok?'

'Yes. Yes. Woke up in a rush, that's all. Weird dream. Sorry if I woke you. C'mon let's get some sleep.'

'Sweetheart. I'm not sure why you're lying to me, but I suppose you have a reason. I know you've had something on your mind for a while and I'm ready to listen when you're ready to talk.'

John twisted around and opened his mouth to speak again, but frowned at the bedroom door as a sensation diverted his focus. In the same instant, Sarah picked up a disturbance and turned in time to see the door swing open.

'Mommy,' Claire's breath came in laboured gasps. 'I'm freezing. I can't get warm.' The violence of Claire's shivering was plain to see, even within the dim glow of a nightlight from the landing. Sarah slid off the bed and stepped towards her daughter. John approached from his side of the bed.

'Claire?' she asked. 'What is it, sweetie? What's wrong?' and she pulled her daughter close. Only then did she realise with shock how cold Claire was to the touch. John grabbed one of her hands.

'Jesus,' he said. 'She's freezing, she's clammy.'

'Where have you been? Why have you been out of bed?' asked Sarah.

'I h … h … haven't,' stammered Claire. 'I've been in b … b … bed. Oh mommy, you must find him. Why is it so … so cold?'

But then the strength gave out of Claire's legs and she collapsed into Sarah's arms. Her eyes turned upwards until only the whites were visible and violent tremors shook her entire body.

'Oh John, she's fitting,' Sarah cried in horror.

'But why? She's cold, not overheated.' John's confusion and dismay robbed him of action.

'Claire? Sweetie?' Sarah coaxed. 'Can you hear me, sweetheart? Talk to mommy.'

The trembling that wracked Claire's body subsided a fraction, and she managed a whisper.

'It's so cold, and wet. The sea's coming in again. Oh mom, my leg hurts.'

Sarah looked at John with horror widening her eyes.

'The sea? Wet? What is she saying?'

'Check her legs. She said her legs hurt.'

The shivering eased a little more as Sarah rolled up Claire's pyjama legs one at a time, checking each limb. There was no sign of injury. But sudden violent tremors surged once more and Sarah sensed John's rising anguish as they both knelt on the floor shocked by their daughter's apparent seizure.

Then amid Sarah's own distress, a feather light touch caressed her brow and without effort or forethought she clutched at the sensation.

Beryl! Help me!

As her mind focussed on her elderly relative, she remembered Claire's own words earlier that evening as they nestled together on the floor of the downstairs toilet. Claire had explained that the psychic shield she used against negative energies was nana Rose. The young girl used the spiritual memory of her grandmother to protect her own spiritual wellbeing. With the power of this memory in mind, Sarah spoke to John.

'John, give me your hand, quickly. Hold on to Claire's other hand.'

With Claire's tremors growing and diminishing in cycles, John and Sarah took hold of a hand each, forming an enclosed circle. *Circle of friends.* In the space of a single breath, Sarah grasped at the image of her mother, Claire's nanny Rose. The shape of her face, the curve of her smile and the colour of her eyes came in an instant to Sarah's mind, as clear as the last time she saw them. Without understanding how to convey her intent, but knowing that was what she needed to do, she projected the vision into her daughter's heart.

'Mom,' Sarah whispered. 'Your granddaughter needs you. Please help her … please.'

Within moments, Sarah sensed a wholeness, the connection as John joined. And when Claire appeared within the spiritual circle hand in hand with Rose, the tremors stopped in an instant.

Claire opened her eyes. 'Mom, dad. I know where Graham is,' and the young girl yawned.

Four

'I could, but what am I supposed to say?' asked John.

Woken by the commotion, Peter and Rachel stood in the kitchen with Sarah and John, each holding a mug of tea. Claire lay safe in her bed fast asleep, as did Sophie and Robert who had slept undisturbed throughout. Still only half past one, they had been discussing whether to call the police.

'Can't you just tell them what Claire said?' suggested Peter.

'Yes, but they'll need more to go on than just a child's guess. They'd need something more concrete than that. Believe me, I've been there. If I ring the police and say my daughter thinks the boy is down near the sea they'll want to know where. There's a lot of shoreline around here, and they'd have searched much of it already. And they'll ask how she knows, what evidence she has, and they may wonder *why* she knows. I can't say "well my daughter has a predisposition to premonitions or visions". They'll tell me to stop wasting time.'

'And every minute we wait is crucial for that boy,' said Sarah. 'We should either call the Police or go looking ourselves, and we need to decide now.'

John glanced across at Sarah, weighing up his choices. Each understood the worry in the other's mind and each guessed the others decision. Almost in unison they said, 'No time to waste. I'll get dressed. Let's go.'

Rachel spoke. 'How about I call the police after you've gone?'

'Same problem,' replied John. 'What would you say?'

Rachel lifted her shoulders and shook her head in resignation.

'Claire's awake,' said Sarah, and a moment later they heard the creak of floorboards on the landing. Sarah walked out of the kitchen just as Claire stepped into the hallway.

'You ought to be in bed, sweetheart. Did we wake you?'

'No. I had a dream about Graham. Are we going to find him?'

'Your dad and me are going out, but we're not sure where to look. It's very dark, and it's raining. The weather's quite bad.'

'I want to come too,' Claire said, walking into the kitchen.

'That's not a good idea. You were quite poorly a while ago,' said John.

'I'm better now and I *want* to come. I can help. I can still feel him, but not like before. I don't hurt anywhere so I'm going to come with you. I might feel him better if we get closer. He's not far from the town.'

Claire's conviction was all Sarah needed to hear, and she nodded. 'Ok. It's an unusual situation, but this is all about finding the boy as quickly as possible. She's a strong girl John and she may be able to help.'

'Ok, but when we get there you both do as I say. This weather's wild and if the tide's high we may have to be careful.'

Sarah and Claire nodded.

'What about Sophie and Robert,' Sarah asked?

'Don't worry about them,' replied Peter. 'You do what you need to do. Rachel and I will stay and make sure the children are fine. But keep in touch. Call us when you can and let us know if we can do anything, if you need us to call the Emergency Services.'

Within twenty minutes, John was driving as fast as he dared along the lanes towards Kirkmichael and Ayr. Sarah sat quietly next to him, eyes fixed on the road ahead, gripping the seat with both hands as John took the corners at speed. Behind, Claire sat strapped into one of the rear seats and appeared to be dozing. Sarah knew otherwise. She could sense her daughter's spiritual exertion as Claire extended her reach out into the darkness, a desperate search for a soul with whom she had developed a strong connection. Sarah marvelled at how tough her daughter had become, how she appeared to have accepted her gifts without question. And she hoped her daughter's strength would continue as she entered her teenage years, years hard enough for those even without extraordinary abilities.

'I hope we've made the right decision, not calling the police,' Sarah muttered.

'I know. But the thing is,' replied John, 'The police will

be inundated with calls about sightings. Some will be genuine and helpful and in good faith, and they all need to be investigated. Then there will be a few from complete idiots who like to waste time.'

'I can't believe people do that?'

'They're out there. Nutters. I've seen it many times. God only knows what motivates them, but they need serious help.'

They fell into a thoughtful silence as John approached the main Ayr to Stranraer road and he eased his foot from the accelerator. With an unobstructed view in each direction and no approaching traffic at this early hour, John shot out onto the road, turned right and headed towards the tiny village of Minishant.

'The thing that worries me is I don't even know if I'm headed in the right direction? What did that last news update say? The police had been searching his favourite haunts. The river in Ayr, the main sea front. He liked a bit of fishing, Claire said, but she also said he like beach combing. How far would he walk? He could be north of Ayr or further south depending on which shoreline he went to.'

A dreamy but clear voice from the rear seat convinced John his daughter was still searching.

'Dad, you need to go to Greenan shore, near the school.'

'Are you sure, sweetie?'

Claire didn't reply, and Sarah turned and saw that her daughter's concentration was complete. She appeared to have little awareness of her surroundings.

When they reached the turning to Alloway and Doonfoot, John swung the car off the main road and headed through the peaceful suburbs of Ayr. Sarah's phone vibrated.

'How are you getting on?' Rachel's voice.

'Claire says we should go to Greenan. Y'know, behind Doonfoot primary school, the beach near the castle ruins? Hopefully, we'll know more in about two minutes the way John's driving.'

'Ok. Call me if you need me and keep safe.'

John drove the last couple of miles in silence. A moderate rain had begun, slashing across the windscreen, driven sideways by a gusting onshore wind. Since the previous afternoon when John and Peter had harvested a variety of late fruit, the temperature had fallen and from the glow of the dashboard John noted a bitter nine degrees, though he knew the wind chill would reduce it still further.

Claire murmured once more, but her voice was distant – a whispered shudder.

'It's so c … c … cold, and wet. The sea's c …c … coming in again. Oh mom, my leg hurts.'

In a sudden panic, Sarah spun around and put a hand on Claire's forehead. She felt cool, but not as cold as earlier. Claire opened her eyes.

'I'm fine, mommy. I'm ok. We need to go along the shore around the headland past the castle.'

'Ok sweetheart. We're nearly there.'

John swerved the car around the last traffic island and then turned left towards the beach car park. At this time of night the car park was empty and in darkness, the distant streetlamps unable to reach this far. John brought the car to a halt, and they clambered out. As they pulled on thick coats and woollen hats, John turned to Claire.

'Ok angel, which way. It's getting chilly and I think the tide's close to high.'

Buffeted by the gale, but heedless of the rain stinging her face, Claire turned towards the beach and the castle that lay invisible in the darkness.

'He's that way,' and she raised a hand pointing across the dunes. 'I think he's trapped somewhere, in a small space.'

Claire turned back to her parents and for a moment John thrust aside his shield. In his mind's eye, he perceived the intensity of Claire's unease, and a flood of nausea churned in his stomach. But he also sensed the magnitude of her spiritual reach as it stretched out into the night.

Claire wrapped her arms around John and he hugged her back. 'Please find him. I know he's on that beach somewhere.'

'With your help, I will. C'mon, let's get going and stay close. Sarah? Got your torch?'

'Yes. We're all ready.'

John led them across the car park and onto a rough path that led through the sand dunes. The rain, though not heavy, was driven straight against them by a gale that screamed from the northwest across the Clyde Estuary from the Mountains of Arran. With the chill rain running down his cheeks and his own torch in hand, John played the beam across the ground, checking his footing with caution. For a hundred yards they weaved their way through the grassy dunes towards the beach, while around them the ceaseless roar of a wild surf filled the night air. A white froth rolled along the shore as they reached the sand, and even in the darkness it was clear the narrow strip of land they had to walk upon was shrinking as each wave rolled higher.

'This is going to be close,' John shouted. 'Come on, stay together. We need to be quick.'

Breaking into a jog, they made their way to where the castle ruins stood upon an outcrop of land high above the sand. Here the headland jutted out onto the beach. At low tide, flat rocks and sand allowed passage around the cliff for walkers and beach combers. At high tide the only way forward was to climb up and over the top, past the castle ruins. But if Claire's guess was correct, and Graham was somewhere on the other side of the outcrop, John needed to stay at sea level and skirt around the cliff. With the added threat of powerful waves, there was little time left to cross the narrowing space.

'Right. This is it,' he said as he halted. 'I don't want either of you going any further. Remember what I said at home? You do as I say. This rising tide is dangerous.'

Sarah nodded. She knew better than to argue, and anyway, she was not going to put Claire at risk by walking around the cliff base.

'Ok,' she agreed. 'We'll climb up and over the top. We can't get onto the beach from up there, but you'll be able to shine your torch at us if you need to and with a bit of luck you'll get a signal on your phone.'

'Ok, but stay away from the edge.' John shot a glance at the water. He'd end up with wet feet, but he needed to get around the small headland. The beach widened again on the other side, but not by much and it was going to be tricky. The waves were very high and from where they now stood, he couldn't see how far up the beach the water would go once he had rounded the outcrop.

He turned back to Sarah and Claire. 'Look,' he said. 'If I find him and I can't get a signal, I flash my torch three times in a row. I'll keep doing that until you flash three times back. That means call the emergency services.'

Sarah could feel tears stinging her eyes.

'Ok sweetheart. Please be careful.'

John gave them both a quick hug and then stepped away onto the rocks. In moments he disappeared around the headland into the darkness, leaving them alone amidst the hiss and roar of crashing waves.

'C'mon angel.' Sarah had to raise her voice. 'Up we go. Stay close.'

Claire cupped her hands around her mouth and shouted up at her mother. 'He's faint mommy, I can't feel much anymore.'

'Ok, try not to worry. Your dad will go as quick as he can. Let's get ready up on the cliff, and then we can try to find Graham together, send him our thoughts?'

Even in the light of Sarah's torch, Claire's nod of agreement was only just visible.

John timed his progress with careful attention to the incoming surf. He knew the layout of these rocks since he had played along this shoreline for much of his childhood. As fast as he dared, and staying near to the cliff face, he picked his way ahead avoiding rocks that appeared slick with weed. He advanced with caution while a spate of smaller waves rolled in, but just as he reached the open beach, an immense wave exploded on the larger rocks and he had just enough time to turn his back towards the chill spray that engulfed him. A thick coat and high collar kept out most of the deluge, but the stinging water drenched his legs. Without hesitating, he made his way from the last rock onto the sand and turned toward the hillside. Ahead and above where he now hurried along, he spotted the tell-tale flash of torchlight and he guessed Sarah and Claire had reached the top of the hill and were now walking parallel to the beach. Though not high, there was no access up onto the hilltop. At the base of the hill lay a strip of greenery, gorse and bramble, which could, he thought, provide shelter, but an ascent was impossible. In amongst the shrubbery lay many large fallen rocks and washed up flotsam making exploration unwise for the less adventurous.

Falling back on his police experience, John used a balance of speed and accuracy as he checked the beach for anything to indicate the boy's presence. For more than a hundred metres he continued, desperation increasing with each slow minute that passed. On a night such as this, he knew that if Graham *was* here, the effects of hypothermia may have already taken its toll and that could prove fatal.

With his spiritual shield still cast aside, John's senses lay open to his family, and though he had limited experience, and his percipience not as extensive as Sarah's, he detected the tenuous thread of psychic energy. However, he sensed only one presence, which, for a moment, panicked him, thinking something was wrong with Sarah or Claire. But then he recalled many a late night conversation with Sarah about voice and song and realised harmony existed in what he sensed—there were two songs and he knew his wife and daughter were safe.

As he continued his search, John became convinced that Graham lay ahead somewhere, his certainty and belief in his daughter unquestionable. He was fearful, though, that he would be too late. But then he detected a sudden change to the song radiating outwards from his family, and he came to a halt. He did not understand what the change meant, there was no conveyed meaning, but in a moment of insight he began playing his torch around his immediate area.

Within moments he spotted a narrow gap in the bushes and hurrying towards it pushed his way into the space. Behind the bushes lay an assortment of driftwood and three large steel drums. Their placement spoke of intention rather than the random effects of the tide, and further beyond, a black space appeared within the general darkness. To pass through the makeshift shelter he had to drop to his knees and crawl, and once on the other side he shone his torch into what appeared to be a cave or shallow depression within the hillside. What he saw made his heartrate quicken. Without hesitation and knowing time was precious, he crawled through the shelter, and back onto the narrow beach.

Now less than ten feet wide and with the heavy surf reaching higher with every wave, John turned and scanned the hilltop. Directly above where he stood, the bright beam of a torch pointed to the ground and the sight gave him hope. Sarah and Claire had come to a halt and were standing still, waiting for a sign. He turned off his own torch plunging his immediate surroundings into darkness. Using the button, he flashed his lamp towards the source of light three times and waited. There was a moment's pause during which the torchlight disappeared but three quick flashes followed. Confident his message was received, he hurried back across the sand and clambering over the rocks, crawled through the makeshift shelter and into the shallow hollow.

Graham Campbell lay unmoving, his legs drawn up in a foetal position, arms wrapped around his small chest. John was competent in detecting basic life signs and within moments found a pulse, though it seemed weak. But what he needed was more, and he tried to imagine what Sarah would do, how she would try to discover the presence of inner strength. Without guidance, all he could think of was to gaze at the boy and try to picture the essence of Graham, his essential being, in the same way he did with those dear to him. Though nausea flooded his soul once more, he detected a vague thread of energy and knew in his heart what he perceived was fragile. The complete lack of coloured aura horrified John as he knelt. Playing his torch over Graham's body, he could see the boy wore only a thin bomber jacket and school trousers. There was an ugly stain on his left trouser leg, what appeared to be drying blood. Convinced that Graham would not survive long without heat and water, John checked his head for injury and finding none, pulled off his own coat and hat and carefully lifting the boy, wrapped the coat around him. He then slid his woolly hat over Graham's head and began rubbing his hands. For many minutes John continued before noticing a flicker of eye movement. Encouraged, he spoke to the boy.

'Graham? C'mon son. Can you hear me?'

More eye movement.

'Graham? My name's John. I'm Claire's father. Claire from school? Can you hear me? Give my hand a squeeze if you can.'

With infinite patience, John held onto Graham's hand and listened for any sound, waited for movement. After long seconds, he detected a tiny change of pressure as Graham moved his fingers.

'Graham? I have a bottle of water. I want you to drink some. Just a sip to start with. Can you lift your head a little?'

Encouraged when the boy tried to move, John placed a hand behind his head and held the bottle to his lips.

The boy took a few small sips before opening his eyes.

'I slipped on a rock,' he whispered. 'Cut myself on that

drum.' Graham tried to raise a hand to point, but the effort was too much. 'My leg hurts and the tide's coming in again. Am I in trouble?'

Despite himself, John smiled at Graham.

'Yes. I expect your parents will have a few words to say, but I reckon they'll forgive you. We just need to get you somewhere warm and dry. Help's on its way.'

While he spoke to the boy, a silent message reached into his soul, and he found himself responding with little forethought. The source of the call came from outside of himself and the message conveyed concern, triggering a response in John similar to that which he would present if he stood in front of the sender. It was clear Sarah and Claire had once more combined their energies and projected their anxiety. Because John felt more at ease now that he had found Graham, his spiritual projection reflected his emotional state, and within moments he sensed Sarah and Claire withdraw. With a disbelieving shake of his head, he guessed he had allayed their fears.

'Now listen,' John said to Graham. 'I want you to stay awake, ok? Promise me. There's no going to sleep while I'm here. Keep having a few sips of water and we'll chat while we wait.'

Graham nodded.

'Now,' said John. 'Tell me about this place. Is this a camp you made?'

As soon as Sarah spotted the flash of John's torch, she responded as they'd agreed. Then she dialled the emergency services, telling them they had found the missing child. Few questions were asked as the Air Sea rescue was scrambled and it wasn't long before Sarah spotted an approaching searchlight from the inky black sky, and heard the distant wail of an Ambulance.

'C'mon sweetheart,' she said to Claire. 'We need to get back to the carpark to direct them when they arrive.'

In the cave, John kept Graham talking, while outside their shelter the rush and fall of heavy waves approached ever nearer. Despite his growing concern, John kept chatting, but after what seemed like hours in his current state, the heavy, thunderous chop of helicopter blades reached his ears. Looking behind, the darkness of the shoreline turned to daylight as the powerful searchlight approached. The force of the downdraft showered a spray of seawater in every direction. Satisfied that Graham was awake and alert, John scrambled out of the cave and with water blowing into his face, shielded his eyes and shone his torch upwards. Moments later, with relief flooding his soul, he saw movement as a heavy winch was set in motion and unravelled its cable lowering someone onto the beach. It was only then John realised that uncontrollable shivers wracked his entire body from head to foot.

Five

'You're a damned eejit,' Duncan McBride hissed. 'You could have been injured or worse out on that beach.'

Duncan stood propping up the wall of an examination cubicle in the emergency department of Ayr Hospital. After a medical examination gave the all clear, John reclined on a chair wearing a sheepish and exhausted expression on his face.

Duncan and John were old school friends, and when John's grandfather passed away, Duncan offered condolences and they had met up often afterwards to share old stories. Duncan and his wife Elise had met Sarah several times. But he and John had more than school in common because Duncan joined Ayrshire police around the time John began his career with West Midlands Police. Duncan was now a Detective Sergeant.

'Why didn't you call me?' he continued.

'And say what?' John said. 'Hi Dunc. I'm sorry it's the

middle of the night, but we think we know where that boy is. Yes, I'm sure you'd have sent a whole unit to search based on what could have been just a whim.'

'Don't be a prat. I know you're not a time waster. If you believed your daughter, that would have been enough for me. I'd have got some people down there.'

John hadn't the energy to argue. 'Maybe,' he said and blew out a long breath. 'But in the middle of the night, everything was crazy. We just did what we thought was quickest. Claire was quite worried.'

'Well the boy's gonna be fine,' said Duncan. 'That's the main thing, so I'm not going to labour the point … that is,' and here he smiled, 'As long as I get an invitation to dinner soon.'

'That's blackmail, isn't it?'

'No, just an incentive to keep me off your back.'

John accepted Duncan's reprimand knowing it came from personal concern. But the rescue was only just in time, for the boy at least. John was confident he himself could have clambered out of reach of the approaching waves, but he would have suffered from the reducing temperature. How Graham would have fared though, he didn't know. By the time Graham lay safe inside the helicopter and the rescue crew were lifting John off the beach, the incoming tide had rolled across the upper shore and the higher waves encroached Graham's make shift camp. The helicopter took Graham and John to the nearest hospital and as the paramedics wheeled Graham towards the main entrance, a newspaper team arrived.

From the carpark at Greenan shore, and after a brief text from John as he rested inside the helicopter, Sarah drove straight to the hospital. While a medic examined John, Duncan turned up and questioned Sarah.

'How did you know where he was? That beach wasn't among the list of places his parents gave us.'

'Claire's idea.' Sarah sat with her daughter in a nearby waiting area.

With a glance at Sarah confirming it was ok to question the child, Duncan turned to Claire. 'Claire? Can you tell me how you knew where to find Graham?'

'I dreamed about him,' Claire muttered.

'Dreamt? How's that?'

Sarah replied for her. 'What she means is she remembered Graham telling her about a den he'd made down on the beach. She remembered it late last night.'

'So you had a recollection?'

Claire answered with her eyes closed, on the edge of sleep. Sarah recognised the signs. After Claire expended a high level of spiritual energy, she often fell into an exhausted slumber. Twenty minutes and she'd be wide awake, during daylight hours anyway.

'I suppose so. I dreamed about him … I felt him.'

Jimmy frowned and looked at Sarah.

'Felt him?' Duncan was shaking his head. 'What does she mean?'

Sarah drew a deep breath and considered whether the truth would make sense to Duncan. But she had met with John's friend and his wife many times and within moments satisfied herself she could tell him everything.

'Duncan, how much do you understand about what we do at the farm?' she asked.

'Sorry. What's that got to do with this?'

'Please, bear with me.'

'Ok. Well, as I understand it, you've continued, or I should say restarted, a business your great grandmother used to run. I remember it because my mother visited several times. In fact, we sent one of our colleagues here. It was ages ago because I'd just started out as a beat copper. The shrink diagnosed this guy with post-traumatic stress. He'd witnessed some pretty shocking stuff.' Duncan dug into his memory before continuing. 'If I recall, your relative's name was Beryl. She used to offer healing sessions and other stuff for those who needed help of some sort. Or even just a massage sometimes. So why is that important?'

'You're right. We offer a range of alternate therapies or a simple massage, though I should say *I* do because John doesn't do that kind of work. But, John, Claire and I have special gifts. Gifts which to us are very real but many people, probably too many, would say are a load of rubbish. Whatever people say, though, doesn't bother me because there are plenty of others who have benefited from our gifts. What would bother me is if the newspapers reported that Claire sensed where Graham was using some hocus pocus to locate him. You know what the media is like. Anything for a big headline. She doesn't need any kind of exposure at her age. So as far as everyone else is concerned, she simply remembered a secret he'd told her. Is that ok with you?'

'Are you saying that's what happened, Claire sensed him? Is that what she meant by felt him?'

Sarah nodded.

'I remember the old tales about the farm above Straiton,' Duncan continued. 'The tales go back years. They tell of a witch who lived up there who could cure all sorts of ailments with the wave of a magic wand or by using some strange concoction ... a witch's brew. More likely herbal remedies. Fantastic stories but people will talk, and there's always some truth behind a rumour, often distorted. I take it you're telling me you have these gifts because you're a descendant of Beryl.'

Sarah nodded again.

'It's hard to imagine,' Duncan sighed.

'Look at it this way,' Sarah said. 'How long have you and Elise been married?'

'What? Let's think. It'll be thirteen years next month.'

'I'm glad you remembered,' Sarah smiled. 'Anyway, quite a while then. This might be a weak way of looking at it, but how often do you start to say something or think of something at the same time as Elise?'

'Ever now and then, I suppose. Often but not all the time, obviously.'

'That's right, but it happens.' Duncan nodded. 'I like to look at it as you're both on the same wavelength. You could explain it as knowing each other's mind and so both guess at the same time what the other is thinking. After so long together you're so close that other times you sense each other's mood by their behaviour or how they appear on the outside. But for me and John, and Claire, it's an extension of that principle. We see deeper into each other. I can't read John's mind, obviously. But I can sense when something's up, even if he looks and behaves normally. What happens is, your emotions will present themselves in your spiritual body. Imagine going through a lot of emotional turmoil. Often it appears as the sufferer losing their hope or drive, their spirit. But with us, we can sense this change from a distance, without seeing the person in the flesh, which is what happened to Claire. She's quite close to Graham because they spend a lot of time together at school. When

Graham was hurt, and the longer he spent alone, his emotions would have run wild and presented themselves in his spiritual body. This energy was powerful enough for Claire to detect.'

'So what happened,' said Duncan. 'Is that Claire woke after dreaming of Graham, after having a vision of him because fear would have made the boy panic … powerful emotions.' Sarah nodded. 'But how did you locate him in the dark?'

'Bear with me, because this'll get more fantastic. As I said, Claire sits next to Graham at school. They're good friends, so Claire has become spiritually connected to him. In a way, the same as you connect with Elise. Because of this connection, she had this vision of him cold and wet near a beach. We took her with us when we went to search for him. We figured her connection would make him easier to find. What we weren't ready for was Graham's spiritual strength weakening by the minute. Anyway, Claire has an obvious connection to John and me, and when John was on the beach and close to Graham, Claire used her father as a conduit to amplify Graham's spirit. When John got closer still, Claire sensed her friend through John and sent a message to her dad to focus on the immediate area.'

Duncan lifted a hand up and over his head.

'Whoosh,' he said. 'I'll have to take your word on that. Sounds like a spiritual text message.'

'That's one way of looking at it. But remember what we said about you and Elise … sometimes you know what the other is about to say?'

'Yes, she's always telling me what to say.'

'I'll tell her you said that,' laughed Sarah. 'But seriously, it's an extension of the same idea.'

'Alright then, whatever you say. I guess I'll never quite understand, and maybe I don't need to. My job is to write up the report. But the official story is, after Claire saw the TV appeal, she remembered Graham sharing a secret about a camp he'd made on the beach.'

'Yes, please. Sounds perfect.'

Duncan nodded his agreement just as a nurse approached with the news that John was ready to go home. Sarah gave Claire a gentle squeeze.

'C'mon sweetie, we can go now. I think a lazy Sunday would be a good idea.'.

Six

'Hi Rachel. We're just leaving the hospital.' Sarah yawned as she spoke into her phone. 'Everything and everyone is fine, but we'll tell you about it when we get home. Are the kids ok?'

A weary John glanced at Sarah and saw her nod. 'Everything ok?' he asked as Sarah ended the call.

'Yes. The kids are fast asleep, and I think Claire will be too before we leave the car park.'

The Macintyre's were nearing the hospital exit when they stopped and turned at the sound of a voice from along the corridor. A woman who looked to be Sarah's age but more rotund hurried towards them, tears streaming down a reddened face. A man followed close behind, and Sarah noted his expression was a mix of anguish and relief.

'Mrs Macintyre … Mr Macintyre. Oh God, I don't know how to thank you … what to say!'

The woman almost collided with Sarah and wrapped

Broken

her ample arms around her in a hug that left Sarah struggling to draw breath. Letting Sarah loose, she launched herself onto John, repeating the intensity of her gratitude. The man, who Sarah assumed was the woman's husband, grabbed Sarah's hand and nodded his thanks. John extended his own hand towards the man and their handshake lingered for several seconds.

'I don't know how to say thank you enough,' the woman repeated. 'If it hadn't been for you, I think we would … we would have lost my boy.'

'C'mon Sue. It's alright now.' The woman's husband was saying. Then he spoke directly to John. 'She is right, though. What you did was amazing. Risking your life like that. The police told us. There's no way we could ever repay you.'

'Please,' John held up a hand. 'It's not necessary. We'd do it again if we needed to. Just happy to help, that's all. But we're grateful for your thanks.'

'Yes,' added Sarah. 'We're glad to help but we have an exhausted little girl here who needs her bed now, as I'm sure you two will after what you've been through. How is Graham doing?'

The man replied. 'He's going to be fine. He was very cold, but you got to him just in time, we're told. He has a broken ankle … slipped on the rocks, it seems, but he told me he dragged himself under cover when the rain came last night. He'll be in plaster for a few weeks but the doctor's say he'll make a full recovery.'

'That's good to hear,' said John.

'But you're right about sleep,' the man said. 'we'd better let you go. If there's any way we can help at all with anything, please get in touch. My name's William and this is

Susan. We both work in social care for Ayrshire Local Authority.'

'John and Sarah,' John said, 'and the yawning one here is Claire. She's in Graham's class at school.'

'Well, take care and thanks again,' William said.

Eager to get home, John pushed the exit button for the emergency department door and they spilled out into the night air. Though the rain had stopped, there was still a strong gale, and they huddled together, Claire in the middle, heads down against the cold. Half way across the empty car park, another voice hailed them from several yards away.

'Mr Macintyre?'

Without thinking John looked up and said, 'Yes?'

Before he'd finished speaking, several brilliant flashlights blinded them as a gaggle of reporters headed their way.

'Oh, for heaven's sake,' muttered John. 'C'mon you two, let's get out of here. Where's the car, sweetheart?'

'Not far,' Sarah answered. 'Over here. I dumped it in a disabled spot.'

A dozen voices began firing questions.

'Mr Macintyre, what's it like to be a hero?'

'How did you feel when you found the boy?'

'Mrs Macintyre, can you tell me why you took your daughter with you?'

The reporters had surrounded them now, scribbling notes or pushing mobile phones at them, trying to record any response. John and Sarah kept Claire between them and without a word made their way to the car. A shout from behind announced Duncan's sudden appearance.

'PEOPLE!' he shouted. 'If you come over here and leave them alone, I can give you a formal statement. Please

... this way!'

'I'll drive,' said Sarah, and John offered no argument.

'How the hell did they find out?'

'The grapevine, I imagine. It only takes one person to speak out of turn, or a conversation overheard and word spreads. It was a big story. We can't expect to get away with it anonymously.'

'I guess not. I suppose anyone in A&E could have called the press, or someone from the Police or coastguard.'

'Well, it is what it is. I just need our home and a decent cup of tea.'

Sarah didn't admit that she *was* a little troubled, hoping no-one overheard her conversation with Duncan. That was just the kind of story the papers would love.

When they arrived home, a thick blanket of cloud lay overhead and dawn was still some way off. Across the yard, a welcoming light in the kitchen beckoned and movement behind the glass spoke of a friendly reception.

'Nearly five o'clock and they're still up ... if they went back to bed,' John yawned. 'It's only been a few hours, but it feels like we've been gone ages. Seems to me like rain's approaching again. A day for staying in, I think.'

Sarah nodded.

'Look. No arguing. We'll take Robert home with us and bring him back later this afternoon. He can play with baby John and Sophie and it'll give you three a chance to catch up with sleep.'

Rachel was insistent, and neither Sarah nor John had the strength to argue.

'Rachel,' Sarah said, masking a yawn with one hand.

'That would be very kind but only if you're sure.'

'Yes, of course I'm sure. The kids will entertain themselves mostly anyway, so it's settled. One of us will see you later.'

By six o'clock, Claire was warm in her room buried in a deep sleep, and John and Sarah climbed into bed. John had tended to the chickens, but that was it for chores. The weather was blustery, carrying with it a light rain with no sign of letting up, and he hastened back across the yard and closed the door, cocooning them inside their sanctuary. With the wind sounding remote as it played across the roof tiles, it wasn't long before they too fell asleep.

Seven

Despite their disturbed night, Sarah and John were up and around by half past ten. Though exhausted, nervous energy interrupted their sleep, so while Sarah headed for the shower, John scurried downstairs to the kitchen. He found Claire sitting at the dining table watched by an attentive Mags and a half empty glass of milk in her hand. The young girl sat motionless, staring into space.

'I didn't expect to see you yet sweetheart,' John yawned.

Claire replied in a voice distant with introspection.

'I think it's going to get busy.'

'Busy? How do you mean busy?'

A knock at the door prevented Claire from answering. Mags barked and trotted out of the kitchen into the hall while John followed and opened the door. A young woman approached with a phone held stretched outward. Behind and at a discreet distance an older man stood nursing a small video camera.

'Mr Macintyre? I wonder if you could spare us a few minutes? We'd like to ask a few questions about how you saved Graham Campbell.'

Taken by surprise, John opened his mouth but closed it again. Without a word, he shut the door.

'Please Mr Macintyre,' a muffled plea. 'Only a few questions – local interest. Nothing too onerous.'

'Damn it,' John muttered as Sarah came downstairs.

'Who was that?' she asked.

'A reporter. It's not that I mind so much, but I'm not even dressed. What do I tell them?'

'Nothing. I'll talk to them while you get showered. I'll ask them to wait. If we give them a few words, perhaps they'll leave us alone. It's hardly earth shattering news.'

Another knock and John shook his head. 'Persistent buggers. I'll leave you to it,' and he disappeared upstairs.

Sarah opened the door and was on the verge of remarking about having little patience when a cheery 'hello' greeted her. To her surprise, Graham's mother Sue stood back from the door. Behind her and to one side, the reporter waited impatiently. 'Mrs Macintyre? Can you spare us a few minutes?'

'Oh hello,' Sarah said, ignoring the reporter. 'Is everything ok. How's Graham?'

'Mom, I'll be outside if you need me.' Claire shimmied past Sue and the reporter and headed across the yard to the hen house.

'Och, he's fine,' Sue replied. 'He'll be coming home tomorrow. He said he can't wait to get his friends to write on his plaster cast. But I'm here to thank you again in person.'

Broken

'Mrs Macintyre … please?' the reporter again.

Sarah retreated inside and spoke again to Mrs Campbell. 'Come on in and make yourself comfortable. The kitchen's on the left, through there. I shan't be a moment.'

Sue Campbell waddled through into the kitchen as Sarah stepped outside and closed the door.

'How can I help you,' she asked? 'Please remember we didn't get home until almost dawn. We've not even eaten yet.'

The reporter persisted. 'We're from the local TV news. We just wanted to share your story with the local community. Y'know … local interest, a bit of feel-good news for a change. I wondered if you and your family would like to answer our questions and maybe let us take a picture or two?'

'Well, we don't want any fuss. We only did what anyone else would have done, but perhaps later. Can you come back this afternoon?'

'Well we wanted to try and get the piece in the evening news. Would midday be ok?'

Persistent buggers, John had said.

'Well yes, ok. Happy to get it over. Now please, leave us in peace for a while.'

'Thank you,' and off they went, though Sarah doubted they'd go far. Maybe the tea room in Straiton. Satisfied they'd have a few hours grace, Sarah went back into the house to Mrs Campbell feeling there was more than extended gratitude on her mind.

'My nana used to talk about this place,' Sue was saying as she lifted a cup of tea. 'She used to say someone with strange powers lived here. A witch, she said, sometimes to scare us wee ones. But my mam put us straight. Said that Beryl was a healer. Funny how things stick in your mind. My mam came here for help a few times and was sad when she couldn't come anymore after Beryl left. Whatever problems my mam had were always better after a visit. Rumour has it that Beryl was a close relative of yours?'

'Yes, she was. My great grandmother. It's a lengthy story, but I knew nothing about her until the end of the year before last when she got in touch. She'd been searching for me.'

'And left you all of this.'

Sarah nodded. 'Yes, bit of a dream come true, though I wished I'd had more time with her. I envy your mom if she met her often.'

'Well, she was not close of course, just came for therapy but my ma told me stories and rumours about Beryl … what she did, how she healed people who'd had no luck with mainstream healthcare.' Sue paused and stared at Sarah, drumming her fingertips across her lips as if pondering how to proceed. Sarah waited for her to continue.

'Sarah, can I ask a question? Actually I already know you're related to Beryl. When working in Social Care it's easy to find some things out so I may as well come straight to the point. Because of what you did for Graham, and what you offer here, I wondered if you could help me.'

'Of course. In any way I can. What are you thinking of? We have a range of services and treatments. And I have a friend who works with me.'

'Sorry. It's not treatment I was thinking of, though I could certainly use some. I was wondering if you would be willing to foster?'

Broken

Sarah was taken aback. She'd guessed Sue had visited with something else on her mind. Gratitude was one thing but an unplanned visit so soon seemed likely to contain an ulterior motive. This however was way past unexpected. Before Sarah could respond, Sue continued.

'Let me explain. There are two boys on my caseload, twins. They've been with me for several years. They've stayed in care homes. They've lodged in foster placements but never stay. They're good boys … give no trouble, but they don't settle down and eventually run away. I've lost count of how many times the police picked them up from sleeping rough or found them wandering the streets. We have to put them back into safe houses. They need a special place because they're both complex in their own ways.'

'But fostering?' Sarah frowned. 'You're asking us to foster? Surely we're not qualified. The authorities haven't checked us out. I thought there were enormous hoops to jump through before you could foster? And anyway, it's not something we've ever even contemplated.'

Sue smiled. 'Being purely subjective and as a parent myself I'd suggest you're plenty qualified, but yes you're right. However, I'm sure I can sort out the legal side because we're desperate, and as a couple I'm confident of your character and stability.'

A quiet creak from above suggested John was on his way downstairs. A distant carefree giggle reached Sarah's ears along with the playful barking of Mags.

'I need coffee!' John called as he entered the kitchen, then, 'Oh, hello. I didn't realise we had … oh, I'm sorry. Its Sue isn't it. How's Graham? How are things?'

Sue stood and opened her mouth to speak, but still somewhat surprised Sarah cut in. 'John, Sue's a social worker … works in foster care. She's asking if we would foster for a while. She seems to think we're just the couple she's looking for.'

'Sorry? Fostering? Did I just hear you right?'

Ignoring John's questions, Sarah turned back to Sue. 'Like I said, we've never considered the notion of fostering, never came up in conversation, but you said they had complex needs?'

'Yes.' She paused again in contemplation. 'Look, I'm sorry to spring this on you. It must seem like a cheek that I'm asking for help when it's me that owes you a debt I'll never be able to repay. Perhaps it's not such a good idea,' and she rose to her feet.

'No, wait please,' Sarah insisted. With her interest piqued, Sarah needed to understand more. 'Perhaps you ought to explain why we are what you're looking for. Please, sit.'

'Are you taking this seriously?' John asked of Sarah.

'Well fostering *is* serious,' she replied. 'But I'm intrigued. I doubt if it's often the authorities come looking for specific people to foster. It's usually the other way around. There's more to this.'

Despite his earlier dismissive remark, John knew his wife, knew it had aroused her inquisitive nature, and she'd need more detail. 'Sue,' he said. 'You do realise we have two children already and a living to make that occupies a lot of our time, a business to manage. We've not been at it that long so its early days for us trying to settle. I guess I'm surprised at the notion but I'm also humbled that you've come out here. Clearly you think we can do this. But I'm not sure we have what it takes to dedicate the time and energy you'd be after.' John poured coffee into a mug and spooned in a little cream.

Sue nodded. 'I understand it's a big decision, but in my job you get a feel for the type of people you meet, and you trust your instincts about them. You see, after you left the hospital last night, William, my husband, and I stayed with Graham for the rest of the night. The wee boy fell asleep around half-past five, but we got to talking. Around seven o'clock I went home, leaving Will to stay with Graham. Working in social care keeps your brain involved even when you're not working. Just goes with the job. I was so moved by how you two helped, I'm afraid I looked you up. That's how I found out what you did for a living, therapeutic support and treatments, and supply of produce from a farm. I discussed it with Will over the phone a little later and he agreed it would do no harm if I raised the subject with you.'

Sue yawned. 'Sorry. It's been a long night.'

'You ought to be at home getting some sleep. I'm sure this can wait,' John suggested.

'No, its fine. This is on my mind now so I need to see it through. But, I'd better start at the beginning, I suppose. The twins, Jamie and Joseph Walker, are eleven years old but they've been orphans since they were five. We tried to trace the father but he's just disappeared, probably out of the country. Their mother, Marie, was an only child to older parents who are now no longer alive. But she herself died in an accident at home. As far as we can tell, Jamie, the youngest by fifteen minutes, was ill at home watched by his mother while Joseph was playing next door with a neighbour's boy. We can only guess that Marie was carrying Jamie downstairs when she tripped and fell.'

Sarah stared in horror at the telling of the tragedy while John paused in the middle of stirring his coffee. Outside,

Claire's giggling had stopped as Sue continued.

'Though Jamie was unharmed in the fall, he lay trapped under his mother until the neighbour found them a few hours later. Imagine his horror, staring at his mother as she lay dying. Social Services took the boys into care where a medic examined them first and then they were seen by a mental health nurse just to assess their wellbeing. Concerned for them as orphans, the nurse met them a few times. Whereas Joseph seemed to get past his grief within a brief period, Jamie hasn't spoken to anyone since that day. Retreated from the world in some ways. He's clever, always has been, and his academic achievement is as a normal eleven-year-old, but he refuses to speak. He was referred to the local mental health service who assessed him several times and finally diagnosed him with Elective Mutism. If you look the term up, you'll find its outdated. They call it Selective Mutism now but whatever the technical term, he just won't talk and we've not been able to help him through it.'

John spoke first. 'Do you think he blames himself? Would he have been old enough to come to that conclusion?'

'That's our view, and some Mental Health practitioners tried to explain that very idea to him. But it makes no difference. The other issue is the effect his silence has on potential carers. Jamie's mutism has an enormous power over people. They're unable to get any feedback from him, any communication of any form. No response. It will take dedication and patience to live with that lack of verbal interaction. He does as he's told at certain times, like washing, eating or school work, probably because he understands he needs to. But that leads me to the other side of the problem, his brother Joseph.'

Sarah and John sat at the table, engrossed in the tragedy Sue shared with them. Outside Claire giggled again and Sarah assumed she was feeding the birds. But the boys' story moved and intrigued Sarah, and her caring nature was shifting towards the possibility of what she, and John, could offer. But she first needed to hear the rest.

'Joseph,' Sue continued, 'has taken on some of his brother's behaviours. He seems to play twice as hard, as if he's playing for himself and Jamie. It's made him a little overconfident as he's been in a few scrapes. He also speaks for Jamie. He says thankyou on his brother's behalf. He asks for things on Jamie's behalf. He voices any discomfort Jamie has such as having a cold or if he's hurt himself. Besides his own, Joseph seems to have Jamie's voice. Identical twins can be extremely reliant on each other and I've seen many twins in my job, but not like these two. As for their knack of running away and not settling, it's as if Joseph is looking for the right place for them both, maybe just for Jamie.'

'So you can understand why I'm desperate and why I considered you, knowing the history of this place, and knowing how you found Graham when all his friends, me and his da and the police couldn't. You have the gift, I guess, the gift that my ma used to talk about. I'm hoping you'd both be able to offer something no one else can.'

John looked at Sarah and for several seconds they were silent. Then John spoke. 'You're asking a lot of us, and I'm sure you understand that. For myself, I'm very cautious about the idea, as I should be. We have to consider our own children as well … what impact or disruption it may have and as I said earlier, we are running a business which is our livelihood. It's clear how desperate you are, but it seems to me the obvious first thing is if we met them ... a formal introduction. How long would that take and where should we meet?'

Sue looked embarrassed when she answered. 'Well they're actually outside in the car. It was very presumptuous of me, but as it's the weekend, I thought I'd take them out for a drive. Graham's at the hospital with his da and I asked them both if I could pick up the boys and visit you. This sounds so awful of me. I'm sorry.'

It was Sarah who raised a dismissive hand. 'There's no need for apologies. Its fine. We understand it was all with good intention. So Jamie and Joseph are outside now?'

Sue nodded.

'Ok,' said Sarah. 'Now's as good a time as any,' and with that she stood and walked toward the doorway. But then she stopped. 'Sorry,' she said as both John and Sue rose to their feet. 'Can we just wait a minute? Sue, you said you understand what we do here. How much *do* you know, because we're just a normal family, really?'

'Normal?' Sue replied. 'I suppose you are mostly, but there is the gift. The ability to help others when normal ways fail. That's why I came here because the usual ways of helping the boys *have* failed. But if I do understand your gift, I think you can see inside a person in some way. When my mother used to visit Beryl, the old lady used to tell her things known only to my ma. Some of the deepest secrets or feelings my ma had, so even though I've not experienced this gift myself, I'm a firm believer. "There are more things in heaven and Earth", as they say.'

'Ok,' Sarah said. 'So on that basis, you'll understand what I'm going to do next without meeting the boys. Before we go outside, I want to grasp, if I can, how much of them

I can sense without their knowledge.'

'Sarah?' John fidgeted. He was uncomfortable with this approach. To him it felt like prying, an invasion.

'It's ok,' Sarah said to her husband. 'All I'm going to do is detect their aura, its colour, as a measure of their emotion. I'm not going to probe into their spiritual layers. Why don't you try? Y'know, like you have with me and Claire? I know you're able to limit your focus.'

'Not sure. This is different, people I've never met … children. What if I go too deep?'

'You won't, because your natural caution won't allow it.'

John gave a half nod and sighed. 'Ok.'

Fascinated by the discussion, Sue sat back down on her chair.

Taking Sue's silence as agreement, Sarah closed her eyes. She lowered her shield, that protective psychic barrier she used to block unwanted spiritual energy, and extended her thought. A short distance away, beyond, she guessed, the boundaries of the yard, she picked up the excited energy of whom she guessed to be the reporters. Perhaps they had driven out of sight and were clock watching, ready to pounce again at precisely midday. Ignoring them, Sarah withdrew the range of her focus and detected two more psychic energies. One was unknown to her but the other she recognised in an instant. This spiritual force represented an unbreakable connection, an energy that was an essential part of her own being and for that matter John's. It belonged to Claire. Mystified, she opened her eyes and with a frown stared at John, looking for understanding, but confusion furrowed his own brow.

'Are you sensing this too?' she asked.

'I did as you suggested and yes. Claire's out there, but why only one more?'

'Ok,' Sarah directed her question to Sue. 'You said both boys were outside?'

Again a nod.

'Well we both only sense one of them, so I think it's time to say hello. Please, after you,' and she stood back to let Sue lead the way.

In a rush Sue stood, confused and a little worried, thinking one boy had run away or was maybe hiding. She hurried into the hall. Once outside, the reason for Claire's giggling became clear. Over by Memorial cottage, Claire sat on the wooden bench next to one of the boys. They were both looking toward the old stone henhouse. While Claire laughed, the boy sitting next to her wore a mirthless smile – his face expressing little emotion. But on top of the henhouse the other boy balanced upside down, performing a very precarious head stand.

'Joseph, for heaven's sake, what are you doing?' Sue hissed. 'Come down from there before you go through the roof.'

Still upside down the boy spoke with humour in his voice.

'But I like it up here. The higher the better. You see different when you get high up. Looking down on things. It's different.'

Sarah laid a hand on Sue's arm. 'It's ok,' she muttered, confusion still creasing her forehead. 'It's quite strong.'

Though Sue had named one of the boys with her words of caution, it was obvious to Sarah and John, which boy was which. But what mystified them was the boys appearance. Not the physical aspects of clothing or hair colour, height or facial features. The appearance that puzzled them was that which would go unnoticed by most people – their psychic aura.

In one fluid motion, Joseph lowered himself back onto his feet. With the confidence of the young and caring little for the danger, he launched himself from the henhouse roof grabbing an overhanging branch in mid-flight. Holding the branch with ease, he swung back and forth a few times and finally dropped onto the ground. He stood still, staring at John and Sarah as if he were sizing them up, figuring out what kind of people they were. He was of slim build, almost as tall as Sarah – tall for his age. With blonde hair and intense blue eyes, his features were striking, and he wore the most disarming of smiles. Cheeky and playful. A happy child despite the tragedy in his life, and Sarah couldn't help but return the smile.

In a heartbeat Sarah took in these physical characteristics and more. To her inner sight, a widespread orange aura surrounded Joseph that spoke of vitality and vigour, good health and excitement. This seemed to depict the behaviour of the boy, backed up by Sue's information.

Joseph remained immobile as if he were waiting for a sign, while Sarah switched her attention to his brother Jamie. Sudden disquiet affected her mood, but its source was not Jamie, even knowing the child's history. Her distress was internal, her own, because Jamie was lifeless to her senses. He possessed no aura she could detect – not even a weak or faded manifestation of one. Neither could she detect any form of spiritual energy, nothing that spoke to her of a mystical life-force. But despite her promise to John and after a moment of probing a little deeper, what troubled her at a metaphysical level was worse, a level so deep that its effects registered only as a disturbance to her psyche. Rather than possessing no energy field at all, it seemed to Sarah there was the faint echo of one, but it had been ripped away leaving an emptiness that was void.

On an emotional level, Sarah felt that Jamie's soul had died.

Eight

'John, what time is it?' muttered Sarah.

'Nearly half eleven?'

'Ok. That reporter will be back in half an hour. We need to decide what we're going to offer them.'

Sue rummaged in the pocket of her coat and pulled out car keys. 'Reporters? Well, my advice is to give them just a brief statement and insist on no photographs. But I've kept you long enough, so I'd better take the boys back.'

'Sue?' Sarah said. 'You understand we can't give you an answer right here and now. We need some time to talk. It'll affect Claire also as she seems to have made friends already.'

'Of course. I'm asking a lot from all of you. It's a big decision and even *I* don't appreciate the full impact on your particular situation. And there's no immediate rush. You must take your time. I'll leave you my card. It's got my work and personal numbers.' Sue called the boys. 'C'mon you two. It's time to go.'

With a quick glance at John who appeared lost in thought, Sarah spoke once more. 'We'll give you our decision in a couple days. We don't want to keep you hanging on.'

'That would be lovely and thank you both again for yesterday, for finding Graham, and for listening to me today.' And with that, she bundled Joseph and Jamie into the back of her car and headed through the gates.

Claire sidled over to her parents and squeezed between them.

'I think we've just met two boys in need of help,' Sarah mumbled.

'Are we going to help them?' asked Claire.

Sarah looked at her daughter while John stared at the cloud of exhaust fumes dispersing beyond the gate. 'Well, that was their social worker we were talking to,' Sarah said. 'Did you understand what she was saying about fostering them?'

'What does foster actually mean?'

'It means that they live with a different family for a while, become a part of that family, until they're found a permanent place. It's meant to give them a safe and secure place to stay that's more like a proper home instead of being surrounded by lots of strangers in a care home. Does that make sense?'

Claire nodded before peering into her mother's eyes. A gentle smile touched her lips. '*Can* we foster them? Have you and dad decided?'

Sarah smiled back. 'That's what I need to discuss with your father, if he comes back to us?'

John continued to stare towards the gate and seemed

not to have heard his wife and daughter. In fact, he was not so much lost in thought as blind to his surroundings. Never once since his gift had awakened had he had any inclination or even dared to navigate the maze of spiritual energies emanating from anyone other than his immediate family. Doing so railed against his personal beliefs of privacy, though he accepted that Sarah was adept at doing so and had a level of control that far exceeded what he assumed he possessed. But his willingness to lay down this self-imposed rule at his wife's suggestion, to see into the hearts of two young strangers had come as a surprise, and perhaps it was his boundless trust in Sarah that allowed him to do so. Maybe guided by Sarah's own gift, he had delved only as far as the outer layers of Joseph and Jamie's spiritual energies to get a measure of their state of emotion. John found it easy to use this simple skill and was accomplished at doing so with his family and expected a similar outcome. However, the emptiness he perceived as he saw Jamie sat next to Claire filled his soul with sudden dread, and he withdrew in an instant. Even to his immature skill, it was clear something was wrong, a desolation where desolation should not exist.

As John withdrew his psychic probing, the vision of an empty soul faded along with his view of the driveway. Unaware of his surroundings, John wandered into a twilight world where memory became vivid recollections – live and unrestricted by time. Amidst the multitude of events that helped shape his life, one memory filled his thoughts, one long since buried. He saw himself sitting in a classroom at school being called out and led towards the principal's office. An unknown fear lay in his heart triggered by the behaviour of the school secretary – one usually chatty but now silent. Once inside the office, the door latched without a sound but his attention was focussed on his father who stood near the window, his face colourless and shocked. Weak and shaking hands grabbed his shoulders and a voice that came to him from a distance told him his mother had died in a car accident. The words held no meaning, had no power – they made little sense but something inside John retreated, searching for a safe place where self-preservation was all that mattered.

John's memory shifted forward to the morning when he had taken himself, along with his father's fishing rods, and spent a day in isolation. His father was beside himself with worry but John strolled in during late afternoon wet and chilled to the bone carrying a single fish that hung limp by his side. With desolation and pleading that turned his face into a mask of heartache, he said. 'I can't do this on my own.' From that day forth John and his father shared their grief and loss, their memories, their tears and laughter.

With the memory vivid in his mind's eye, John returned to the world of Manseburn and became aware that Sarah and Claire waited in silence. Staring through the gates and along the empty driveway, he understood that Jamie needed help in the same way that he needed it when he was a similar age. Joseph supported his brother as much as he could, but an eleven-year-old boy had limits. Now that John had seen a soul in need, he could not turn aside. His inherent caring and empathetic nature rose up, those motivations that led him years ago into a career where he'd hoped to use his energies to support others less fortunate. Put simply, he wanted to help, and more so now he understood the background and hardship the boys had endured.

'Earth to John,' Sarah said.

'What? Sorry. I was just wondering.'

'Wondering or wandering?'

'Come on, let's get some proper breakfast … or lunch.'

But Sarah wasn't going to leave it at that. 'You started to say something? Come on, what's on your mind.'

'I was going to say yes, lets foster.'

'Wow, that was a quick decision.'

'You just said it yourself, we've met two boys in need of help. I guess both boys have been shunted from one place to another, never settling, not having much chance to be outside, y'know having a garden. Isn't that what we enjoyed as kids, being outside in the fresh air? I know it's only one aspect of raising any child but they can get plenty of that here and perhaps I can teach them something about where food comes from, give them some skills, create better choices for them for the future. Plus,' and here John smiled. 'I'll need a bit of extra help in the coming weeks, some free labour.'

'You mercenary.' Sarah gave John the benefit of a steely gaze, but it soon gave way to a smile. 'So it's a yes then? Claire?'

'Yes please,' Claire said. 'I like them and I'd like to help.'

'Ok, its unanimous. Just imagine,' John said after a moment's pause. 'If Graham hadn't got himself in a fix, we wouldn't have gone looking. Sue wouldn't have come here. We wouldn't have met the boys.'

'Of course daddy.' Claire was serious for a moment as if John's inference was unnecessary. 'It was meant to happen.'

John nodded his agreement. 'I guess it won't be straightforward. We may even get turned down. But I guess we can offer them what they need. I know just having all this space isn't the be all and end all, the answer to their problems, but there's an opportunity to give them something a little different. Perhaps they'll feel safer and settled while they're here. And it horrifies me that Jamie has no aura. What's that all about? How can that be? I've not much skill but …'

'Yes, I know what you mean,' replied Sarah. 'and perhaps that's something else we can help with. But I don't think we should call Sue until tomorrow. I don't want to interrupt her Sunday any more than it already has been. Plus, it'll give us more time to talk it over. Tomorrow will do, so she can kick start what she needs to and let us know the final decision. Oh, damn it. That reporter's on her way back. I can sense it.'

'I'm making toast,' muttered Claire.

'Would a bacon sandwich be better?' asked Sarah. 'And the smell will drive those reporters crazy.'

John laughed. 'I'll cut the bread. You two always cut it too thin.'

Their ordeal with the reporter was less than they feared, though it delayed their breakfast still further. They answered a few questions and allowed the photographer to take photographs of the property but refused video or portraits. John insisted Claire stayed inside the house. By the time they left, breakfast turned into lunch so they gathered around the table with a full English. After tidying away and setting dinner to slow cook, a cooling breeze had sprung up and a steady rain began, isolating them with its grey blanket and blocking out the views. John made a quick trip into the greenhouse and then they settled for the rest of the day in front of a warming fire. September was drawing to a close and though October often brought mild weather, the shadows were lengthening and sunset would come earlier as each week passed.

Later that evening, they sat and watched the news broadcast in silence, and after it finished glanced at each other. Claire hadn't spoken throughout and John sensed her attention had wandered out of the room.

'Sweetie?' he asked. 'Do you have something on your mind?'

He waited for Claire to speak – experience had taught him she would only do so when ready.

'Something's going to happen,' she muttered. 'I wish we hadn't talked to that reporter.'

Nine

Jimmy Gillespie was irritated. In fact, his mood was worse than that. Raging may have been a better description. His Sunday evening lay in ruins. The unwelcome phone call from the care home where his aged mother lived, meant he'd had to leave Ayr Racecourse early missing a planned celebration of the winnings he'd collected.

His afternoon hadn't quite gone according to plan. After an early win, dead cert's failed to fill his pockets and what little cash he had left he invested on a tip off. Falling lucky for once, he'd expected to be in the club for the rest of the evening aiming to leave with one of the female bar staff. But the phone call wrecked his plan. So, leaving his friends in the bar with a story that one of his 'many' female acquaintances needed his help or, as he put it, was gagging for it, Jimmy screamed out of the carpark in his rusting VW Golf and headed towards Girvan. *For fuck's sake. What's the stupid cow done now?*

Broken

Jimmy was an only child and thoroughly spoilt by Linda, his mother. As a miner, his father Malcolm provided well for his unintentional family, but apt to remain distant, and demonstrated little of the paternal behaviour of a responsible father. Malcolm married Linda when she was twenty-nine, Malcolm being two years younger, but it took Linda four years to have a child.

A young Jimmy spent much of his early years alone with his mother who was overprotective and overtly affectionate. Since Malcolm worked long hours and varied shifts, Linda had little companionship. When her husband took extended time off work, he expected a lot of food, fresh clothes and time alone with his wife, though for Linda, this intimate time was never enough to satisfy her. Hence a frustrated Linda expended much of her desire for companionship on her son, gushing with overbearing motherly love.

The boy was comfortable with the attention until his father's death when he himself hit puberty. At forty-six, Malcolm's death certificate only confirmed the dangers of an excessive lifestyle, a poor diet and too much alcohol. After an acceptable period of mourning, Linda took the occasional lodger to help pay the bills, much to Jimmy's disgust. At the tender age of twelve, he took to burying his head under the pillows in both embarrassment and loathing at the sounds emanating from his mother's bedroom whenever she became over friendly with her guests. But worse was to come. Word soon spread of the free flowing nature of Linda's affections, and Jimmy found he either had to learn to use his fists at school or try to join in the jokes levelled at him. But one day enough was enough, and he floored a boy at school who stood several inches taller and was two years older, but it left him hating his mother for putting him through the pain.

Despite the triumph, Jimmy had few friends his own age, and those he did he found dull and weak. So to fit in with older boys he began fabricating tales. Anything to lift him into the upper echelons and help him run with the crowd. His tales involved fishing, swimming off the coast, earning excessive amounts of money from local farmers so he could buy himself the best and biggest, and of course girls. The latter had no name and conveniently went to different schools. But Jimmy was caught out in a lie all too often, though it didn't stop him. He just learnt to be more creative with his stories.

When Jimmy left school, he followed his father into the mine, but didn't stay long. The work was heavy for which Jimmy didn't have the stomach as he'd never had to lift a finger for himself during his childhood. Instead, he looked for something less exertive and began earning a wage in local shops before moving to a supermarket.

Though short in stature, he'd grown into a bright and blue-eyed young man with a shock of red hair that woman, young and old, found attractive. With a twinkle in his eye Jimmy discovered he could flirt with most woman with ease using a little cheek and a disarming smile. He also found that with little effort it was easy to seduce enough woman to satisfy his needs. Picking his targets with care, he developed a keen eye for those who he knew would fall easily to his charms. But being self-centred and shallow, Jimmy didn't have the capacity for commitment and so moved on if anyone threatened his independence.

His entry into gambling at the age of nineteen occurred when an uncle, his father's brother, took him to Ayr

Broken

Racecourse on a Saturday afternoon and lent him two twenty-pound notes. His uncle was a regular and introduced Jimmy to many of the bookies and runners, and everyone liked the bright-eyed young man for his attentiveness and enthusiasm. Luck was with Jimmy on that day, and he increased his forty pounds to a respectable four hundred. Jimmy made no offer to share the winnings or even return the stake, but he was hooked. Here was a place where he felt he belonged, and as often as he could he wangled a visit with his uncle or entered the place on his own to build his circle.

After a lucky streak, and with a back pocket bulging with money, Jimmy moved out of his mother's house, renting a furnished flat near Ayr town centre where he kept himself to himself when he wanted, answering to no-one. He used a local launderette for his laundry and lived off convenience foods. Jimmy had few visitors and seldom extended invitations, keeping his flat as his sanctuary and just clean enough to keep his landlady satisfied. With a disarming smile and a close fitting tee shirt, he found other ways of keeping her happy.

Once settled into his bachelor pad, Jimmy seldom visited his mother.

As time moved on, he became ever more adept at telling tales, sensing how best to weave a believable story to buy comradeship. For several years into his mid-twenties he continued on this path, working by day, pleasing woman by night, making money most weekends at a variety of gambling venues, and laughing with his drinking buddies at the Racecourse.

His lifestyle caught up with him one night, however, when after too many beers and with untimely bravado he crept into the back garden of a woman he'd been seeing for a while. Aiming for the place where the back door key lay hidden he let himself into the house. Many would have said that the beating he got from a suspicious husband lying in wait, a police officer with South Ayrshire Police, was less than he deserved. Jimmy ended up in hospital with suspected broken ribs, but an official complaint was far from his mind – he stood to lose too much. He also ended up with a police record, since a little extra focus from the 'wronged' husband discovered that Jimmy's car had expired tax and no MOT certificate and hence no insurance.

Raging best described Jimmy's mood and he convinced himself he was the victim. If the stupid copper was unable to satisfy his own wife, then why should he suffer for it. He was offering a service, one that seemed to have plenty of demand. But despite his anger, Jimmy was more careful in selecting his future conquests, staying clear of married women or aiming at those his own age. He joined a local gym, deciding that a few extra muscles would be helpful if he ever found himself in another difficult situation.

But as he approached his thirtieth birthday, a call from his mother's neighbour brought him to Ayr Hospital. The neighbour had driven Linda to the emergency department, and when Jimmy arrived, she explained that she'd heard screams from next door. The latest lodger, a man whom Jimmy met just once, had severely beaten his mother. No-one knew his name since Linda kept no record of those who passed through her doors. Linda's reputation was consistent over the years, but despite her continuing need for passion, her looks and energies were not what they once were. At the time of the attack, she had reached her fiftieth birthday and after speaking to his mother Jimmy put two and two together. It seemed she'd tried to become too friendly with the new lodger whose revulsion he took out on Linda.

Jimmy felt little emotion while sitting waiting for the nurses to dress Linda's wounds. Any affection or respect for her had long since gone, and though he harboured no specific ill will, he possessed no loyalty towards her – she was simply the woman that gave birth to him.

He stayed long enough to drive her home and then went on his way.

Life drifted on uninterrupted until two years later, another phone call brought Jimmy to hospital once more. This time, however, his mother had suffered an event from which she wouldn't recover. A stroke took her independence and affected her speech. With limited mobility, she was at least able to feed and clean herself, though managing her life without help was not an option. Conversation improved, if the listener had patience which didn't apply to Jimmy. He was more than happy to place his mother in local authority accommodation, spinning a good tale to the support agency why he was unable to manage her care. And so, with no guilt and no regret he devolved his responsibility to social services.

As Linda's health deteriorated still further, the authorities moved her to where she could receive more focussed care. She ended up in Girvan, in a compact and manageable room near the dining room of the same care home from where a cryptic but compelling note drew Sarah and her family into a new life.

Soon after Linda moved in, Jimmy received notification that any assets his mother possessed, her home, would need to be sold to raise a part of the funding. Even his inheritance, it seemed, was being snatched away. Once more he was raging. The stupid cow couldn't even die soon and leave him something. Infuriated at what he saw as life's injustice, he just left the legalities to a local agent.

Once the sale was complete, the agent called Jimmy into the office to take possession of a number of documents that were found at Linda's house. Jimmy had instructed his representative to sell everything, he wanted no reminders of his childhood years, but in his wisdom the agent recovered papers that looked important and handed them to Jimmy. Thanking the man without enthusiasm, Jimmy took them home and threw them into a cupboard where he all but forgot about them.

Jimmy paid a short visit to his mother on birthdays and at Christmas, but seldom at other times and when he hit his thirty-third birthday, he responded once more to a call from her carers. He hoped with little compassion it would be for the last time.

Ten

Later that Sunday evening, while Sarah, John and Claire settled in front of the fire, sheltered from the gusting wind and driving rain, an irritated Jimmy Gillespie slammed his car door and ran across the car park to the main doors of the care home. Margaret, the receptionist who greeted Sarah almost two years earlier on the day she found Beryl, looked up and groaned to herself.

'Hello Jimmy,' she said with a forced smile.

'Hi Margaret. Y'know the one thing about not seeing you very often is that I keep forgetting how pretty you are.'

'Jimmy Gillespie, the one thing about not seeing *you* often is that fortunately I forget what a terrible flirt you are.'

'Me?' Jimmy said with hurt surprise. 'I don't know what you mean. I'm just expressing my pleasure at your charms.'

'Behave or I'll have you thrown out. I take it you're here to visit your mother.' Jimmy confirmed with an abrupt nod. 'Well, around tea time she became rather agitated so we thought it best to call.'

Jimmy didn't care much, but the chance of staring at Margaret's jumper softened his earlier rage.

'Nae bother,' he replied. 'A chance to see you is always welcome.'

Margaret had had enough so pointed along the corridor. 'Be off with you. You know where she is, and be kind for once.'

Jimmy turned away, believing the only kindness would be if the old woman died. He made his way toward her room and with a sigh of irritation opened the door.

Inside, Linda sat lopsided and leaning forward in a chair staring at the television with such intensity, Jimmy thought she would bore holes in the screen. He banged the door shut with little consideration to the noise he made. Linda jumped and turned toward him with sudden animation.

'Jimmy,' she slurred. 'Thank god you've come. You won't believe it. You won't believe it. Come … come … sit down. The news is coming on again.'

'What news. What are you on about? I was busy, you know.'

Linda stared at him, her head nodding from side to side and a slight tremor shaking her hands. 'Listen to me. The news. It's nearly on.'

'Yes, you said that. So what's so important about the damn news?'

Linda's reaction took Jimmy by complete surprise. For years, even when he was young, she tended to be subservient and accepting of her social position, expecting nothing grand from life. But tonight she summoned aggression from somewhere within and rounded on him.

'Jimmy, you fucking eejit, shut your mouth for once and listen to me! Show some patience and you might hear something useful! The news will be on again in a few minutes. You'll see for yourself why you're here!'

Despite her infirmity, she glared at him and banged her fist on the arm of her chair. Jimmy was so taken aback he found nothing to say and in exasperation collapsed onto the edge of the bed.

In the distance, the hall clock chimed just as the theme for the local news began. Linda returned her intense gaze to the television and muttered, 'Wait, just wait, Jimmy. Wait.'

Jimmy checked his watch and rolled his eyes as the newsreader gave a rundown of the day's headlines. A heartwarming story of a family who risked their lives to save a missing young boy. A severe crash on the A77 came as no surprise. Job losses at a local store as a national retail company closes a number of its outlets, and a school expanding their vegetable growing plans for the autumn.

'There it is,' said Linda. 'Wait and listen.'

The theme music stopped, and the newsreader kicked off with the item on Graham Campbell, a head and shoulders school photograph displayed on screen.

Ten-year-old Graham Campbell from Ayr, reported missing yesterday, was found in the early hours of Sunday morning by local hero John Macintyre with the help of wife Sarah and daughter Claire. Graham sustained minor injuries to his leg and was discovered in a homemade camp down on Greenan shore. A keen angler, Graham told police he had decided to go fishing on Saturday afternoon but had fallen and cut himself on scrap metal washed up by recent storms. With strong winds and rising tides, Graham had been unable to walk to safety and had hidden under the cliffs. The Macintyre family went in search for

Graham following advice from daughter Claire who, as a friend of Graham, guessed where he may have gone. Rescued by the coastguard, our correspondent was told that a few minutes later and both Graham and Mr Macintyre could have been swept away by the unusually high tide.'

'It is unclear why the Macintyre family did not call the authorities, but Graham's parents told us they are just happy and grateful to have Graham back safe and sound,'

At this point, a picture of Manseburn taken from the driveway entrance replaced the photograph of Graham.

'Interviewed at Manseburn, their home and business premises near Straiton, the Macintyres' declined to make any comment other than to say they only did what any other caring parent or local citizen would have done.

'Manseburn is reputed to be a place of mystery and is something of a local legend, with the Macintyres' taking up ownership only last year. The business running there today continues a longstanding and traditional health and well-being service set up by generations of the same family, though services ceased some twenty years ago when the then resident retired. The current owners have revitalised the local alternative therapy services and along with a small market garden have already built a successful livelihood.

'Legend has it that in the seventeen hundreds the original owners of Manseburn were descendants of paganists offering services similar to those offered today.'

At this point, the newsreader smiled.

'Maybe the finding of Graham Campbell owes something to this legend and the mysteries surrounding Manseburn.'

Linda was beside herself, but Jimmy just stifled a yawn.

'You see ... did you see?' she yammered.

'I don't see anything. Just a story about some kid who was dumb enough to get himself almost drowned. So what?'

Broken

Linda jabbed at the remote and the TV screen went blank. She turned to her son, but once more her head and hands shook. When she spoke it was with extreme effort and concentration – an attempt to get her words out and make her Jimmy understand.

'Listen Jimmy. Just listen. There are things I need to tell you. Things I've kept quiet all these years because there was nothing I could do about it. I didn't know what to do even if I could.'

Jimmy figured that the quicker Linda got on with her tale, the quicker he'd be able to leave, so he stayed quiet.

'I've got letters. They're in a big envelope. You probably never saw it. Letters, I say, ancient ones. Not written by your dad or his dad. A lot older. From way back during the war, the great war. Your grandad gave them to me because he couldn't trust your dad. He gave them to me to give to you if one day they would help. Now listen. I remember what he told me about your past, where your great, great grandpa used to live. He used to live there.' Linda pointed to the television.

'What,' asked Jimmy. 'Where did he used to live? What are you on about?'

'There at that farm, where that family live.'

'The family who saved the boy? So what if he did? What's it got to do with me?'

'Be quite and listen. A hundred years ago, your great, great grandpa William was master of that house. He lived there with his family. I have letters. I read them years ago, but I still remember what they said. I couldn't do anything about it. I didn't know how, but you can. My life's over, but you have a chance.'

Linda stopped for a moment to catch her breath and

take a drink, but then in a quiet voice continued.

'The letters were love letters to a mistress he had. His mistress is why you are here because she got pregnant with your great, great grandpa. She started off your family. And because your great, great grandpa was master of the farm and you are his great, great grandson, you have rights. You have a claim on the farm. It's partly yours or even all of it because back then everything was passed down to sons. Don't you see? You need to make a claim. Your Grandfather gave me the proof because there's more than just love letters. There are other letters you need to read, but your grandpa didn't know how to claim and it was too late for him. You must do something. It's part of your inheritance. You can make something of yourself. Jimmy, do you understand?'

For the first time since he was a child, Jimmy Gillespie began to pay attention to his mother. For the first time for years she appeared to be making sense, if only because what she said involved the possibility of making some money. But he was cautious. The old lady had said nothing of any interest to him for years, and he had questions.

'Ok,' he said. 'I hear you, but how do you know it's the same place? There must be hundreds of farms around here that look like that one. It could be anywhere.'

Linda became excited once more, her expression urgent. 'I read the letters remember, and there are photographs too. The letters spoke of a farm above Straiton. Find them Jimmy and read them before it's too late.'

Still sceptical, Jimmy wondered if his mother was rambling and heading for another stroke. 'Ok so what did you do with these letters then? Where did you put them?'

'I told you. In a big envelope. They were in the house.'

Jimmy convinced himself his mother was confused. He'd found no large envelopes when he emptied the house, he was sure of that. Surely the crazed old woman was wrong. But then he cast his mind back over a year to when he'd been told he needed to sell the house to support his mother's care. He'd passed responsibility for the clearance and sale to a solicitor. The solicitor kept him informed of every stage of the proceedings which included handing Jimmy an envelope that contained what he, the solicitor, felt were important and personal papers. With the return of that memory, Jimmy's interest increased. All he wanted now was to escape, go back to his flat and hope he hadn't thrown the envelope in the bin. He stood and opened his mouth ready to give an excuse to leave, but Linda hadn't finished.

'Wait,' she said. 'There's more.'

Jimmy raised his eyes and sighed. 'What else. I need to go home and find those papers.'

'Margaret,' Linda said.

'Margaret who? Margaret on reception?'

'Yes, that tarty girl you're always chatting too.'

Jimmy thought that was rich coming from his mother. 'What about her?'

'Ask her about Beryl.'

'For Christ's sake, who the hell is Beryl?'

'Talk to Margaret. There used to be an old woman staying here. She stayed here for years before I came. Her name was Beryl. Funny old witch. Had lots of stories she'd tell to anyone daft enough to listen. But she used to be the owner of that cottage until she died, or so I was told, and she'd passed it on to her family. The news said the farm had been in the same family for years and that must include your great, great grandpa. Which means whoever is there now will be related to you. Work it out.'

Jimmy's hopes took a leap. 'Ok, that figures if it *has* been in the same family for years. But what has Margaret got to do with it?'

Linda was shaking again, her hands unable to stay still, and she yawned, her efforts making her tired. 'She used to spend hours with the old woman. She must know a thing or two that might help.'

Jimmy remained standing and stared at his mother. His mind was racing now. If this Beryl had indeed owned the farm and one of his relatives owned the place a hundred years ago, then it was likely he did in fact have a claim on the property. He needed to search for the letters, but before he left, he'd speak to Margaret.

Linda was now silent and still. Having related her tale and drained herself of energy, she appeared to have fallen asleep. This suited Jimmy because he could leave without having to impart any pleasantries – time he'd prefer to spend chatting to Margaret. Within his sordid mind, he warmed himself with fantasies of Margaret, who, in his narcissism, would tell him everything he wanted to know. He slipped out of the room and hurried towards reception. But his anticipation soon turned to irritation when, instead of Margaret, an older woman lounged behind the counter, sprawled across it like a heap of discarded clothing.

'Oh. I was expecting to see Margaret. Has she left?' he asked, trying hard to be polite and light hearted.

The woman glanced with little interest at Jimmy and blessed him with a one-word answer. 'Yes.'

'Ok. Well maybe I'll catch her tomorrow.'

'No, you won't. Not here at any rate.' Then the woman

appeared to liven up a little and shared a piece of information that, she must have thought, would raise her standing as a source of knowledge. 'No, not here but she'll be working at that place that was on the news. Did you see it? The one where that family lives … the ones who saved that little boy. What was it called?'

'What, Manseburn?' Jimmy had paid attention to the news report.

'Yes, that's it. She does reception there a few mornings a week. She used to know the owner.'

A voice called through from the office behind reception.

'Alison! What have I said about personal information?' A well-dressed woman appeared in the doorway, a woman Jimmy surmised as management. 'You must not give out any personal information about staff or residents without knowledge of who you are talking to. Not without the proper authority. It is against the law, for heaven's sake.'

'Sorry Mrs Kendrick.'

'And who are you?' Mrs Kendrick questioned Jimmy.

'Gillespie. Linda is my mother.'

'I'm sorry, Mr Gillespie. It's not policy to give out information about residents or members of staff. I'm sure you understand.'

'My fault,' Jimmy feigned an apology. 'I'd asked about Margaret but I can catch her later in the week.' And at that he turned and left, thinking 'silly cow told me enough anyway'.

Eleven

Half an hour later, after racing home along a dark and often hazardous A77, Jimmy ran into his flat and headed straight for the cupboard where, some eighteen months previously, he thought he'd thrown the envelope.

Typical of thick-walled stone buildings, inset cupboards lay either side of the fireplace in the living room of his one-bedroom flat. Built into the wall itself due to the depth of stone, the storage areas had open shelves at the top and doors at the bottom. Jimmy used the shelves to keep spirits and a few glasses, but the cupboards were blocked at one side of the fireplace by the TV and the other by an armchair. Unsure of where to begin, Jimmy wrestled the armchair out of the way and yanked open the doors. Amidst the dust and cobwebs he found nothing but an old rucksack bulging with hard core porn magazines. Muttering obscenities, he shoved the rucksack back and slammed the door.

With more care, he rolled the large screen television out from the opposite corner and pulled at the doors. The hinges were rusty and stiff from lack of use but withstood his aggression and the doors creaked open. Inside were papers he recognised. These were documents relating to the tenancy of his flat, and to the sale of Linda's house. The sale documents were familiar because the solicitor insisted he read and understand them before he signed them. Along with his tenancy agreement, he grabbed them and threw them into the middle of the living room.

Then a smile creased his lips.

Half buried under an old coat, he spotted the corner of a large brown envelope that in fact looked more like a padded jiffy bag. He reached inside and pulled it onto his knees before standing.

'Gotcha, ya wee bastard,' he muttered.

Jimmy crossed the room and placed the packet onto his armchair before reaching for a glass and a bottle of single malt. Before settling, he placed the discarded papers back in the cupboard and rolled the TV into place. Taking a large gulp of whisky, he savoured it for a few seconds before swallowing. As the heat hit his throat, he breathed out through pursed lips.

'Huh, who'd have thought it. Now ... what have we got?'

An hour and three large whiskies later, Jimmy's face wore a drunken smirk. On the floor lay the love letters he'd found. He'd read through them in case they contained information of use. Most, however, were just that – love letters. Sentimental crap. There wasn't even anything pornographic in them he may have found interesting. Not like the texts he sent to girlfriends. But on his lap lay what he thought important. To begin with, as Linda had recalled, there was indeed a photograph. Black and white, creased and faded around the edges, but it showed a cottage at its centre, with a small derelict croft and an even smaller stone building to its left. The photographer must have been some distance away, maybe where the entrance to the property lay, but fixed to a post in the foreground, a clear hand painted ornate sign said Manseburn.

Jimmy inspected the photograph with care because there were differences. He recalled the news item, and the photograph shown on television. That image had shown a brick porch attached to the front of the main house, with a new barn erected to the right. But in his mind, and comparing it to the photo in his hand, there was little doubt it was the same place. And confirming his conclusion, on the back of the photograph a printed stamp marked the image with the name of the printer and the words 'Manseburn Farm, Straiton, February 1912.'

The letters nestled on his lap included several from a William Gillespie addressing a solicitor named James Abernathy of Abernathy and Castellaw. William Gillespie was the man Linda hinted at as Jimmy's great, great grandfather. These letters were hand-written and dated between 1914 and 1915. Jimmy read and re-read them but the final letters contained acknowledgement from the solicitor that Mr Gillespie had the right to claim ownership of Manseburn, and Mr Gillespie's instruction to begin that claim against the current owner, Mrs Celeste Gillespie nee Drummond. The forwarding address that Mr Gillespie gave for correspondence was not Manseburn but one stating c/o Mrs H. Dowie.

Jimmy puzzled over this address for a short while until he remembered what his mother had told him, and he laughed. The dirty old bastard was shacked up with another woman, and the claim was against his own wife. But then Jimmy didn't understand why Manseburn belonged to the wife Celeste and not his great, great grandpa as the head of the household. But he gave it little thought because the claim never happened, otherwise he, Jimmy, would be living it up in the sticks instead of a poxy one-bedroom flat overlooking a railway yard. The only reason, Jimmy guessed, that the claim had not gone ahead was because the old fool kicked the bucket.

Jimmy now knew what he needed to do. In the morning, he'd put the feelers out for a cheap solicitor who'd take up his claim based on information in the letters. As for now, and fired up with confidence and lust, he grabbed his mobile and called his female friend from the Racecourse. Right now he needed a woman, and he didn't care how late the hour.

Twelve

The following morning, Sarah and John packed Claire off to school and slipped routinely into the day. The weather hadn't changed, though the strength of the wind had increased still further and the rain now flew in horizontally from the northwest. John insulated himself and headed outside while Sarah checked her appointments for the day.

The first client wasn't due until ten o'clock, so she had time to call Sue and give them their decision. During their lazy afternoon both Sarah and John had at times thrown in a comment about the negative side of fostering, playing devil's advocate to be sure they were making a measured decision. But by bedtime they'd not changed their minds, and Claire had said nothing. The ten-year-old made her decision from the moment she understood what fostering meant. Sue's response, it appeared, was a mixture of delight, gratitude and guilt. Sarah, John, and Claire had done so much for her already but Sarah understood the reason Sue had considered them in relation to temporary care for Joseph and Jamie. They were the perfect caring family who could offer a stable environment, especially since there was a measure of urgency to the case.

As Sarah finished her conversation with Sue, Margaret arrived for her early shift, followed by Rachel. As always, they gathered in the kitchen for tea and a chat before heading for the barn and the therapy rooms.

Rachel was quiet, just stood at the sink holding a mug and staring out at the rain while Sarah asked Margaret how things were at the Care Home.

'The same really,' Margaret said. 'Except for Beryl. I still miss chatting to her, even though it's well over a year since she left us. She was there when I first started as a teenager, and even *then* she used to talk about missing relatives. It took ten years to find you.'

Sarah nodded. 'I believe it took ten years for the time to be right. Beryl was ill, she needed to bequeath all that she had, so she needed to find me. But this is where it gets intriguing. Was I mugged to make it easier for Beryl to sense me? Or was she aware of me, anyway? In which case, why didn't she contact me beforehand.'

'Ripples,' Rachel muttered.

Sarah laughed. 'Oh you're awake then.'

With a smile, Rachel turned her attention back into the room.

'Ripples,' she repeated.

'What do you mean?' asked Sarah.

'If I've learned something from you over the past eighteen months, its cause and effect, coincidence versus destiny, action and reaction.'

'Deep. Go on.'

Rachel glanced outside at the rain and for a few seconds said nothing. She appeared preoccupied.

'Well,' Rachel said after a short pause. 'There's a big puddle over by the old cottage? I was watching the rain landing in it. There's a leaf in the middle and it keeps floating this way and that according to the ripples. Our lives are like that leaf. We're moved according to things that go on around us.' Rachel turned back to her friends. 'Sometimes when you ponder your life and remember the things that've happened to you, you realise and … well, perhaps accept that the course of your life is a mix of choice and destiny. Many things happen through choice, like the kind of work you do, where you live, who you marry. You can choose these things, but then, for example, what *is* it that makes a person choose a line of work. I was happyish, doing what I was doing back in Wolverhampton until your gift awoke, Sarah. And choosing where you live. I wanted a modern apartment in the city until stuff happened and I realised it was actually soulless. Also who we marry. We fall in love with people we like the look of and sometimes decide to marry. But then what is it that brings us together with someone.' Rachel paused and looked at the floor. Sarah and Margaret waited for Rachel's thoughts to continue unravelling. 'I know I'm rambling,' she said. 'But I wonder if our choices are only presented after some divine intervention has set us on a course. Something happens in life that presents the opportunely to take a particular job. You're looking for a place to live just when the right place comes up for sale. Events happen that lead you to the person you marry. Do we really have much choice, y'know, choice that's based utterly on what we *want* to do, rather than what's laid before us?'

Sarah replied with a blunt question. 'You may be right but does it matter?'

'Does what matter?'

'If you ultimately have choice, or if your choices are forced upon you after events put you in a particular situation.'

Rachel opened her mouth to reply but clamped it shut again.

Sarah continued. 'Just rambling myself, because it's down to personal belief which no one has a right to question. Some people will argue blindly everything they do is their choice … end of. Others would say yes, but you only have that choice because this or that happened first. For example, I couldn't live in a London apartment unless I had a good salary. And that would be countered by, how did you get to the position where you earned a load of money … fate or choice. You see, it all comes down to belief structure. You can be a fatalist, you're on a predetermined path and there's nothing you can do about those major life changes, or you can believe that everything you do comes from within, wholly as your choice. The arguments for and against are endless. I believe it's a mix, but then I'm philosophical about it … it is what it is and I don't think too much about the reasons why things happen. Anyway, what brought this on?'

'Not sure,' Rachel replied as she glanced out of the window once more. 'Maybe the rain. It's a bit bleak out there and winter's getting closer.'

'And?' Sarah asked. She could sense by her friend's mood there was more to it than just Monday blues.

'Well, I was thinking about my little family unit this morning. How it all came about. I was thinking about what a brilliant father Pete is. Then I began wondering about *my* father. Why he left, what he's doing … is he still alive?'

'Wow. In all the time we've known each other, you've never spoken about your father. Why now?'

'I guess it's being a parent. It focusses the mind.'

'Have you any notion of trying to find him?' Margaret asked.

Rachel shook her head. 'No. I know nothing about him at all. What's the point. We're talking thirty years plus. We'd have nothing to say to each other.'

'Seems to me you'd have a lot to say,' Sarah said. 'A lot of questions.'

'Maybe. But after all this time?' Rachel peered at the clock and drew in a deep breath. 'C'mon, its time I was over in the barn getting ready.'

Margaret drained the rest of her tea and stood. 'Yes. I'll nip over and open up. See you in a minute.' And with that, she draped her coat over her shoulders and disappeared outside.

'Are you ok, hon?' Sarah asked.

'Yes, yes, I'm fine. Just having one of those pensive moments. It'll be fine once I'm busy. You coming over?'

'Yes. I'll just wash these things up and join you.'

'Ok. See you in a minute.'

Just after lunchtime, before a two o'clock client arrived, the house phone rang. John answered. He'd finished eating and was contemplating his choices for the afternoon with a view on the weather when a voice at the end of the phone spoke.

'Mr Macintyre? I'm sorry to trouble you. This is Mrs Abernathy, one of the school secretaries. I'm afraid there's been an incident during lunch break.'

'An incident? What, with Claire? Is she ok?' Sarah, who was eating a bowl of minestrone, looked up, her spoon in mid-air. 'What's going on?' she demanded.

'Yes, Mr Macintyre. She's fine but there's a boy who isn't. Could you come in to discuss it with the principle? Better done face to face.'

Without hesitation, John agreed and cleared the call.

'What's happened?' Sarah asked again.

'She wouldn't say over the phone except that Claire's ok but another boy isn't. I'll go down and bring her home. You've got a client arriving soon, anyway.'

'Yes, otherwise I'd go myself.'

'No worries. I've done most of what I wanted and the weather's getting worse.' Grabbing his keys and a coat, John headed out into the rain with a 'Won't be long'.

The incident, as Mrs Abernathy put it, occurred in the school playground during lunch break after the children had eaten. A lull in the rain meant everyone headed outside for some welcome fresh air.

Claire was minding her own business chatting to a group of friends when from behind a loud voice jeered.

'Look here, it's the witch. Yah! Where's the broomstick, witch?'

Caught mid-sentence Claire stopped talking. She noticed her friends shift their focus and the slight widening of their eyes didn't escape her attention.

'Hey. Witchy. What did you eat for lunch? Bats or frogs.'

A smattering of laughter arose in response. For the benefit of her friends, Claire raised her eyes and shook her head. She recognised the voice. It belonged to Fraser Anderson, a boy known for his bullying, his scheming and his record of poor behaviour. It was only by chance he hadn't been excluded by the school governors. Fraser was in the same year as Claire but a different class. Until now Claire had avoided him, mainly because she'd sensed with innate intuition that he would be a drain on anyone's wellbeing. But something must have happened and here she was, the centre of his attention.

'What's up witch, afraid to turn round in case everyone sees your hooked nose and warts?' Another spate of laughter.

There was no escaping the inevitable confrontation so she turned to face Fraser.

The stocky boy stood a few inches taller with a broad chest despite his junior years. With an aggressive sneer distorting his face, he stood with feet apart. Half a dozen other boys stood behind, each laughing at the joke, though in reality they knew how good-looking Claire was with her blond hair, piercing blue eyes and soft features. Claire stared straight at Fraser and held his gaze for many moments. Then she shifted her attention to each of his followers. With her inner sight she sized each boy up, measuring their strengths and motivation and what she saw made her smile. Of the six boys tagging along for sport, Claire understood that four would rather be elsewhere. They had not their leader's conviction, but joined in simply to conform.

'What are you smiling at?' Fraser demanded. 'I know you. I saw your house on the telly last night. That old place up in the hills. My dad says there's been witches there for ever. He said back in the old days they used to burn witches … or drown them cos they were evil. You ought to drown cos you're ugly. And how come you found that kid that got lost. No-one knew where he was, but you found him. Only witches do that. What you say lads, shall we dip her in the swimming pool see if she floats?'

Fraser took a step towards Claire and with a large grubby hand shoved her backwards. He spoke in quiet tones now, more threatening.

'I bet your mom and dad are ugly too, covered in warts. How bout I catch you after school and dip you in the Loch.'

Claire recovered her balance and stayed silent, just stared at Fraser with a half-smile still on her face.

'Oi!' Another voice, but one that Claire recognised. She turned, and her smile broadened. Flying down the steps from the school entrance came Joseph followed in a more sedate manner by Jamie.

'Leave her alone!' Joseph yelled and headed for Claire. Jamie strolled over and stood by her right shoulder as Joseph came to a halt by her left.

'Butt out you two,' Fraser said but then recognised the twins. 'Oh look who it is. Newcomers. What is it? Do you fancy witches?'

Joseph took a step towards Fraser but it was only then that Claire spoke. 'He's not worth it. Just leave him, and anyway I don't need any help.'

Joseph retreated as if he understood and accepted that his recent acquaintance knew what she was doing. Jamie did not move but simply stared at Fraser as he sneered again.

'Ah, chicken shit. What you gonna do anyway. Save the ugly witch and her ugly family.'

'Y'know, there's only one ugly here,' Claire sighed, staring straight into Fraser's eyes.

'You saying I'm ugly, you bitch. You'd better not be

alone after school cos your friends won't help you, especially that freak.'

'What did you say?' Claire demanded.

'Him. The freak that won't speak. He won't help you.'

It was only then that Claire reacted. This was tiresome and pointless. She hated this behaviour, couldn't understand it. She cared little for name calling. It only reflected a weakness in the person responsible, so she had always ignored it when aimed at herself, albeit rare. But labelling Jamie as a freak annoyed her and with little forethought she lashed out.

Maybe it was easy to blame Claire's actions on too many TV fight scenes, or perhaps she understood there was only one shot at getting rid of Fraser, but with her antagonist so close and leaning toward her she reacted. With her left fist balled she drew her arm back and threw a punch straight into his stomach. When a grunt of foul breath hit her in the face, she stepped back and brought her right arm around with as much force as she could muster and followed through with a satisfying crunch to Fraser's nose. The pain flared in her knuckles and she jumped backwards bumping into Jamie while rubbing her hand with the other.

Fraser howled in agony while gasps of surprise and not a little admiration rang out from the crowd of onlookers. When a teacher emerged from the building Fraser began to cry.

'You broke my fucking nose you bitch!' he wailed.

'Fraser Anderson. We'll have none of that language here. What's going on?' It was Mr Wilson, head of sports.

Claire stopped rubbing her hand and lifted her voice.

'It was me sir. I hit him. He was being nasty about my friend.'

Broken

When Mr Wilson saw the blood, he turned to one of the playground attendants and said, 'Mrs Barron, would you ask one of the secretaries to open up the first aid box please? Fraser, go inside and get fixed up while I sort this out.'

Mr Wilson descended the steps and approached Claire as she stepped forward, while Joseph and Jamie moved in and stood beside her, an action that signalled unconditional support. While he had a chance, Joseph whispered in her ear. 'That was awesome!'

On her other side, Claire felt searching fingers touch her own and without hesitation grabbed hold of Jamie's hand.

Thirteen

By the time John had driven to school, spoken to the principal and returned home, it was almost four o'clock. He and Claire had spoken little on the way, lost in their own thoughts. John had listened to a retelling of the incident at school but decided he'd wait until they were home before talking to Claire. This was the first time his daughter's behaviour had ever warranted a phone call from school and John found himself wandering in unfamiliar territory.

Claire sat staring out of her side window engrossed in the drops of rain skidding backwards across the glass, tracking random patterns before flying off into the unknown. She was reflecting on the situation as her great grandfather Hamish would have done. Her hand still ached and though her action wouldn't be her usual chosen course, what was done was done, so she put the incident to one side and with quiet detachment watched the water dance beside her. However, her spiritual layers blazed with activity, her senses firing off in every direction. For a brief moment she touched her father, but he was quiet, as he concentrated on driving and she understood he preferred to keep his spiritual gift closed – maybe guarding. She stretched beyond the confines of the car towards her mother but only detected mild concern. Little Robert was also quiet. Though he was too young to communicate using normal means, he and Claire were linked by more than blood. They were the product of an extensive line of spiritually aware ancestors, with gifts still untapped. But from deep within Robert, she detected a deep understanding of her actions and took it as support.

But one thing that kept coming to the forefront of Claire's more earthly senses was Jamie's unexpected behaviour. Though they had met only briefly when Sue brought he and his brother to Manseburn, Claire had developed a connection to the twins. Joseph, with his playful and friendly nature, was a young boy that everyone would take to with ease and Claire was no exception. But Jamie was different. Without knowing what he had been through, she sensed his pain and with natural empathy wanted to help. But he was almost invisible to her. She had tried to touch his soul with delicate probing but there was little to touch or so it seemed. However, Jamie must have felt something within Claire that inspired his need to offer his hand after Claire punched Fraser. Within a corner of his heart, he must have decided it was a way he could show support – a tentative physical touch. Whatever Claire did or said, or her behaviour during their visit to Manseburn, had reached beyond Jamie's voluntary shield and maybe triggered an emotion. Whatever the reason, his sensitivity puzzled and touched Claire, and his action brought her comfort.

'Almost there sweetie,' John said. 'We've got egg, chips and peas tonight. Something simple. Are you ready for it?'

As if rising out of a dream, Claire blinked her eyes as she realised where they were. She turned towards John and loosening her seatbelt a little, stretched up and kissed him on the cheek. 'Yes please. I'm hungry now. Is there some apple pie left?'

'Yes, enough for a big piece each.'

'Dad?'

'Yes,' John wasn't sure how he felt about being called dad after years of daddy, but had to accept his daughter was getting older.

'I'm sorry.'

John reached over and squeezed her hand as they approached the driveway. 'It's ok angel. I understand as I'm sure your mom will too. Do you want to tell her or leave it to me?'

'I'll tell her.'

Claire relayed the entire event to Sarah only leaving out the part where Jamie had offered his hand. Once she'd finished, John added, 'I'm afraid she's excluded for two days as a lesson. She didn't break the kid's nose. Just blooded it and I guess given him a black eye. But they have strict rules and said they can't tolerate behaviour like that, even though they had witnesses to Claire standing up for the twins. But if you remember we've heard of this kid from other parents and the troubles he's caused. It's just a damn shame he saw the news last night. I did wonder if an interview would be a bad idea.'

'C'mon John, keep things in perspective. You saved a

boy's life, its local news. You can't diminish it all because of one badly behaved child.'

'So, sweetie,' Sarah turned to Claire. 'Neither your father nor I are going to lecture you because what you did was for a reason. You know you should never start a fight but on this occasion you certainly ended it. How's your hand?'

'It still hurts. Did I break it?'

'No, otherwise you wouldn't be able to move your fingers. It's only bruised. I'll sort some arnica out to put on it for a few days. Anyway it's time for dinner.'

It was past six o'clock when they had finished eating, and while John ran a bath for Robert, Claire helped Sarah wash and dry.

'We ought to get a dishwasher like we had back in Penkridge,' Sarah said. 'On the other hand, I don't mind the view out of this window and washing up gives me time to think. What do you say, sweetie?'

Claire picked a plate from the drainer and dried it with a tea towel. 'I think we're going to get some news.'

'News?' asked Sarah, then the phone rang.

Shaking her head at her daughter's occasional and unnerving precognition, Sarah dried her hands and picked up the phone. A familiar voice greeted her with a cheery 'hello?'

'Mrs Macintyre? Sarah?'

'Yes. Is that you Sue?'

'Yes. Sorry to call at this hour but I wanted to tell you straight away that we've got the go ahead to plan the twins placement.'

'Oh wow, that was quick.' A sudden nervous pang

fluttered in Sarah's tummy despite their agreement to help.

'Well no time like the present and best before they wander off again,' Sue replied with a laugh. 'What we need to do first though is an arranged supervised visit … bring the boys to stay for a few hours, a proper visit so we can all see how everyone interacts.'

'Ok, that makes sense. If you're in a hurry how about this coming Saturday … a non-school day.'

'Yes, if that's ok with you. I'm sure I can arrange it and confirm it with you tomorrow.'

'That's wonderful. I'll talk to John and Claire. There's plenty to do around here so we can keep them busy.'

'Wonderful and thank you so much. I'll call tomorrow. Bye.'

'Bye, bye.'

'Are Jamie and Joseph coming to live with us?' asked Claire as Sarah closed the call.

'Well, it's not confirmed but they're spending the day with us on Saturday, to see how we all get on. Then if that works ok … well, I don't know what happens next but we'll soon find out. Now, I think your dad's finished in the bathroom so how about you get showered or bathed and we'll settle in. I think this weather's in for the night. Time to light the fire.'

Fourteen

'Sweetheart?' called Sarah. 'Are you ready? We need to get to Ayr and back before the twins arrive.'

It was early the following Saturday and everyone was up and ready for the day even before the sun rose.

'Coming,' shouted Claire, thundering down the stairs.

John wandered into the kitchen with Robert secure in his arms.

'Won't be long,' Sarah said. 'Just need school shoes for Claire. I'll be back well before they arrive.'

It was just before eleven when Claire announced, 'they're here'. She had been waiting in the kitchen, peering out of the window every few minutes. John was in the utility room pulling on wellington boots while Sarah was placing an online order for therapy products.

Claire trotted out of the kitchen and opened the porch door with a smile. A gust of wind threatened to drag the door out of her hands but she pushed it back and slid the door stop against it. A spattering of rain blew in but she cared little. Sue drove through the gate and brought the car to a halt in front of the barn. Almost before the car stopped, Joseph threw open his door and launched himself out, a smile spreading across his face. Jamie waited a few moments for Sue to apply the handbrake and turn off the engine. Only then did he open the door and climb out.

Sarah and John joined Claire, and they stepped outside to greet their guests. Joseph sauntered up to Claire and raised his hand in a high five gesture. Clare responded in kind.

'That punch of yours is the talk of the school,' he said. 'No-one's gonna mess with you again.'

'Joseph,' Sue chastised. 'We said we wouldn't talk about that didn't we.'

Ignoring Sue's remark, Joseph turned to John. 'So what are we doing today? Can we help?'

John smiled at the boy's enthusiasm. 'Yes I'm sure you can. There's always work to do, even in the rain.'

'Great, we've got wellies. We were bought them. Jamie wants to pick veg. He likes carrots. Weird if you ask me because he likes them raw.'

Joseph turned to speak to his brother and found he had walked away. Jamie stood gazing at the garden spread out within the stone walls of Memorial cottage. Many of the plants had faded but other late flowering varieties were still attracting a few bees. Claire approached and stood next to him. To Sarah and John's surprise and with obvious tenderness Jamie touched Claire's hand and opened his fingers for Claire to take. It was clear Joseph also witnessed the moment, but he kept quiet—just smiled.

Broken

Touched by the gesture Sarah cleared her throat and spoke. 'Well c'mon everyone, shall we get out of this weather and decide what to do? Sue, can we offer you a drink? Will you be staying all day?'

'No. I'll leave you to it. I wouldn't normally leave under these circumstances and please keep it to yourselves but I'm sure you won't have any problems. If you need me, call.'

With that, Sue jumped back into her car leaving a somewhat dazed Sarah and John alone with two young boys who were in essence complete strangers.

'C'mon everyone,' Sarah repeated. 'Let's get inside and we'll make some plans.'

By the time Sue returned at four o'clock, the boys were showered and hungry waiting for an early dinner. Claire and Joseph were playing a game of Jenga while Jamie sat on the sofa holding a playful Robert on his lap.

Despite the lowering cloud and stiff breeze, the two boys had helped around the farm. Apart from a few heavier showers, the rain had eased long enough for Joseph to help John harvest late potatoes and carrots and clean them ready for delivery. They kept some for their own use. The boy chatted constantly as if, as Sue suggested, he had conversation enough for two people – himself and Jamie. And he was a keen and a quick learner, unafraid of getting dirt under his fingernails. Jamie, on the other hand, and in quiet contentment helped Claire with other chores – feeding and clearing out the chickens, hunting for eggs and checking over the two pigs they kept. Without understanding the cause of Jamie's silence, Claire was, nevertheless, at ease with holding one-sided conversations with him, realising early on that though the young boy chose not to speak, he understood and reacted to whatever Claire said.

When the rain finally settled into a steady downpour just before three o'clock, they retreated to the house and to the smells of fresh baking and a stew simmering on the Rayburn.

Once everyone had cleaned up, Sarah asked if either of the boys wanted to help in the kitchen. With a passing glance at his brother, just long enough for a single breath, Joseph nodded. Jamie stood and followed Sarah. Remembering Joseph's comment about raw carrots, Sarah gave Jamie a knife and a handful of carrots and asked if he would prepare them for dinner while she washed and prepared potatoes. She worked over the sink leaving the boy to his own devices but once she had peeled and dropped the potatoes into a pan and submerged them in water she said, 'How's it going? Are you all done?' With a smile she saw a large pile of carrot chunks ready to steam, and a handful of carrot strips in a separate pile.

'Oh wow, that's brilliant. How did you know we preferred chunks rather than slices? Not sure if you've ever tried broccoli but would you chop that for me please? Oh and I'll get you a glass for your carrots.'

Sarah placed a large broccoli in front of Jamie and asked if he wanted a drink. Jamie looked into her eyes and held her gaze for a moment. Still blind to his inner self, Sarah wondered if the boy was performing his own subconscious analysis, checking her out, wondering, perhaps, if she was someone he could trust. With sudden dismay, she imagined for a moment what Jamie had been through and the horror of it made her shudder. Maybe on a subterranean level she picked up a spark of raw spiritual energy. Whatever the source may be, it left her with a now familiar and unwelcome nausea. But the light in the boy's eyes calmed her spirit – made her wonder if underneath Jamie's chosen withdrawal lay a boy aware of the motivations of those around him, aware and cautious, but also desperate – desperate to belong.

'I think,' she said, 'you would like to try some of our own elderflower cordial. It's a drink we made a few months ago from fruit we foraged. Its fresh with a little tang to it, but it's worth a try.'

Sarah made the drink and dropped ice cubes into it before handing it to Jamie who had already prepared the broccoli. Jamie took a cautious sip and then downed the rest in one go.

'I call that a success,' and Sarah smiled. 'Right, as we have apple crumble keeping warm, I could do with some help to make up the custard. You up for it?'

A glint in the eye was all she needed.

When Sue arrived, Sarah and John ushered her into the living room while the twins and Claire ate dinner. The three adults sat with tea and biscuits and discussed the day.

'How has it been then,' Sue asked?

John was the first to reply.

'Easier than I expected. It's one thing to have one of Claire's friends around for a few hours or even overnight but another when you're contemplating fostering. I wondered if it would make me behave differently but I don't think it did. Without any agreed plan we split them up, unless they did that themselves. Joseph helped me out in the fields while Jamie stayed with Claire. She's quite taken with him, and I found being with Joseph easy. He's keen to learn and quick at it. It's clear he enjoys being busy with his hands. I'd like to believe I gained his trust too.'

Sue said nothing to lead either of them but turned her focus to Sarah who was silent for a while as if gathering her thoughts. Once more she pondered how spiritually invisible Jamie appeared to be but also reflected on the message she'd seen in his eyes.

'Well, I spent less time with both boys. Less than John and Claire but I found them both to be polite and friendly, courteous, keen and very likeable. To go deeper into the question, Joseph is so confident and direct it's easy to like him. What an amazing boy for one who's only just a little older than Claire. He seems very protective of his brother but doesn't pamper to him. He encourages but seems to respect Jamie's need for silence and simply relays what he understands his brother wants. He has a strong character which I guess is not surprising. But Jamie is closed to me. I can't read him or see him with my gifts which concerns me. He's locked himself away so deep, to protect himself from further hurt I guess, and again that comes as no surprise. However he's also a quick learner and keen to please. There was a moment when I suspected he was checking *me* out but of course the twins will have trust issues. John said it went easier than he expected. I'd agree with that. You'd have to ask Claire how she got on with Jamie but I felt relaxed around him. Even though he refuses to speak, he appears able to communicate simply by behaviour or expression. I like them both enormously, and knowing what we are all capable of, I'm sure we're in a good position to help.'

Sarah looked across at John who nodded his agreement.

'I take it this means you're happy to go ahead?' asked

Sue.

'It does,' replied John. 'And from whenever you can make it happen.'

Sue drained the rest of her tea and rose from her chair.

'I need to discuss with the boys what they want and then make a few phone calls. Until I've done that I can't say much more but it sounds like you've all had a wonderful day. Can I see the children on their own?'

'Yes, of course,' answered John. 'You know where the kitchen is. Help yourself.'

When Sue had left the room, Sarah asked John for his thoughts.

'It doesn't seem like five minutes,' he said. 'When I scoffed at the idea of fostering, but I'm so used now to change and shifting beliefs that I'm not surprised to say I'm looking forward it. These two have had a terrible start yet it's not turned them into troublesome kids. Y'know ... wayward. Troubled maybe. Joseph may have more of a wild streak but in essence he's harmless. Just a typical boy but he was so interested today, so keen, and I repeat what I said earlier in the week, we *can* offer them something a little different.'

'Glad you said that because I agree, and I'm really concerned about Jamie, well and Joseph but for different reasons. Joseph's future may be in jeopardy if he's not able to make his own life because of caring constantly for his brother. And if Jaimie doesn't get help, how will his life work out?'

Sarah stared at John but her focus was on the kitchen. 'Y'know,' she continued. 'I can sense three people in the kitchen, just three.'

'Yes, I know. Last weekend when Sue brought them

here, remember you lost me for a minute just as they left? Well I was searching the car as they drove away and I only sensed two souls. It was that experience that settled my mind ... made me wonder about helping. These boys are special and different in a way that makes them stand out to me. What did Sue say? They'd diagnosed Jamie with Elective Mutism. If I understand the term, that means he's chosen to be the way he is and maybe the only way to help a boy like that is to place him with people like us. And Claire can help perhaps more than we can. It's obvious she's connected with them already, more so to Jamie. And dare I say it? It's almost like fate has brought us all together ... that old destiny thing again. Right place, right circumstance, right time. Huh. And all because of a young boy lying hurt in a cave with the tide coming in.'

'Oh my, what has happened to you?' laughed Sarah. 'Well, we're both of the same mind and Claire is too. Let's hope the boys want to give us a chance.'

As soon as Sarah shared her hope, the living room door opened and Claire ran through dragging Jamie behind. Joseph followed on their heels.

'Mom, dad. Guess what?'

'Yes sweetheart,' asked Sarah.

Claire turned to Joseph and nodded.

'Mrs Macintyre? Mr Macintyre?' he asked with exaggerated but sincere formality. 'If it's ok with Mrs Campbell, me and Jamie would like to come and stay here.' And then his face lit up with a cheeky grin. 'We've had a wicked day.'

Knowing his wife, John stepped up behind her and took her hand. Sarah had to bite her lip to keep the emotion from spilling over and left John to answer.

'Joseph, Jamie, we'd be happy to have you stay for as long as you want. Oh … and it's been a pleasure having you here and thanks for your help.'

Claire turned, grabbed both of Jamie's hands and pulled him around in a crazed dance. The boy turned on the spot though his face displayed little emotion, just the traces of a smile. But Sarah noticed his eyes were fixed on Claire's, staring without blinking.

Sue had followed the children somewhat more sedately and spoke with caution.

'Now listen boys. Joseph, Jamie? I need to clear this with the authorities. I know they'll listen to my recommendations even though it's going against all the rules about careful vetting and choice of foster carers. So it's not yet certain. I can't say yes or no at this moment but I'll make some phone calls while you're at school on Monday. I can't do it any quicker than that.'

Joseph fell quiet and glanced at his brother before noticing his hands, hands that clung to Claire's as if he did not want to let go. Joseph nodded his head once.

'Jamie understands,' he said. 'And he's grateful for everything you do for him. And so am I of course. We know you'll do your best.'

'Why thank you young man. I will do my very best. Now, it's time to get you back. Let's leave these good people to talk.'

Half an hour later, Claire was reading to Robert who, now fed, watered and bathed, lay tucked up in his room ready for sleep. John and Sarah had stoked up the fire and sat quiet, busy with their own thoughts. Sarah was drawing her focus inwards trying not to become too hopeful, but

John appeared unable to settle and had become restless.

'Would you like a drink?' he asked. 'Alcoholic or would you like some tea?'

'It's bleak out there tonight so how about a wee dram to warm us. Let's celebrate the success of the day?'

'Brilliant idea,' John replied and wandered into the kitchen to fetch a small jug of water.

Due to a mix of the late season and the blanket of heavy cloud, dusk was well underway, and he flicked on the kitchen light as he entered the room. Taking a jug from one of the wall cupboards, he half filled it with cold water from the tap, but as he turned the water off and lifted his head to gaze out of the window, something caught his eye.

Across the driveway, a few feet inside the entrance gate and half hidden within the shadows stood a figure. So immobile was the silhouette that John blinked thinking the half-light and his imagination were creating a vision. But then a thin stream of mist escaped from the top of the shape. Whoever was out there wore a hood, and with hands thrust into deep pockets as protection against the wild weather appeared not to care about being visible.

In a moment of clarity John recalled his dream and a surge of adrenaline punched him into action. He banged the jug onto the kitchen table and with sudden and irrational rage rushed into the hall. By the time he'd yanked open the front and porch doors and stepped outside, the figure had disappeared.

Seconds later and disturbed by the noise, Sarah walked into the hallway and found John standing a few yards away from the house, drenched by the pouring rain.

Fifteen

Earlier in the week, on the day Claire had defended the twins and bloodied the nose of Fraser Anderson, Jimmy Gillespie called in a favour.

Over the years he'd used his skills of charm and negotiation, and when that failed, his threats, to get co-conspirators out of trouble or supply them with whatever dodgy stuff they needed via other co-conspirators. This meant he'd built a network of associates who owed him, and Jimmy took care to keep this balance of favours on his side. With little deliberation, he knew who had contacts within the legal system and who could source a cheap consultation – a no win no fee arrangement. The result was an hour with a junior solicitor who took copies of the letters and indicated there appeared to be merit in raising a case. With inherent arrogance, Jimmy took this to be confirmation that he would make money out of the claim and after receiving agreement to investigate further, walked away wearing an enormous grin. He did not hear, or chose to ignore the solicitor stating that though a case could be made, property claims were far from simple and the results even less certain.

Following what he felt as a successful day, Jimmy was on a high until the following Friday when he received a phone call about his mother. This time it was a voice he did not recognise.

'Mr Gillespie, this is Heather McGee, care home manager. I have some news for you but it would be better if you came to see us. I'd rather not talk over the phone.'

As always when it came to his mother, Jimmy had no patience, and compassion was a concept unfamiliar to him. Despite Linda's revelation about Manseburn, he had no interest in sharing any of the proceeds. The money would all go to him anyway because his mother was tucked away safe and sound in the care home. The only thought that passed through his mind was 'for fuck's sake, what now?'

'Can't you just tell me? I am very busy,' he replied.

'Mr Gillespie, I'm sorry but I'd prefer to speak to you face to face.'

'Look,' Jimmy said. 'I could make it tomorrow evening. No earlier.'

'I'm afraid it won't keep that long.' When Jimmy didn't reply, Heather sighed. 'Mr Gillespie, I'm sorry to say that your mother passed away a short time ago. Since your last visit, she'd been unsettled, quite agitated, and because of her weakened state suffered a heart attack. It was all over in a few moments. Please accept our condolences.'

Jimmy lowered the phone for fear his jubilation may escape. A smile spread across his face. *This week's turning out to be great.* But then a squawking voice brought his attention back. He tried to soften his tone.

'Ok ... well, thanks for letting me know. What do I need to do?'

'Well, if you come in to see us, we can discuss the next steps and offer advice or contacts for funeral services. I know how hard this can be but is there anyone else you would like me to contact, perhaps another family member?'

'No,' Jimmy was abrupt. 'There's no one else.' He paused for a moment before continuing. 'Look, I'll re-arrange things and drive over now.'

'That would be very helpful,' Heather said. 'And once again my sincerest condolences.'

Jimmy didn't hear the final words because he'd already ended the call.

Collecting Linda's belongings, of which there was little, obtaining copies of the death certificate and arranging the funeral didn't take Jimmy long and he'd finished just past lunchtime. He agreed with the Funeral Director, more for appearance, to a single line in the local newspaper and a small wreath to go with the coffin. A cremation was agreed, and the service set for the following Friday, just a week away.

Later that afternoon, Jimmy received a call from the solicitor who told him that a letter of intent to claim against the current owners of Manseburn had been posted first class and that he would keep Jimmy informed as soon as any news was forthcoming. It was only after the phone call when Jimmy sat propping up the bar of his local hostelry, that the thought occurred to him a visit to Manseburn might be a good idea. The television news had revealed its location as near Straiton, fifteen miles from Ayr, but Jimmy needed to see it for himself, on the quiet. The day was getting on and he'd already drunk too much, so he made plans to sneak up under cover of darkness on Saturday evening.

With anticipation and arrogance, Jimmy drank more beer and celebrated with a curry.

Twenty four hours later, Jimmy waited until after sunset before leaving the flat. He was in no rush and for once drove with care around the lanes from Ayr through Kirkmichael towards Straiton. Slowing the car still further as he entered Main street, he noticed the pavements were devoid of life, the inclement weather keeping the inhabitants indoors. He drove past the Black Bull, making a mental note to have a pint on his way back, and crawled out of the village, passing a school on the left and a cemetery on the right. A few hundred yards past the cemetery, he rolled past a layby and then appearing out of the gloom reflecting the glare from his headlights, he spotted a sign just before a driveway on the left. 'Manseburn', it read. Jimmy grinned, put his foot on the accelerator and drove past looking for a convenient place to turn. After a few hundred yards and having no other choice, he pulled into the entrance to a field and looped around, bouncing the front wheels up the grass verge on the opposite side of the road.

To make as little noise as possible, he kept the car slow, labouring in high gear, and crept back to the layby before pulling into it and coming to a halt. It was only a short walk back to the driveway so Jimmy climbed out of the car, flipped the hood of his coat over his head and pulled the zip up to his chin. At a brisk trot, he arrived at the driveway entrance in less than a minute and turned up the hill.

Lined with sturdy fencing, the drive was longer and steeper than he expected, and by the time he reached halfway, he gave up running and stopped to catch his breath. At a more leisurely pace and listening for any sound of a vehicle, he continued at a steady walk and after five minutes spotted the glow of a light. With a furtive glance around, he backtracked a few yards and made his way to the right, crossing the drive and climbing over the fence. Skirting around a field to keep out of sight, he made his way to the rear wall of a large barn. One step at a time he crept around to the front, and scrutinised the courtyard and the rest of the property.

For the first time he understood the scale of Manseburn. The main double story croft, the huge converted barn and what looked like the ruins of an old cottage.

I could flatten that, he thought, *and use it to park the cars.*

The light he'd spotted from the top of the drive came from a small lamp that lit up the entrance to a boot porch at the front of the large house. The entrance faced the barn, positioned as such to shield the front door from the prevailing winds. To its right he saw the warm glow of soft lighting from one of the rooms. A living room, he guessed. In one of the upstairs rooms a similar glow shone, but dulled behind drawn curtains. As he watched, a woman appeared in front of the downstairs window, raised her arms and pulled heavy drapes across to seal out the wild autumn weather. Silhouetted against the lighting, for a moment he saw straight through the clothing Sarah Macintyre wore and a familiar thrill quickened his heartbeat.

Fuck me, Jimmy thought. *I could use a bit of that.*

With the occupants now sealed inside, Jimmy crept closer to the house and circled around it, noting every detail. He memorised the position of every entrance – peered through each window to get a sense of what rooms lay where and scanned around the property as far as the darkness would allow. Deciding that enough was enough, he walked without concern towards the ruined cottage, only pausing long enough to urinate inside the old entrance. He then strolled back across the courtyard and stopped at the top of the drive by the entrance gate, turning around to survey the property one last time, convinced that soon it would all belong to him. But as he stared back, bright lights appeared in a room on the opposite side of the entrance, a room he now knew to be the kitchen. Into the glare of overhead spot lighting walked a tall man, blond hair, heavy set. Jimmy guessed who the man was based on information he'd seen on the television. But as he sneered, the man glanced up out of the window and stared straight towards Jimmy.

For a moment, the man seemed frozen in surprise, unmoving, and at this distance, Jimmy knew his own face remained hidden. But then, as John Macintyre broke free from inaction and raced out of sight, Jimmy understood it was time to disappear. Before John had crossed the hallway and opened the door to the boot porch, Jimmy Gillespie was fifty yards along the driveway, running downhill like the wind.

Sixteen

By Tuesday evening, three days after Jamie and Joseph spent the day at Manseburn, and while Robert lay asleep in his bed, Sarah, John and Claire began tidying one of the spare bedrooms in readiness for their guests. Sue telephoned earlier that morning with the news. She told Sarah that because of the urgency of the case – there was a danger Joseph would take Jamie on walkabout again – she managed to convince the local authority safeguarding team that the Macintyre family could offer them a safe and caring home for as long as required. The recent news item concerning Graham Campbell's rescue only supported Sue's argument as it indicated the caring nature of the family. The only question requiring an answer was when the move could take place, and John had mouthed 'next Saturday?' to Sarah who relayed their eagerness.

And so, later that day, they began clearing out one of the unused bedrooms which had become a dumping ground from the day they moved in over a year ago. The bedroom was sizable and had plenty of space for two single beds, which the local authority would donate.

'Should we give the walls a coat of paint?' Sarah asked John.

'Well its clean and bright anyway, as it was when we moved in so let's not get too carried away. You still have clients and I have work to do. Anyway, for the twins I suspect it'll seem like a mansion compared to other places they've been in. If everything works out well, then maybe we can ask them what they want later.'

As a family, they worked on the room as time allowed, but by Friday evening, the makeover was complete. Bright blue curtains, plain but heavy enough to keep out the winter chills with matching bed linen. The carpet had been in the cottage when they moved in, but it was clean and thick with a comforting underlay. Neither Sarah nor John knew what personal possessions the boys possessed so made no attempt to dress up the room. When they were settled in, John suggested, they could ask if there was anything they wanted. The only additional items were those Claire suggested. The first was a Celtic Shield Knot she'd made at school and woven onto a paper stencil from strips of leftover wool. This, she explained, was to ward off evil spirits. A large Rose Quartz crystal was the second item Claire donated and she placed it on a chest of drawers they'd brought with them from their house in England.

'But isn't that the piece Nana left for you?' Sarah asked.

'Yes,' Claire replied. 'But I want to share it with the twins, especially Jamie. It was a gift from Nana, and now it's a gift from me. You know what it's for, don't you?'

'Of course. To promote deep inner healing and

feelings of peace. That's very thoughtful of you, sweetheart. I think it'll make a lovely gift.'

Just before eleven on Saturday morning, Claire carried Robert into the kitchen where her parents sat waiting rather nervously.

'They're here,' she announced, which freaked John as it always did.

'How do you do that?' he asked. 'I haven't heard a sound yet.'

'Dad, I can sense them. You know that. They're driving through the village. Oh, and the postman's here too.'

'Surely you can't sense Archie driving through the village!'

'No silly. I've seen him coming through the gate.'

Sarah stifled a laugh and stood to greet Archie as he pulled his red van up to the house. She walked out onto the yard.

'Morning Archie. How are you today?'

'No bad, hou's yersel? Hou's yer man and the wains?'

'They're good. Anything interesting today?

'Maybe. There's a brown envelope from a solicitor. In court again? Caught at last?'

'Och aye,' replied Sarah, slipping into local dialect. 'It's because of the drink.'

'Och, there's no crime in a wee dram,' and they both laughed and bid their farewells.

Sarah wandered back indoors carrying the mail but left the door open as she herself sensed Sue and the twins as they turned into the driveway. She dropped the pile of letters on the hall table and called to John and Claire who joined her outside under the terrace roof.

Once more Joseph opened his door and stepped out almost before Sue brought the car to a halt.

'Hello again.' A flash of white teeth and eager eyes. 'It's great to come back. Are you really going to let us stay for a while? Hope so. Jamie's talked of nothing else all week. Hard to keep him quiet, even at bedtime.' There was a twinkle in his eye as he teased.

'Joseph, please.' Sue rolled her eyes in exasperation as she climbed out and opened Jamie's door.

'It's true,' Joseph exclaimed. 'He talks to me all the time.'

Sarah probed the twins as she had done when she first met them, but there was no change. Joseph was alive with psychic chatter, which matched his vocal conversation in intensity. Jamie however, remained hidden.

'Claire?' she said. 'I think Joseph's impatient to see his room. Would you like to show the boys where they'll be sleeping?'

'Ok mama,' she replied, slipping into local dialect herself.

Sarah took Robert from his sister and raised her eyebrows at Claire's use of a new family label. *Mama? Oh my, she's getting more Scottish by the day.*

'Come on you two. I'll show you around,' said Claire, and leaving her parents alone with Sue, raced Joseph up the stairs while a more sedate Jamie paused long enough to stroke Robert's head before heading for the stairs.

Sarah and John exchanged a glance.

'See how affectionate he is?' said Sue.

'So it seems,' agreed John. 'Ok, so what do we need to do now.'

Broken

There was in fact little to do. Sue went through the legal papers, but John had the feeling she played lip service to the process. Mindful of the need for safety regarding child placement, in this case her confidence in the Macintyres' was without question. From what John understood of the twins situation, this was almost their last chance before the possibility of being separated. With sudden realisation, he understood the enormous responsibility they were undertaking – all three of them.

An hour later, after Sue left, the three children headed outside to wander around the farm and explore every corner and beyond. Before letting them loose, John mentioned two rules, the first to stay away from the road. Even though it was a minor road, some drivers still used it as a racetrack, driving at inappropriate speeds. The second comprised of two rules rolled into one – stay within earshot and enjoy themselves.

Claire acted as guide and explained everything to them, including Memorial cottage and the part it played within their family history. Joseph appeared taken by it and fell quiet for a few moments.

'We don't have a family history,' he said without emotion. 'I don't think we had a Nana or Papa.'

'You must have at some time. Maybe they don't know about you,' Claire said.

'Who knows,' and Joseph paused for a minute. 'But anyway ... what's next. Shall we race up the hill?' And off he shot without waiting for an answer, running through the gap between Memorial cottage and the main house. With a shout, Claire took off in hot pursuit.

'Cheat,' she yelled. 'You didn't warn me.'

At the sound of Claire and Joseph's laughter, Sarah

glanced through the kitchen window and spotted Jamie as he walked through the entrance to the old croft and into the garden. He wandered to the rear and came to a halt in front of the Celtic Cross and the plaque that lay at its base.

For Rose.
For ever.
Mama, the search will never end.

Amber, 1701 to 1802

With no sign that Claire and Joseph were returning from their antics, Sarah strolled out of the house and across to Jamie.

'Hi sweetheart. Has the plaque caught your eye? It's very interesting, isn't it? Has Claire explained the history? We only found out about it last year and it came as a complete surprise. Maybe one day I'll tell you more, though there's lots we still don't know.'

Jamie hadn't moved. His eyes were locked on the inscription as if it was important, though why Sarah did not know. But then she knew little of Jamie. He may be given to moments of introspection, but for a moment Sarah was at a loss of what to do next. She didn't want to touch him in case she disturbed him, but instead turned away meaning to wait by the entrance in case he needed her. But as she turned, searching fingers caught at her own and clasped them. Sarah sensed affection and need in the grip and without hesitation took Jamie's hand and held it. Five minutes later, Claire and Joseph found them when they returned from the hillside out of breath and at a more leisurely pace than when they left. Then at the same moment, two voices disturbed Sarah and Jamie, and in unison they let loose their grip on each other and turned.

The first voice was from a breathless Claire as she called, 'Is lunch ready yet?' The second from John, who stood at the front door and called with a voice full of surprise and annoyance.

'Sarah, you need to see this. That letter Archie delivered, the one he joked about? Well, he's right. It *is* from a solicitor.'

Seventeen

'But how is this possible?' Sarah said, waving the letter in the air. 'Who is this, and where has it suddenly come from?'

They sat at the kitchen table after sending Claire and the boys out onto the terrace with a sandwich. John was dismissive and surprisingly calm, considering the content of the letter. 'Just some bullshit.'

'John,' Sarah chastised. 'The kids.'

'Well look at the header. It looks as if it came from a back street solicitor than a practice of any standing.'

'Doesn't mean its fake. What if it's legitimate? What would we do? This is our home and livelihood.'

John reached across the table, grabbed Sarah's hand and subconsciously lowered his shield as on a deep level he sensed the disturbance in Sarah's wellbeing. Though he understood little of his gift, he opened his soul and felt the chill surrounding her heart dissipate.

She stared at him. 'What did you do then? You never

did that before.'

'What? I just held your hand.'

'You did more than that.'

'Ok. I wasn't really aware of what I was doing. But isn't that what you do when you love someone?'

'Who'd have thought it. That you would turn healer.'

For a moment they sat as they were, basking in the wonder and strength of their spiritual energy. But then Sarah sat upright and stared once more at the letter. It contained an official legal intention to make a claim on the ownership of Manseburn by a James Bryce Gillespie. Based on a dispute concerning entitlement to profit from property, where the claimant was not the same as the legal owners, the claim had its basis on recently discovered documentation dated between nineteen fourteen and nineteen fifteen and written by a former resident. The original resident's name was given as William James Gillespie, who lived at Manseburn between eighteen ninety-four and nineteen sixteen. Late in nineteen sixteen William Gillespie passed away, and the letter claimed that ownership should have passed to William's son John, and not remained with William's wife Coral Mary Gillespie.

As Sarah re-read the letter, recollection triggered deep within her memory – recollections from a conversation she'd had with Beryl as she listened with amazement at a tale she had never imagined. Beryl spoke of her own grandmother Celeste and her mother, though she hadn't named the latter. Maybe the family tree would help.

'I need to check the names,' she muttered.

'Sorry?' John said.

'My side of our family tree. One of these names, Coral Mary,' and here Sarah pointed at the letter. 'is familiar. I just want it clear in my head who this Jimmy is?'

'Why? Are you taking this seriously?'

'I don't know. Aren't you? We can't just ignore it. ' Sarah stood and left the room. 'Wait here a minute,' she said from the hallway.

They'd kept both family trees in a large and secure metal box at the back of John's wardrobe. They'd discussed whether to have them placed with the family solicitor for safe keeping, but decided they wanted easy access so kept them in the house. Sarah returned within a few minutes and rolled open the precious paper. John held onto a corner while Sarah traced her finger over the list of names.

'Yes,' she said. 'Here she is. Coral Mary was Beryl's mother. William James was Coral's husband, and they had two daughters, Beryl herself and her older sister Amber. So the names make sense, but who is Jimmy? How does he think he has a property claim?'

'The best thing to do is hand the letter to our own solicitor. They're the experts, and will know what to do. *We* need to consider what to do if the claim is legitimate. What you said earlier is true. This *is* our home, our livelihood. If necessary we'd have to buy him out but what that entails who knows.'

'But this doesn't make sense. William James had two daughters and the family tree mentions no-one called Jimmy. There's Amber who didn't have children of her own. Instead, she raised my grandmother Jade. Jade had one child who was mom, and she's the only one with two children.'

John shrugged and shook his head to acknowledge his own confusion.

'But hang on.' Sarah closed her eyes and frowned with concentration. 'Beryl told me her dad wanted a son. What was it she said? He wanted a son and heir and became embittered that he'd never had one. She also said he was older than Coral ... quite a bit older, so maybe had old-fashioned ideas, y'know needing a son to carry on the family name. Well, old-fashioned as we would think it. Beryl said he and Coral drifted apart.'

They fell silent for a few moments while outside the care free chatter of young voices drifted through the open doorway. But then John spoke in little more than a whisper.

'Oh my God. Sarah, you realise what your suggesting.'

Sarah shook her head. 'What?'

'If they were drifting apart, perhaps he had a mistress. It would have been commonplace then. If he didn't get what he wanted from his wife, maybe he tried elsewhere and had a child, or more than one. There could even be a string of relatives lurking around!'

Though a shocked silence fell between them, their minds raced with unspeakable possibilities. Was it possible a related family member possessed a legitimate claim to Sarah and John's inheritance? If so, was there a chance of losing their home if the courts upheld the claim. And how many otherwise unknown relatives could they have?

John eventually broke their silence.

'Look. We've got to stop this. This isn't helping. Outside, there are two boys who have only just arrived. We need to give them our full attention. There's nothing we can do until Monday when we can hand the letter to the solicitor. So to save us from going mad, and I know that'll be hard, I think we should load up the car, take a trip to the beach to clear our heads and give the kids some fun ... wear ourselves and the boys out for their first night.' John managed to raise a smile. 'And if that doesn't work, we can always open a bottle of wine.'

Sarah sucked in an enormous deep breath and took several seconds to exhale. 'Mr practical as ever. And makes sense, though I'm not counting on much sleep tonight.'

'Well, perhaps there's something else we could try?'

Sarah raised an eyebrow and shook her head. 'As always, I admire your optimism.'

Eighteen

Joseph gripped the front door key and rotated it anti-clockwise until it met resistance. With infinite care borne out of experience, he turned it against the stiffness of the lock, making no sound as the tumblers revolved in the barrel unlocking the door. That had always been the easy part, Joseph thought. The next part was harder. Pulling a door handle downwards to disengage each security bolt ran the risk of groans or metallic screeches depending on how well the door was maintained. He and Jamie had been caught before because of noisy locks. Others slipped open as if made of nothing more substantial than the wind. But luck was with him on this occasion and as he pulled down the handle using both hands for minute control, the door unlatched and moved towards him. Joseph turned towards his brother and only then noticed there were two additional spectators to his escape activities.

A few feet behind and with a smile on her face stood

Claire, one hand resting on Mags's head who sat quite still. For a moment Joseph thought the dog also wore a smile, and maybe that was true. But before he could react, Claire moved close and whispered, 'What are you doing? I hope you're not running away.'

Joseph shook his head and pointed towards the outer porch door. He turned away from Claire and stepped into the porch. Slipping on his shoes and a coat, he motioned for the others to do the same. With as much care as he had taken with the inner door, he unlocked and opened the porch door, revealing a world of mystery and shadow. Stepping to one side, he let both Claire and Jamie outside but before he had a chance to close the door, Mags scurried out too, refusing to miss out on the fun. Only then did he speak in hushed tones.

'The dog won't make a noise, will she?'

'No. She'll only bark if she senses danger. So what are you doing?'

'Jamie wanted to explore at night? Me too, I guess. Where's best to go?'

Claire thought for a moment. 'The hilltop,' she suggested. 'Where we raced to this morning. Jamie, would you like that?'

Claire turned to Jamie who had moved a few feet away from the house and stood with his head tilted upwards. In a rare physical gesture Jamie lifted an arm and pointed to the heavens. Claire knew without looking what had captured his attention but stepped towards him, took his hand and pulled him back against the house.

'Not here,' she hissed. 'If we step out any further, we'll set off the floodlight. Come on. Follow me. Mags, come on.'

Still holding Jamie's hand, she led her friends along the

wall of the house and through the gap between it and Memorial cottage. A chill breeze from the north west greeted them as they moved into the open and away from the shelter of the trees. The tall scots pine behind Memorial cottage sighed and creaked in time to the rhythm of the wind. Out of the reach of the lights, Claire headed up the hill, Jamie by her side, Mags roaming ahead wondering if there would be food somewhere, and Joseph walking behind with an excited smile lighting up his face.

The brow of the hill stood a few hundred yards from the house with a towering electricity pylon upon the summit. A young moon as thin as eggshell lay low in the east, and the surrounding landscape was as dark as it was mysterious, while the pylon loomed against the sable sky like a giant, immobile beast.

After ten minutes brisk walk, Claire stopped short of the summit and they huddled together.

'Now,' she said. 'We can take a proper look,' and once more Jamie raised an arm and pointed skywards.

'Come on,' said Joseph. 'We can see better if we lie down,' and without hesitation he dropped to the ground and stretched out, eyes staring at the spectacle. The others followed suit, even Mags who settled next to Claire and lay her head on her paws.

Above their heads, from north to south and east to west, a wondrous vision presented itself. A myriad of multi-coloured pinpricks of starlight spread out and appeared to fill every available space. Across the middle, running almost north to south, a brighter and more densely packed band lay – a glowing smudge that defied description.

'Awesome,' Joseph whispered as he too pointed upwards. 'Jamie says that's the Milky Way in the middle. We did it in school.'

Still holding Jamie's hand, Claire felt a tremor course through his body and his grip tightened. She returned the squeeze.

'There are things they call constellations,' she replied. 'Like Orion and Pegasus, but there's so many stars I can't find them.'

With so little light pollution and wondrous clean air, each star stood out clear and bright. Even close to the horizon, hardly a twinkle disturbed their clarity. To young eyes, every colour of the rainbow presented itself. Red, orange, blue or white – bright and faint, all laid out for their wonderment.

'This is so wicked,' Joseph muttered and then fell silent.

For many minutes they lay together, staring this way and that, taking in each moment and storing the memory away until Claire spoke once more.

'Y'know, some people believe each light is the spirit of someone who was alive once. They rise to heaven when they pass on.'

'Dunno about that,' replied Joseph. 'Seems to be too many. Maybe just some people. Maybe good people.'

'Maybe,' said Claire.

After a few moments, Joseph spoke again, but this time his voice was a faint whisper.

'Maybe you're right, bro. And why not? If you want to believe then why not? I guess it's possible. Ma could be right up there over your head shining down saying buck your ideas up. And listen to your brother. Yes … why not?'

Claire chose not to reply to what she heard, but instead asked a question. 'It's only your first night but do you want to stay here? You're not going to run away, are you?'

Joseph raised himself on one elbow and looked over his brother at Claire.

'Run away? No way, man. It's too cool. Loads of room and space to run around. We stayed in some small places. Some were ok but Jamie always said they wasn't right so we left. And we've seen stars before, but not like this. I like it up here. The higher the better. You see different when you get high up. Looking down on things. Everything's different. And your mom and dad are nice people. And I guess,' and here Joseph laughed. 'I guess Jamie fancies you.'

'Joseph,' Claire exclaimed with mock annoyance. 'Remember, I broke someone's nose a few days ago!'

'Ha … you'd have to catch me first.' And they shared a laugh.

Once more they fell silent, but a sudden gust of chill air found its way around the hilltop and they shuddered. Mags stood up, and glancing towards the pylon lifted her nose and snuffled into the wind. Raising a leg, she pawed at Claire's arm.

'Yes, Mags, it's time to go. Look everyone,' and she pointed towards the north. 'The stars have gone up there. I think the rain's coming back. We'd better hurry. But remember the flood lights when we get by the house. And be quiet.'

Hidden within the darkness, the children rose to their feet, brushed the dust from their clothes and with Mags roaming ahead once more, scurried down the hill, eager for a warm bed and sleep.

Nineteen

Three days later, John sat in one of the offices with their family solicitor concentrating on every word the senior partner relayed. Despite his blasé comments to Sarah at the weekend his anxiety had grown, but the partner took pains to allay his fears.

'John, listen to me. I'm confident there is no claim to answer. No transfer or sharing of ownership to make, no settlement regarding historic contracts, no losses due to unacknowledged contributions to original purchase, no unfulfilled promises of ownership. Nothing. This intent letter has no basis in anything factual.' Sam Mackie paused and waved the letter in the air. 'In fact, it's something of a joke in legal terms. I checked out the firm behind it and they're essentially an on-line group with one or two offices dotted around South Ayrshire involving newly qualified solicitors. For newly qualified, read inexperienced. Anyone with any understanding would have checked first with land registry or the historical Sasine registers here in Scotland, which would answer the initial question of title deed and ownership. Maybe they have but they should state that they have done so in their communication and only if they believed there was a historical claim to make should they have sent you a letter. That letter should detail the argument. But whatever their argument, whatever information they think they have, I can assure you there is no claim.'

'I don't mean to question,' John said, 'but I need to understand everything so I can relay this back to Sarah. You know how she is. What you're saying is, even if this Gillespie fella proves to be some distant relation, it still means he has no claim?'

Sam nodded. 'Precisely.'

John had done as she and Sarah agreed on Saturday afternoon and delivered the letter to the solicitor as soon as their office opened on Monday morning. Mackie and Macintyre had been the legal representatives who succeeded in tracking down Sarah, upon Beryl's request, even before the assault upon her took place in Wolverhampton. As soon as Beryl became aware of her terminal illness, her need to ascertain the precise whereabouts of her young relative had become urgent and she had set them the task. Sam Mackie and Donald Macintyre were the current senior partners of the law firm that had been a part of Beryl's life while her parents were alive and her ancestors before that, though they never represented Beryl's father William. William possessed an air of grandeur and chose to use the services of a well-known and upmarket solicitor in all his legal dealings. The expense did not deter him. But Beryl knew from conversations with her Grandmother Celeste that the relationship Celeste had with their own legal agents, and indeed throughout the female line, could be traced back to Rose whose name lay etched for eternity upon a brass plaque fixed to a slab of granite within the garden of Memorial cottage. Celeste had shown Beryl a copy of the land title deeds where Manseburn now stood – title deeds drawn up by the very man and Sheriff who loved Rose in the seventeen hundreds and fathered Amber and Hamish. Sarah had yet to see this document, but the original still sat secure with Mackie and Macintyre, the firm used by Amber and Hamish's father. It was definitive and unambiguous in relation to the covenants held therein.

'You see, John,' Sam continued. 'In the UK under the Inheritance Act, a child can make a claim against the estate of their father even if that father was not married to the mother. So adopted children and illegitimate children have the same legal rights to the estate of a deceased person as legitimate children. However, within the deeds to Manseburn there are covenants, binding agreements unchanged since they were first written stipulating that the property will only be passed to descendants of direct lineage. As the document dates back generations we'll never know the reason for this inclusion. What it means is that unless there is a direct blood connection to the original owner, the deeds cannot be passed on. This applies to Jimmy Gillespie. He has no blood connection to the original owner. Haven't you seen the deeds, as Beryl certainly had a copy?'

John shook his head. 'No, neither has Sarah, but there's still a lot of Beryl's belongings she's not gone through yet. But anyway, isn't it still possible to make a claim as an illegitimate child or grandchild ... however far down the line?'

'In this case no, because there is more.'

'More? What more?'

'There's no proof that Jimmy Gillespie is who he says he is?'

'How come? Does that mean it's a scam?'

'Not necessarily, but we're solicitors remember. It's a simple matter for us to search the register of births and deaths. On the register we found Jimmy Gillespie and his mother Linda, who coincidentally passed away just over a week ago. We traced back his family to the period we're talking about, around a hundred years ago, but found no connection to a William Gillespie who died in 1916. William Gillespie was, as I'm sure you know, Sarah's great, great grandfather and married to Coral Mary. But Jimmy Gillespie's lineage stops at John Gillespie, *his* great grandfather, who lived between 1905 and 1942. John Gillespie's birth certificate shows a Heather Dowie as his mother and "unknown" as his father. We'll never know if the unknown father was William Gillespie and thus meaning that Gillespie has a claim to make as the relative of an illegitimate heir, but as there is no documented proof of direct line to William, then ... well, game over.'

'That's clear enough, but it's puzzling that this Gillespie has the same surname as William but is descended from the Dowie family. How does that work?'

'Any number of reasons could explain it but it's irrelevant. The simple fact is, whatever the name, without that proof of lineage to William there is no claim.'

John took a moment to digest this information, but another idea raised its head. 'One other thing, what about DNA proof, could a DNA test prove lineage?'

'For heaven's sake your determined to think of every

negative aspect aren't you? I understand little about DNA testing to connect to distant relatives, but what I *do* know is that technically, an ancestry test is not recognised as legal proof of paternity. And anyway Gillespie would need a DNA sample from you or Sarah and well ... he's not going to get it, is he?'

John blew out a relieved sigh and shook his head. 'You do know what a relief it is to hear Sam?'

'Yes. I guessed it would be.' Sam smiled at his friend. 'John, get yourself off home. Tell Sarah there's nothing to worry about and carry on with your lives. Manseburn is yours and yours alone. Oh, and I'd appreciate an enormous cake as a way of a thank you.'

John laughed and rose to his feet. 'Thanks Sam. You've lifted a weight off and I'll talk to Sarah about a cake *and* a pie.'

Five minutes later, John moved through the traffic heading out of Ayr, while Sarah sat in the kitchen at Manseburn waiting for her first client. She was sharing recent news with Rachel, who was covering reception for the morning before seeing clients after lunch. Until two o'clock on Tuesdays, Margaret worked a morning shift at the care home in Girvan.

'What?' Rachel wore a horrified look on her face. 'A distant relative? Are you sure he is? Is it a hoax? Has he given any proof? I thought your only relatives were in direct line from Beryl. And that doesn't include John's relatives.'

'That's where John is now. At our solicitors hopefully getting the answers. He took the letter yesterday and they called last night asking for a meeting. John's gone into Ayr to get an update.' Sarah slurped at her tea. 'Rachel. You know me. I'm pretty philosophical about life. What will be will be sort of thing. But I don't mind admitting I'm worried. On a scale of one to ten for stress, this is around one hundred.'

'I can imagine, after all you've been through to get here and set this all up. But what will you do if he has a legitimate claim?'

Sarah fell silent as she explored her feelings. Surely Beryl would have known if there was any question concerning inheritance to her estate – been aware of any hidden relatives. Beryl's spiritual reach, Sarah believed, had been extensive, especially where a connection to family blood line existed. But at that thought, it occurred to Sarah maybe Beryl knew nothing because Jimmy Gillespie wasn't in fact a blood relative. She recalled John's suggestion about Sarah's great, great grandfather having a mistress. If that was true, then any offspring wouldn't be of any direct relation, though Sarah wondered if she was simply grasping at any notion to refute the claim.

'Sarah? What's in your head ... you've disappeared off somewhere again.'

'Sorry,' Sarah said. 'I was just running away with myself. Look, let's wait until John gets home. We both need to focus on clients when ... they ... arrive.'

Sarah's voice stuttered and faded, and she closed her eyes. Rachel sat still and said nothing. She recognised the signs. Her friend had received a spiritual message and had withdrawn from what Rachel classed as the real world. With patience Rachel waited, knowing Sarah's temporary sojourn could last from a few seconds to five minutes. Because Rachel didn't experience these messages, Sarah once tried to explain. She said it was similar to a smell or a sound that triggered a reaction within the brain, and that reaction, after being processed, resulted in an emotional response. Much like the smell of baking often created a nostalgic connection to childhood memories. Spiritual messages, however, brushed the outer layers of a person's aura, in particular the sixth layer called the Celestial layer. This layer was where, amongst other things, spiritual awareness and intuitive knowledge existed. Sarah said there was a permanent connection linking herself, John, Claire and Robert, and indeed her departed loved ones. With learning and practice, she and John had become adept at focusing an emotional thought into a spiritual message to transmit across the Celestial plane into the Celestial layer of the recipient. This would then translate, while traversing the auric layers of the receiver, into an emotional response. The first time Sarah gave this explanation, Rachel crossed her eyes in utter confusion. 'What have you been drinking?' she cried. But as the months rolled on, Rachel experienced the proof first hand. Sarah or John had often responded to 'something' sent from the other which then proved to be the truth when they met.

Of course there was nothing specific in these messages, nothing shared with words since that was impossible. Put in simple terms, they created a happy thought or a concerned one, and this was what Rachel had learned and why she waited. But this time a smile spread across Sarah's face in less than ten seconds.

'What?' Rachel asked. 'Tell me.'

'I've no specifics, but John seems less tense than when he left this morning. In fact, I get a rush of tranquillity.'

'Does that mean good news?'

'I guess so. I can't imagine any other reason he'd feel

that way.'

Rachel breathed a sigh of relief. 'Thank God for that. Please don't frighten me again.'

'Not jumping to any conclusions, but I'll do my best not to make you redundant.' Sarah looked toward the kitchen window. 'First guest is not far away. Shall we share a moment of peace before they arrive?'

Rachel always looked forward to their shared healing – clearing their souls before work began.

An hour after midday, Rachel pushed her chair back from the kitchen table where she, Sarah and John were sharing lunch.

'Well, can we get back to normal now please because I need to prepare for a new client. A man for once. One that Margaret booked in for me last week.'

John shared Sam's news as soon as Sarah had finished her first session. There was just enough time to let both Sarah and Rachel know the claim was a none starter and he gave more detail over lunch. When John explained the reason, the lack of evidence of lineage, Sarah blew out a sigh of relief. 'Thank heavens. I must remember to thank Sam.'

'Oh yes, I almost forgot,' John said. 'He asked for cake by way of payment and I said a pie as well if that's ok?'

Sarah laughed. 'It's a good price for saving our home.'

'Yes it is, but on the drive back something occurred to me and now the thought won't go away.'

'What's that?' asked Sarah.

'Well, this claim is bound to be a big thing for this Gillespie fella. He won't be happy when he finds out he has none to make.'

'Obviously, but the law is clear.'

'Yes, but some people get so wound up over these things they never let it go. I mean, he has the same name as Beryl's father which is a bit of a coincidence. And why now, out of the blue?'

Sarah frowned at John. 'Aren't you worrying over nothing? Yes, I admit he's not going to be happy but we're not responsible for that. And what can he do about it? Yes, he might have the same surname as my distant relative but so has half of Scotland. As for why now, I guess he spotted Manseburn on the TV. After a bit of asking around, he probably saw an opportunity. This place has plenty of history amongst the locals. Anyone could have fed him wrong or distorted information and given him the notion of making a bit of money. You *are* worrying over nothing. It'll all die down soon.'

'Hmm, maybe your right. Maybe the whole thing troubled me more than I realised.'

Sarah opened her mouth to confirm her agreement, but closed it again when a momentary darkness cast its shadow across her soul. It took only moments to pinpoint the source. John. She studied his face and probed for a few seconds before drawing back and letting it go. She knew something was troubling him, something she'd picked up at random moments over the past few weeks, but now was not the time. Rachel was in the room with them, and both she and Rachel needed to focus on their next clients. Making a mental note to talk to John that evening, she drained her cup and switched her attention to her friend.

'New client? Well that's good. Always helps to increase our number of regulars. What's he after, aromatherapy or reflexology?'

'Full body aromatherapy. A long appointment with the

questionnaire and history to run through.'

John took a sudden and unusual interest. 'A man? Are you comfortable with that? We don't get all that many male clients and those we do get tend to be older with stiff joints. Any idea how old he is.'

John's sudden concern puzzled Sarah, but Rachel answered. 'Not yet, but it'll be fine. Why wouldn't it? And you know perfectly well I can handle stiff men.'

John all but spat out a mouthful of tea. 'For god's sake! You women. Far worse than men!'

Sarah and Rachel laughed at John's attempt at outrage.

'Sweetie,' Sarah snorted. 'You ought to be used to it by now, spending most of your days in the company of women.'

'Huh,' said John with mock embarrassment. 'I'm going back to my fields where it's a lot safer. The fairer sex, they used to say. There's nothing fair at all,' and after blessing both Sarah and Rachel with a kiss, he made his way to the door. But before he left the kitchen he paused, stopping with his back to the table.

'John?' asked Sarah.

It took a while before John answered, but then he turned and stared at Rachel.

'You will make sure you have your personal alarm with you, won't you?'

'Yes of course,' Rachel said. 'It's always with me, always charged and tested. Now bugger off and get back to work.'

John gave a half smile and walked out of the house.

Twenty

Rachel's client arrived ten minutes later, a little before Margaret's afternoon shift began.

'So, Mr Barrie.'

'Call me Craig.'

'Ok, Craig. First, I need to get some background information, find out what you're having difficulty with and what it is you need before I decide what oils to mix. If you could fill in this questionnaire for me, please. It shouldn't take long.'

Rachel handed over a pen and a clipboard with a printed form attached. While Craig busied himself with the questions, she laid warm towels on the couch and flicked through her collection of tranquil music.

'How did you hear about us?' she asked selecting a compilation of pipes and flutes.

'Friends,' came the short answer. 'But you've been on the telly.'

'Oh, the news, you mean? We try to play that down.'

'Why?' Craig looked up and stared at Rachel with such intensity that she felt momentarily uncomfortable. Something in his eyes maybe, or just the fact that she noticed the quick shift of focus as his gaze roamed over her body. He turned back to the questions. 'Free advertising, good for business.'

'Not our preferred method of encouraging people to visit, but I understand what you mean. It has made no difference, really.'

'Shame,' he said and glanced at her again. 'All done,' and he handed the pad back.

'Ok, let's have a look,' said Rachel lowering herself onto a chair.

She scanned the information Craig had provided, nodding to herself.

'Lower back pain and tension in the shoulders. You've not said for how long?'

'Months.' Again a short answer as his eyes flicked up and down. Responding to his unwelcome attention and her own subconscious alarm bells, Rachel crossed her legs.

'Do you know of any specific reason why it began? Any injury or trauma or emotional event?'

'No. Just thought a massage would help.'

'Well, as its just your back you're having a problem with, we could save you some money today rather than do the full massage.'

'Not very good at business are you,' and Craig grinned.

Looking up at Craig as he lifted himself up onto the couch and sat down, Rachel's discomfort increased, but this time she spotted what appeared to be a leer behind the grin.

'We only provide what we feel our clients need rather

than taking money unnecessarily. But, if you want the full massage, there are warm towels ready for you. I'll give you a few minutes to undress.'

Once more the grin and for a moment she imagined a wolf – leering, slavering.

She left the room and sauntered over to Margaret, who sat behind the desk they used as an informal reception.

'Hi,' Margaret said. 'How are you today?'

'Oh hi. I'm good. I've got this new client. The one you spoke to a few days ago.'

'Ok.'

'Did he say how he heard about us?'

'No. Just said he needed a massage for aches and pains if I recall. Why, is everything ok?'

'Not sure. He's strange. A bit of a sleaze, I think.'

'We can always ask him to leave.'

'No ... no. Let's see how it goes. He should be ready by now. I'd best get on.'

Rachel tapped on the door and entered the room. Craig Barrie lay face down on the couch, head resting on his hands and a towel draped from his waist to his feet.

'Ok', said Rachel. 'I'll mix some Eucalyptus and Chamomile. These are good for pain and inflammation, and Lavender which has a calming influence.'

'So how long have you worked here?' asked Craig.

'Almost as long as the current owners,' answered Rachel. 'Around a year.'

Rachel poured a quantity of oil onto her palm, rubbed her hands together and worked it onto Craig's shoulders.

'And did you massage before?'

'No. I only qualified earlier this year. I just helped out before that. Reception and child minding.'

Craig fell silent for a few minutes as Rachel worked around his shoulders and back. When her fingers probed the base of his spinal column, she noticed a shift in his hips.

'Well, you seem like a pro to me,' Craig muttered.

Rachel drew a silent breath through her teeth. *Christ. C'mon Rachel, let's just get through this.*

Craig continued his questioning.

'What about the owners? How did they get to own such a big place.'

Rachel pondered the question before answering. There was no secret, especially after John's heroics on the beach and the television news report.

'Inherited. It's been in the family for generations, but the last owner had to leave a few years ago when she became too frail to be here on her own.'

'She left a few years ago? Does that mean it was empty?'

'For a while, until the current owners were traced.'

'That must have been a challenge. Who traced them? I guess whoever it was had proof they're related?'

'Of course.'

Rachel moved around to the end of the couch, poured more oil on her hand and began massaging Craig's calves. She was feeling uncomfortable now, in part at the line of questioning, but mostly at how this man affected her wellbeing. Once more he shifted his position as Rachel moved up to his thighs.

'So,' he continued. 'What if there was someone else in the family, someone else that the solicitor missed?'

This was getting beyond what Rachel considered appropriate conversation.

'You're supposed to be relaxing.'

'Ok, ok,' he replied. 'Just interested because you often hear about people who rob a relative of their inheritance. Especially when there's loads of money involved.'

Rachel said nothing, just worked on the other leg, hurrying as much as she dared, keen to end the session.

'How about you?' he continued. 'How well do you know the owners?'

Rachel chose not to answer, and they both fell silent.

While Rachel pressed her thumbs into Craig Barrie's calf, pondering the notion that added force may put him off arranging any further appointments, John walked through the entrance and came to a halt outside the door to Rachel's treatment room. A minute later Sarah entered the building and touched his arm, but his focus remained on the door. Sarah recalled her husband's earlier concern, a concern she now shared.

'You too?' she asked.

'Yes.'

'Did you actually go outside?' she asked.

John sniffed and smiled without humour. 'Yes, but only to the greenhouse. Something's wrong.'

Margaret listened to the exchange with mild puzzlement. 'What's going on?'

'Not sure yet,' Sarah replied. 'But I'll tell you later. John, it's not always easy to sense, but we sometimes have clients that carry a lot of spiritual disturbance. They're really not well. It may be nothing more than that.'

Only then did John turn to Sarah. 'If that's the case, why have you followed me here?'

Sarah did not answer because she too had felt Rachel's increasing tension. Her wellbeing was under attack, and as close friends John and Sarah had responded. But still they waited.

'Ok, let's change the subject,' Craig suggested. 'You're very good at massage but what else do you provide?'

'Provide? Well we offer a range of treatments. Reflexology, crystal therapy, sound therapy, Indian head massage.'

'Yes, but something special, perhaps?'

'Well, Sarah, one of the owners, she can offer deeper spiritual healing like energy therapies, extensions of Reiki.'

Craig shifted once more and lowered his voice.

'C'mon, don't be coy. You know what I mean. Personal service, perhaps at home. Skimpy clothes. I bet they'd suit you.'

Rachel yanked her hands away from Craig Barrie as if she'd received an electric shock. She stepped back a pace and froze. Sudden fear filled her soul as old terrors returned. How could a situation descend to this in so short a time? Craig Barrie rose from the couch dressed only in a pair of black underpants. As he stepped toward her, his semi-arousal was plain.

Rachel closed her eyes and retreated towards a corner of the room, knocking a pile of towels to the floor and fumbling at her waist for the alarm.

'Come on, missy. I bet you could use some of this,' he whispered.

But as he took a step closer to Rachel, the door burst open and slammed against the wall. John filled the doorway, eyes blazing and face dark with aggression.

'You fucking pervert,' he hissed.

Without hesitation, John strode across the room and

grabbed Craig's wrist. In one fluid motion and with confidence borne of long practice, he spun Craig around, and pushed an arm up his back. With a sharp kick at his feet, John brought his victim to the floor.

'Give me one good reason why I shouldn't kick you in the bollocks you fucking bastard!'

'Go one Macintyre. Do it and see what you get,' Craig yelled into the carpet.

'John, be careful' Sarah warned as she crossed the room to stand as a shield to Rachel. 'Rachel, honey. Are you ok? Did he touch you?' Rachel shook her head.

'How do you know my name,' John demanded?

Recognising the voice, Margaret entered the room. 'Jimmy?'

'You know him?' Sarah asked in surprise.

'Yes, it's Jimmy Gillespie. His mother was in the care home at Girvan. She passed not long ago. He said his name was Craig Barrie when he rang up. Jimmy, why would you do that? What are you doing?'

Still holding Jimmy by the wrist, John spoke again. 'Hang on … Jimmy Gillespie. You're the misguided prat who tried to take our home?'

'You're breaking my fucking arm.'

'John,' Sarah repeated. 'Let go. None of us want to see him dressed that way anymore. Just get him out of here.'

John realised his grip but stood over Gillespie. 'Ok everyone, out of the room. I'll wait here. Shut the door behind you.'

'John?'

'No arguments,' John insisted.

Sarah took Rachel's hand, ushered Margaret out and followed, drawing Rachel behind. With a worried glance back at John, she did as he instructed.

'Ok Gillespie. Get your clothes on,' he ordered. 'You've got two minutes to get off my property.'

'But it's not your property is it. It's mine. Grandparents to parents. Parents to son's. I'm in line as a son and there's nothing you can do about it.' Jimmy Gillespie grinned as he dressed.

But a smile spread across John's face.

'That's where you're wrong, you fucking moron. I spoke to my solicitor today. He's told me you have no claim.'

'Piss off,' Jimmy spat back. 'I've got the letters. I've got the proof, and there's nothing you can do,' he repeated.

John shook his head. 'You don't get it. Talk to that joke of a solicitor you hired. You have no claim because there's no proof you were ever related.'

Jimmy's grin had faded. 'What are you talking about? I have proof.'

'No, you don't, because your birth certificate doesn't show the name of your father.' John gave a single laugh. 'Ha. Not only are you a perverted bastard, you're a real bastard.'

Rage contorted Jimmy's features. 'You're a fucking liar!' and he took a swing at John who fielded the punch, grabbed Jimmy and laid him out on the floor once more.

'Right.' John was calm now. 'I'm going to take you to your car and put you in it. I'll be talking to the police to press charges for indecency. And I suggest you visit your solicitor. He should get a letter soon from our solicitor, proper solicitors. And if I ever see you here again, no amount of caution from my wife will prevent me from kicking you in those weedy nuts of yours. Give me the car keys.'

The fight had gone out of Jimmy Gillespie. He

recognised he'd lost any advantage and needed to retreat. And anyway, he wanted to see his solicitor as soon as possible. It took a while longer than two minutes, but true to John's word, he led Jimmy to his car. Leaning inside, John spoke for the last time. 'You'll be getting a visit from the Police soon, now get lost.' John inserted the key and started the engine, and with a mixture of satisfaction and relief watched Gillespie leave the property in a cloud of dust and gravel. Only then did the after effects hit him, and making his way to the nearest porch chair, he collapsed onto it and tried to still his shaking hands.

Twenty One

Unsure of her husband's intentions, Sarah found it hard to leave him alone. But for once she realised arguing wouldn't sway his insistence, so she headed back to the house. Rachel was subdued and pale but didn't want a fuss, though she accepted a brandy.

'I'm ok,' she insisted. 'Just came as a shock, behaving like that.' Rachel paused in thought for a moment, and sipped her drink. 'But I felt something was wrong as soon as I walked in the room. His eyes and his grin. Vile man.'

'Shall I call Peter?' asked Sarah.

'No need for that. No need to worry him and anyway nothing really happened.'

'Maybe nothing physical, but what he did is a form of abuse and not acceptable.' Sarah paused a moment, studying her friend before turning to Margaret. 'How do you know him again? You said his mother was at Girvan?'

'Yes. Around three weeks ago I called him because his

mother had become agitated about something on the television. Then the manager had to call again a few days later because she'd passed away suddenly. Her heart, they said.'

'Three weeks ago on the TV,' said Rachel. 'That was when you and John saved that young boy on the beach.'

'Yes that's right,' Sarah replied. 'Margaret,' Sarah continued. 'What else do you know about him?'

'Not a lot. He didn't visit his ma often and when he did he seemed annoyed, like visiting was an inconvenience. Terrible flirt too. Really fancied himself, always coming on to me. But just the same as with anyone else I had to be polite.' Margaret turned to Rachel. 'I'm sorry, it's my fault. If I'd known it was Jimmy, I would have put him off somehow.'

'Don't apologise,' Rachel said. 'You weren't to know and anyway, no-one would expect that kind of behaviour. And how he thought he'd get away with it, I don't know.'

'I don't think Jimmy Gillespie cares what he does or what people think,' replied Margaret.

'Margaret,' said Sarah. 'Could you give us a few minutes, please? I just need to speak with Rachel.'

'Yes, of course. I've got work to carry on with so I'll leave you to talk.'

As soon as they were alone Sarah sat in front of Rachel and closed her shield. She did not want to pry, but wanted Rachel to talk.

'The truth now. How are you, really?'

Rachel drank the rest of the brandy in one mouthful and drew a sharp breath through pursed lips.

'How am I? Shit is how I am. But you know I've been through worse. I know what you're concerned about … did it bring back memories. I'd be lying if I said no but it was more of a surprise than anything. He's obviously a man with a deluded opinion of himself. He's made me feel like I need a shower, the sleazy little bastard. Yes, he reminded me of the past a little, but now I'm just fucking angry. How dare he come here and behave like that. I hope the police can do something. Where is John by the way?'

Sarah knew John wasn't far away but then they heard his voice drifting in from outside and a few moments later the front door opened.

'I've just spoken to Duncan ... south Ayrshire Police,' he explained to Rachel. 'I told him what happened but there's little they can do. Duncan says he'll pay Gillespie a visit, warn him off.'

'What's that mean, little they can do?' Sarah said.

'Just that,' muttered John.

'But why?' Rachel asked. 'That's ridiculous and surely what he did is illegal.'

'Well Duncan says because there's been no actual physical contact, there's no assault or offence. Indecent exposure doesn't apply because it didn't happen in a public place. And the problem is, he says, Gillespie could claim *you* encouraged him because there's no witness. I'm sorry, Rachel. Really I am, but the law sometimes doesn't give us the result we know to be right. What Duncan *did* say, however, is that he's well known to the Police. He has a record for a number of petty and not so petty crimes ... some of them violent. So what he'll do is have a few informal words and warn him to stay away.'

'Great,' Rachel replied. 'If he comes here again, I'll kick him where his delusion begins and ends. Animal. I can't believe he thinks he's a part of this family.'

'Neither can I,' said Sarah.

That evening, after the twins, Clare and Robert were settled in bed for the night, John and Sarah sat in the living room with a mug of tea. The log burner glowed with a heat that drew them into its embrace, enticing them towards sleep. Outside, a gusting wind roared through the trees behind Memorial cottage, driving a stinging rain across the yard to rattle and skitter against the windows.

'John?' Sarah said.

'Mmm?'

'I'm only going to ask this once because you're going to give me the truth.'

John pulled his eyes away from the flames. 'Truth? About what?'

'What is going on with you? For over a month you've been waking during the night. You think your quiet about it, but I see and hear you. I sense there's something in your head but though I can gauge how it's affecting you, I can't read minds. You were twitchy this morning about Rachel treating a man on her own, warning her to be careful. You didn't go far from the house and you were out in reception when it all kicked off. And I thought *I* was the one who had random premonitions. So talk to me. No hiding anymore. What's going on?'

John sighed, smiled at his wife and shook his head. 'Y'know it's impossible to keep anything from you. And maybe after today it's time to come clean.'

'Tell me what?'

'I've been having a dream.'

'A dream?' Sarah frowned.

'Yes. Do you want a wee dram?'

'Aye,' Sarah replied.

John busied himself with glasses and whisky and when he wandered into the kitchen for a jug of water he shot a quick glance out of the window, suspicion aroused. This night though, there was little to see but a film of rain obscuring his view. Beyond, there was just an interminable blackness.

Back in the living room he explained.

'I've been having a recurring dream. Well it's a bit of a nightmare, actually.' He paused, but Sarah said nothing, waiting for John to continue. 'In the dream I kill someone and after today I think its Jimmy Gillespie.'

John said no more, leaving Sarah to respond.

'Kill Jimmy Gillespie? You're worrying me. Why would you do that?'

'It's only a guess and remember I knew nothing about him until we had that letter last week. And … I've been having this dream for several weeks before all this began. How do you explain that?'

'What happens in the dream?'

John hesitated as if reluctant to continue, or unsure of how to say the words.

'John, what happens.'

'Sarah, try not to worry but someone breaks into the house, attacks me and threatens you and the kids. The dream is always the same. The only thing I can do to stop him is kill him. Stab him.'

Sarah found the detail horrifying, the specificity disturbing.

'Stab him? John …' but words failed.

'Yes, I know,' John said, and he took hold of Sarah's hand. 'It always follows the same course, the dream, always the same detail. It's very specific. What worries me is that it seems like a premonition. But premonitions aren't real, surely. I know you had a premonition about Dave and me, the day before he died. But that was just a feeling. There wasn't any detail, was there?' Sarah shook her head. 'My dream has detail. It's clear. That's why I'm concerned. At any moment, I feel as if tonight will be the night when the dream comes true. It seems utterly farfetched, but the whole idea disturbs me.'

John dried up and sipped at his malt. Sarah tried to gather her thoughts.

'No wonder you've kept it to yourself,' she said. 'And I'm not surprised you're worried.' Sarah rose from the sofa, walked to the window and peered out, moved maybe by John's comment about tonight and his dream coming true. But outside there was little to see. The gloom greeted her sight. An impenetrable darkness that ate up even the light escaping from the living room window. With her head resting against the glass she peered from side to side but her action was futile. The lack of light was overwhelming.

Drawing the heavy drapes, she crossed the room and sat next to John once more.

'Ok,' she said, feeling her way forward. 'From personal experience I know the reality of a premonition can be disturbing and consuming. They seem an impossible notion, but for us they are a reality. I guess they only occur when there really is something to worry about, which horrifies me. As you said, my premonition was just a feeling but it came true. Yours has specific images which fill me with dread. What can we do with such an unknown? And is it to do with Jimmy Gillespie or someone else?'

'Too many questions and not enough answers,' John

replied. 'I've spent weeks thinking about it and not come up with any answers … and the dream keeps coming.'

John's protective instinct kicked in and with it his practical nature. 'Right,' he said. 'Here's the plan. We're going to prepare, however outlandish it seems, preparing for something that may never happen based on a dream. But I'm willing to run with it. We'll make sure all the security lights work. We'll make sure the locks are secure or get new ones. We'll get an alarm installed to cover all the buildings. We'll each have a torch to hand. And of course Mags hears anything out of the ordinary, even though she's getting on now.'

'She's almost twelve, remember. We had her before Claire was born.'

'Ok. We'll factor that in. Maybe we should keep her safe. But I'm going to have a word with Duncan. See what he can do or suggest about keeping tabs on Gillespie. What did I say earlier today, some people get really wound up when their hopes are gone? Well it seems Gillespie may be one of those people. If he's willing to come here and behave the way he did, I doubt if he cares what he does, or the consequences. That makes him a psychopath and maybe unpredictable. So if we're prepared and nothing happens, fine. If something does happen, well these are all sensible security precautions.'

Sarah nodded her agreement but then locked her gaze on John. 'You do know what they say don't you?'

'What?'

'If you remember your dream, it wasn't a dream, it was a message.'

Twenty Two

'I'm sorry Mr Gillespie but yes, that's the truth.'

Jimmy paced back and forth across the consultation room where his solicitor proclaimed the news. Simmering inside and barely controlling his rage, he hissed, 'You've got to be fucking joking. What about those old letters from that solicitor?'

'The letters may have had some value if proof of birth was evident, but without that they constitute no legitimate bearing. Whatever you may have been told or believe, we cannot indicate any ancestral connection. That, along with the covenant contained within the title deeds, the agreement that states that unless there is a direct blood connection to the original owner the deeds cannot be passed on, you can make no claim.'

At that, Jimmy lost control. He turned and banged a fist on the table in front of the solicitor. The young man recoiled and raised both hands in a conciliatory gesture.

Broken

'It's a crock of shit!' Jimmy shouted. 'You and your fucking people! You're all the same. Take money off the poor punter, make promises and don't deliver.'

'Mr Gillespie, I made no promises. I just indicated the case had merit and was worth investigating. And no win, no fee remember. You have paid nothing.'

Jimmy lunged around the desk and grabbed the solicitor by the throat, tightening the knot of his tie until the man's face began to redden.

'Don't be fucking clever with me you smart arse bastard! Well, it's not over. You watch. It's not finished!'

Jimmy shoved the man backwards until his chair tipped, spilling its occupant to the floor. Then with a sweep of his hand he cleared the desk of its contents and hurtled out of the room.

Five minutes later, while the police responded to a call from the solicitor's secretary, Jimmy Gillespie raced out of town and headed towards Straiton and Manseburn. With no plan other than to vent his rage, he drove with mindless intent until he arrived at the layby under the hill below the farm. Swinging the car onto the gravel surface, he skidded to a halt and turned off the engine. In the silence that followed, he sat gripping the steering wheel and stared unseeing through the windscreen. But as his racing heart slowed, a plan formed in his head while grim determination spread across his darkened features.

Twenty Three

The following weekend bought a welcome change to the recent unsettled weather. The last few hours of Friday afternoon and early evening proved what the west coast of Scotland was renowned for – a magnificent and breathtaking sunset. When Claire, Joseph and Jamie arrived home from School, John and Sarah squeezed everyone into the car and along with Mags headed for Girvan beach, an impressive stretch of soft sand.

For an hour, kicking a ball and chasing the dog, they ran along the water's edge, now more sedate after the recent heavy tides,. Then tired and hungry, they headed back to a hot dinner and a warm fire.

In mid-October, cloudless skies promised a crisp Saturday morning but with layers of clothing the weather was perfect for a morning in the fields. Joseph volunteered with enthusiasm to help John. Jobs for the morning included planting out and protecting seedlings for an early crop the following year, harvesting late crops of beetroot and parsnip, and laying a mulch of manure around the many soft fruits that thrived on the farm. And so, after a bowl of porridge, eaten before nine o'clock, and leaving Sarah, Claire and Jamie still in pyjamas they headed out the door.

'Shall we shovel shit first?' asked Joseph. The boy was so innocently cheeky that John found it impossible to resist laughing out loud.

'No,' John chuckled, 'and don't let Sarah hear you say things like that. The manure we can start on later. We need to get the new stuff in the ground and protected first.'

'Ok. Can I plant some?'

'I was hoping you'd say that. We can start at opposite sides and work our way along. Get finished quicker. Then we can harvest some veg.'

'I don't mind planting on my own.'

'Let's do it together, we can talk easier.'

Joseph squinted at John. 'You're not going to lecture me, are you?'

'What ... force my years of extensive wisdom on you?' He laughed again. 'No. No lecturing. Just chatting.'

Armed with a trolley laden with trays of established seedlings, they began at one end of the plot and worked their way towards the other.

'So,' asked John. 'It's only been a week since you and Jamie arrived but how's it going? Can you tell me about it?'

Bent closer to the ground Joseph was getting ahead of John but caught up with the question, paused and stood upright. 'It's cool. There's loads of space. Lots of cool stuff to do instead of just watching tele. Me and Jamie got our own room.' A glint of humour shone in the boy's eyes. 'And the food's great.'

'Well that's good all round. You seem ok with Claire. How about Rachel and Margaret. You've met them a few times.'

'Yeah, they're cool too for old people.'

'Old! We're only in our thirties y'know,' Joseph sniggered at John's indignation but John joined in with the humour. 'So, how many other places have you stayed?'

Joseph bent once more to resume planting. 'Twelve,' he said without need to consider.

'Twelve?' Joseph's lack of hesitation and his surety in remembering the number astonished John. 'Must have been hard. How come you never stayed at any of them?'

'Too many rules … telling us what to do. Some weren't very friendly. They shouted at Jamie cos he didn't speak. I mean, if he doesn't want to speak, what's the problem? And anyway,' again the humour cheered his voice. 'I shout at him enough.'

'How was it in the beginning?' John was probing because he wanted to see how comfortable Joseph was discussing subjects that for others would remain buried.

'The beginning? When ma died?' Joseph lowered his voice. 'It was shit.' He continued without breaking his rhythmic planting. 'I remember the ambulance took us away. They had to check Jamie over. We didn't know where they'd taken our ma, and our dad had pissed off after we were born. We had a nana and papa, but they were ancient. At the hospital, a policewoman told us our ma was dead.' Joseph stopped talking for a moment and John kept silent, leaving the child to continue if or when he chose. Joseph raised his eyes towards John. 'Jamie never made a sound all the time we were there, and he's not made a sound since. Not that he needs to with me around.'

John smiled. 'And how long is the longest you stayed with anybody?'

'Dunno. A few months. There was one family that was ok but the man became ill and we had to leave.'

'And do you know where your mum is? Have you been to visit?'

'Yes, she's in Ayr graveyard. We went once, but Jamie wouldn't go past the gate. Not been since. Don't see the point. Do you go to your ma's grave? Does Sarah?'

'Good question and, no. My ma died when I was around your age. Road accident. After that, my dad took me to live in England, so I was miles from her grave. As for my dad, he died a few years ago and I used to take flowers until we moved back to Scotland, but I've not been to ma's grave since we've been back. Sarah used to take flowers every couple of weeks to her mom and dad's grave when we lived south. But of course that's stopped now. But you ask about a point? For us it's about remembering who they are, the people who raised us. Churchyards are peaceful places, not places of death and sadness, and when you sit there for a while it's easy to take a moment to remember things that just pass you by day by day. Memories that you forget about. Perhaps we all ought to visit. I could visit my ma, my nana and papa, and you could visit your ma. But it's your choice. For some folk it's important, for others it isn't.'

Joseph raised himself upright once more and fixed a questioning stare on John. 'Is that a lecture?'

John laughed once more. 'Not at all. Just a suggestion. Sometimes visiting a churchyard can make you feel better.'

Joseph smiled. 'Maybe it would help Jamie. Especially if Claire went with him.'

John nodded.

Joseph resumed his planting. 'They like each other. I talk to him and he listens, but he still won't talk back. Maybe he'd talk for Claire. He holds her hand, and he's never held mine.' Jamie sniggered again.

'Yes I noticed,' John laughed back, and they fell quiet for a while, concentrating on the job in hand and feeling comfortable in the silence. After five minutes during which John lowered his spiritual shield and listened to the hectic chatter emanating from the boy, Joseph asked a question which stung at John's heart and revealed a sensitivity that lay hidden underneath the child's confident and cheerful nature.

'Can we stay here forever? I like it and Jamie feels safe.'

John took a moment to draw breath. 'Jo, I'll be honest with you. It's not entirely up to either of us, Sarah and me. There are the authorities who have a say, and you know Sue is trying to do her best. But I think I speak for us all when I say that even after only a week we'd be pleased if you could stay with us.'

With a quick glance up at John, Joseph blessed him with a flash of white teeth, a glint of excited eyes and a single word. 'Cool!'

While Joseph and John were sharing thoughts out on the back fields, Claire and Jamie explored the farm buildings. After a hearty breakfast, they wandered outside with a few chores of their own. Sarah asked if they'd make a start at tidying up the garden inside Memorial cottage and afterwards clean out the henhouse.

Claire took Jamie into the converted barn first, where they changed the flowers Sarah kept in several vases set around reception.

Broken

'This is where mom and auntie Rachel see their patients,' Claire spoke with a lowered voice. 'There's other rooms upstairs where people can stay, but mom and dad haven't started using them yet. Auntie Rachel's in the room at the end with someone now, so we need to be quiet.' Claire took a moment to ponder what to say next. 'They treat people who have special illnesses like being extra sad or worried. They use oils like those we burn over a candle in the house, but they mix them together and massage them in. Rachel does reflexology, which is a special treatment for feet and sometimes hands.'

Jamie listened with intent, eyes bright and focused on Claire.

'Mom does different stuff though, because we all have a gift,' Claire continued. 'You've heard of witches. Well, that's what we are, but nice witches not horrible story book witches. That stuff's ok for little kids. We can see what people look like on the inside cos everyone has colours and other stuff. Mom knows what to do when people are ill in their hearts and heads.'

Apart from the shine in Jamie's eyes, there was little indication he understood Claire, but with intuition she knew he had absorbed her meaning. Closing the door behind them with care, they left the barn.

'Let's sort out the chickens first,' Claire said and raced Jamie across the yard. The henhouse stood to one side and towards the rear of Memorial cottage. Made mostly of stone but with a wooden roof, frontage and a caged run, it stood on old foundations raised above the ground. The ancient trees of the windbreak sheltered the henhouse from the worst of the Scottish weather, and behind, the ground fell away down into the coniferous planting that bordered the road to Straiton.

Claire opened the cage and the inner door and let the chickens spill out where they fluttered away in search of insects, worms or any other scraps they could find. Handing a pair of gloves to Jamie and pulling on her own, they began to rake out the old straw and paper from inside the house, dragging it into a pile where they could wheelbarrow it away for composting.

'Did I tell you about Memorial cottage?' asked Claire. Jamie blessed her with a slow shake of his head. 'Well, it's been here hundreds of years before the big house or the barn. Its where one of my great, great, great, great, great grandmothers lived in the seventeen hundreds, Nana Rose. We don't know who lived here before, but she died because people hated witches. There were some horrible people back then. Anyway, she had two children, Amber and Hamish, who were separated when Nana Rose died. They never found each other again, even though they looked for each other all their lives. Amber had a daughter and so did her daughter and so on until mom was born. Hamish had a son and his son had a son and so on until dad was born. So my mom and dad are related to Nana Rose and from the same family but hundreds of years ago. So we always think Amber and Hamish found each other in the end, even though it took a long, long time.'

While Claire told her story, Jamie listened with intense concentration as if his life depended on each tiny detail. Though he made no sound, Claire could see by his eyes the tale moved and excited him.

'C'mon,' she continued and turned to leave. 'We need the wheelbarrow.'

Jamie grabbed her hand and shook his head before

walking away. Claire understood his meaning – he would fetch the barrow.

A few minutes later he returned and began scooping up the spent straw with a shovel. As he stepped back into the henhouse for the last load, his boots thudded across the wooden floor and he stood still, peering at his feet.

'What is it?' asked Claire.

Jamie banged the floor with his foot, interested in the hollow sound.

'Is it the noise?' Claire said. 'It's a bit loud isn't it but its wooden and dad says there's a gap underneath so it doesn't sit on the wet ground.'

Jamie kicked the floor once more and then looked up at Claire, who raised her eyes and stared back. She fell silent and held her breath, transfixed by something in his gaze, or maybe something she sensed beyond.

Across the yard, back in the house, Sarah entered the kitchen and switched on the kettle. Glancing up and out of the window she spotted the chickens roaming around the yard. Further beyond and inside the henhouse she saw Claire and Jamie standing immobile gazing at each other. Drawn into the spectacle, Sarah stayed as she was and watched the two children for many minutes. Their immobility puzzled Sarah, but she sensed no disturbance coming from her daughter and Jamie's soul as ever remained invisible. When Claire turned away and reached for a handful of shredded paper, Sarah smiled. She felt there was nothing to worry about. Maybe the children were simply sharing a moment and all would be revealed when the time was right.

But during their shared moment, Claire was drawn out of herself, pulled firmly into a different existence by an irresistible force—into a plane where past, present and future held no meaning. There was no then and now, since every moment existed one and at the same time. A plane where spiritual movement was unrestricted and memory was accessible without limitation. Though she could see Jamie, hear the world of Manseburn around her, even sense her mother watching from the house, she also perceived a moment in the future, a tenuous breath – a wisp of something yet to take place. Though the sensation held no substance or detail, a perception that Sarah called a premonition, Claire knew there was something imperative she needed to do. As the vision faded, so that only Jamie and the henhouse remained to her sight, she spoke without hesitation.

'I need to show you something. It's very important, but it's a close secret. You can never tell or show. Ok?'

Jamie nodded his understanding.

'Good,' Claire breathed. 'Let's finish and I'll take you there straight away.'

Twenty Four

'Sarah?' John called. 'Who put the chickens to bed last night?'

'Sorry?' asked Sarah as she entered the kitchen and yawned. It was early Tuesday morning, still dull outside and a week following Jimmy Gillespie's visit to Manseburn.

'The hen house, who closed it last night, or didn't close it because the gate's open.'

'Oh no. Can you see anything?' Sarah hurried to the window and peered out. 'Are they ok?'

'I can't tell for certain. I don't think we've had a fox around, but I'd better check.'

'Well Claire usually sees to them but she seemed preoccupied last night so I did it. I know I locked the gate with the bolt.'

'Well its open now,' said John and headed into the front porch to pull on his boots. 'I'll go take a look.'

As John wandered away from the house, his motion

triggered the floodlight fixed high on the front wall and the yard and henhouse appeared stark and in contrast with dark shadows stretching away. Over to the east, the sky paled as the distant sun, still beyond the horizon, made its presence known.

John crossed the yard and squeezed inside the cage of the henhouse, fearing the worst, but there were no signs of damage or destruction. A fox would have killed indiscriminately if succeeding in gaining entry. Lifting the access door, he counted eleven chickens and frowned. There should be twelve. Puzzled, he counted again and with a frown closed the access, bolted the gate and walked back to the house. By the time he re-entered the kitchen, Claire and the twins were just settling down to a bowl of cereal.

'Well?' asked Sarah.

'Odd,' said John. 'There's one missing. No damage. No feathers. Just one missing. I even counted them twice.'

'One missing. Well, the obvious thing is, I missed one last night when I locked up. Could still be wandering about.'

'Hmm. Maybe, but you always count like I do … like Claire does.'

Claire looked up from her bowl. 'What's happened?'

Sarah replied. 'The hen house gate was open this morning. I mustn't have shut it properly last night, that's all. We're lucky a fox didn't turn up.'

Claire stared at Sarah, but it was obvious her focus was elsewhere.

'Sweetheart?' Sarah asked.

'Nothing,' the girl whispered. 'But you did lock up.'

For a moment silence filled the kitchen. Even the twins stopped eating as if they sensed something important had happened. Sarah glanced at John who peered back – a shared moment that had become commonplace, ever since their daughter's other worldly percipience had manifested itself.

'So how is it open now, sweetheart?' John asked.

'I'm not sure but someone else must have opened it,' replied Claire, stating the obvious.

'Ok,' said Sarah in an attempt to end the moment. 'Well, let's not worry about that now. We need to get you three ready for the school bus.'

Just before midday, after Rachel arrived with little Scott, and both she and Sarah were with clients, John wandered over to the henhouse, still puzzled and disturbed by Claire's statement. Taking advantage of the brightness of midday, he scanned the ground nearby, looking for any sign he considered out of the ordinary. Falling back on his police experience, he covered the ground in segments – small areas mapped out in his head, but found nothing of interest until he moved to the rear of Memorial cottage.

Behind the stone walls, the ground lay at least twelve feet below the highest point of the old croft, while the hillside fell away only a few feet from its base. It was possible to hide behind the walls without being seen from the house. Close to the right-hand corner, within the gap between the croft and the henhouse, John found a single boot print, adult sized, a shallow but distinct indentation left in the damp ground where little direct sunlight fell. There was no reason for anyone to be here, nothing to see or do, even for the children, so it was obvious someone had stood there out of sight of the house. John continued to scan the area even to the edge of the sharp slope that fell down the wooded hillside. It only took a few minutes, but he found more evidence of an uninvited visitor. There, a few yards down the incline, lay a discarded, half-smoked cigarette. Taking care with his footing and to steady his descent, John made use of overhanging branches as a hand hold, until he reached the cigarette. Gathering a few large pebbles he marked the spot, then scrambled back up to the rear of the cottage, and hurried over to the greenhouse. Armed with an empty seed packet he headed back to recover the cigarette.

He had a plan. He would ask Duncan McBride, his friend in the police, if he could gather a DNA sample from it. Suspicion formed in John's mind, driven by their experience of Jimmy Gillespie. The event with the henhouse was no accident, no forgetfulness by any of his family. John was sure of that, given his daughter's reaction, which he trusted without question. This meant that a deliberate act of intended vandalism had taken place and there was only one person, he felt, with the mind-set to carry out that act. That was Jimmy Gillespie, and as he had a police record already, the police would have data on file.

The problem was, Duncan would need to justify a request for expensive DNA profiling and without evidence of a possible or proven crime, that wasn't going to happen. So John decided to keep the cigarette safe for future use if needed, but doing so raised a difficult notion in his mind. Future use meant waiting for something else to happen – more attacks on their property. Only then would he approach Duncan.

Damn it!

The question was, how much should he tell Sarah, though the answer came as soon as the question formed. She would know something was on his mind, as she had done before he revealed the essence of his dream. So he would share his suspicions straight away rather than risk her wrath if something else happened and he'd kept his concerns secret.

With the evidence secured in his pocket, John made his way back towards the cottage, intending to use the hosepipe to clean off the ground around the henhouse and wash out the bowl they used to provide drinking water for the chickens. Permanently connected to a tap under the kitchen window the hose lay coiled on the ground ready to use. John grabbed the spray gun and turned the tap. To his annoyance and discomfort, a jet of water spurted from somewhere in the middle of the coils. With high pressure from a natural supply fed straight off the hills, the icy water sprayed straight over John, soaking his head and shoulders. Quick as he could, he closed the tap.

He wiped a hand across his face and stared at the last dregs of water as they escaped the hosepipe. Under close examination, John saw a clean cut on the hose, a neat incision that passed almost through the whole pipe.

Fucking Gillespie … it has to be that little bastard.

At that moment there was little John could do except repair the hose, so he padded around to the store at the rear of the house in search of strong tape. On his way back he met Sarah, Rachel and Margaret as they left the converted barn heading towards the house. They seemed puzzled.

'What's up?' asked John, noticing their shared confusion.

'Well, neither of our appointments have turned up this morning,' said Sarah. 'And we've had three other no shows since Thursday. Never had that happen so often in such a short space of time. In fact, I'm not sure we ever had anyone just not show up … cancellations or re-arrangements maybe, but no shows – none. Why are you wet?'

'No shows?' John paused for only a second before continuing. 'Ok. We need to talk, but first, I need a towel.'

Half an hour later, over a bowl of soup, the four adults sat at the kitchen table while Robert and Scott sat in high chairs attempting to feed themselves pasta.

'Are you sure about this?' asked Rachel.

'Yes,' replied John. 'I know there's no concrete evidence, but who else, and for what reason.'

'It's not just some kids mucking about?'

'Doubt it. There aren't many teenagers around in the village and I can't imagine them walking all the way up here just to do some damage.'

'Y'know, I've known Jimmy for years,' Margaret said. 'Ever since his mother came to stay at the care home. And I think he'd be capable of anything if he was angry.'

'Ok, so what's next?' asked Sarah.

John considered his response for a few moments, but then falling back on his primary reason for becoming a policeman many years earlier, that drive to protect, he spoke with assertion. 'Most important, keep an eye over your shoulder. He knows all of you. That may sound overdramatic, but if what Margaret says is true about his mood and temper, I guess he could turn up anywhere just to vent his anger. Duncan said he's had assault charges in the past and though I'm not suggesting he'd do anything stupid, he may still try to intimidate us. But I'm certain Sarah and I are going to be his targets because he's lost what he hoped he had a claim to. When he was here, I told him he had no claim and to talk to his adviser. He would have had the same answer from them by now. So yes, he'll be angry, and he'll take his revenge out on us. But Rachel, Margaret, I still want you to take care.'

'Could he be responsible for the no show appointments?' asked Rachel

Margaret answered. 'It's possible. We had a few calls last week from withheld numbers and it was always a male voice. And they were all for names we haven't got on record … new clients.'

'Ok,' said Sarah. 'We'll have to work out a check on new patients for a while till this resolves. Address maybe … I don't know – something.' Sarah turned to John. 'You said there was no proof it was Gillespie. It seems to me the only way to *get* proof is if something happens again and hope he leaves evidence behind.'

'I'm sorry to say that was my thought too.'

'That's not a very comfortable notion.'

'No,' John said. 'And this is how he gets to us, petty destruction, annoying disruption to spoil our life here and keep us on the lookout, affect our peace of mind.'

Sarah stood to take her empty bowl to the sink. Outside, the chickens roamed uncaringly around the yard, while spots of rain skittered across the window pane. Sarah shivered, and in a rare moment of negativity muttered, 'I hate Jimmy Gillespie.'

Twenty Five

Later that afternoon, after Claire and the twins were back from school, John stepped outside to gather the chickens and close up the henhouse. 'Not that I don't trust anyone else to do it,' he said. 'It's just for my own peace of mind.'

Though sunset was still over an hour away, heavy cloud brought an early dusk and the outside world had lost its colour. Half way across the yard John stopped and turned to look back at the house, a frown creasing his brow. Glancing up towards the eaves to where the floodlight clung to the wall, he realised it had not turned on in response to his movement. Its infrared sensor had not detected his body heat, and he was certain the lamp would have triggered in the half light. But a closer inspection revealed the reason. The glass cover was shattered and despite the shadows that lurked under the eaves, the small hole in the back of the casing was clear to see.

'What in God's name?' he cursed, and retraced his

steps until he stood underneath the remains of the lamp. On the ground he found shards of glass, which he gathered with care into a pile, and, to his consternation, a twisted and crushed pellet – one he suspected was fired from a small gun or rifle. John took a moment to take control of his anger. Here was proof positive that someone was intent on creating destruction but his immediate concern was that the damage had occurred during daylight. As he crossed the yard early that morning, he recalled triggering the floodlight, so whoever the culprit was had been around during the day and had kept out of sight.

There was nothing he could do now, so returned to the task in hand. Making his way to the henhouse he counted the birds, and satisfied they had all settled down to roost for the night he closed the door, rattling the latch to make sure it was secure. There were still only eleven and he pondered the notion that Gillespie had taken one.

Once back inside, he called Sarah into the utility room at the rear of the cottage out of earshot of the children.

'The floodlight's broken,' he whispered. 'Or rather someone's deliberately broken it.'

'Broken? But how, when it's so high up?'

'I guess an air gun,' and John showed her the tiny lead pellet.

The shock on Sarah's face was clear. 'A gun?' she said and John nodded. 'But who would have such a thing?'

'Who do you think? Gillespie. It's only a small air gun pellet, though it can cause serious harm, and these guns are easy to get hold of. You can buy a license for just a few pounds a year, but someone like Gillespie wouldn't want to be on record. And of course they don't make much noise.'

'Should we call Duncan about it?'

'Yes. I'll call him in a minute and arrange to meet. I know what he'll say about needing evidence, but he may have some thoughts.' John paused a moment and lowered his voice still further. 'I don't think we should mention this to the kids, but we need Rachel and Margaret to be aware. I want them to be cautious wherever they are.'

Sarah nodded. 'Ok. We can talk to them tomorrow.'

Two days later, John stood with his elbows on the counter of the bar in the Chestnuts Hotel, a favourite drinking hole that lay a short distance from Ayr town centre. Duncan McBride stood next to him and handed John a folded sheet of paper.

'I shouldn't be doing this as you well know so read it and get rid of it.'

It was early evening, and a handful of couples indulging in dinner littered the lounge. John and Duncan stood alone away from prying eyes and inquisitive ears. John unfolded the paper, scanned it then stepped over to the fire and tossed it into the flames.

'So,' he muttered, returning to Duncan and picking up his glass. 'Gillespie has quite a record.'

'Yes. Before he'd reached legal age, he'd had a string of minor convictions, mainly for petty theft. But his illegal activity finally led him into a twelve month sentence for burglary, though it's been said someone inside the force who held a grudge fitted him up. Who knows, but there's no doubt he lives off crime. When he was twenty-three, a conviction under section 47 for ABH put him away for two years. Since then his record's been clean, but only because he's as slippery as a Teflon frying pan. He's even been charged with rape, before the complainant dropped the accusation. We've charged him with car theft and assault, the latter often sexual in nature but again he wriggled out of them in one way or another. One thing for certain, he's dangerous and unpredictable. Be warned John, I don't know what he's capable of and I don't want you or your family to find out. Stay well clear.'

'Try telling him that.'

'So what's this all about? Why the need to see his record.'

'Just wondering what kind of person I'm dealing with.'

'Dealing with? In what way?'

'We've been having some trouble but there's a possible family link.'

'Family?'

'You remember Beryl? We told you about her connection to Sarah. Well, Gillespie claims to share Sarah's great, great grandfather.'

'Claims you say. Any evidence?'

'None. Nothing legal. It's a long story which I may tell you one day, but there's no legitimate evidence such as a birth certificate that links him. He claimed a share of Manseburn, but his claim was denied because there's no proven link and I guess he's pissed off about it.'

'So these acts of vandalism are his way of getting back at you?'

'Yes … well those are my thoughts, but I have no evidence apart from a discarded cigarette.'

Duncan raised his eyes and leaned towards John. 'A cigarette butt? Do you still have it?'

John fished in his pocket and pulled out a small sealed bag.

'You realise I can't promise anything. If it has skin cells

or saliva and hence DNA, I need to have a reason for getting the labs involved.'

'Yes, I understand. There's not much of a case unless something bad happens or at best just something else.'

'You know the process and sometimes it's shit. If things escalate, I'll take it to the labs and see what I can do. One thing I will stress again. Be wary. If it is Gillespie, I don't know how far he'll go. He has a temper, we know that. He's not afraid to threaten any potential witnesses to his crimes or call on favours for alibis. Be careful, John. Don't frighten your family but warn them to be on the lookout. Anyone associated with Manseburn may be on his radar. He's unpredictable.'

John nodded. 'This may be the wrong thing to say but he'd better hope I don't catch him first.'

'I don't give a shit if it is the wrong thing to say, but if you do find him, make sure he starts it. Now,' and Duncan emptied his glass. 'A fella could die of thirst.'

Twenty Six

All Hallows Eve dawned cheerful with cloudless skies welcoming the morning hours. John leaned over the kitchen sink and cast his eyes upwards, reading the signs.

'Perfect morning to get stuff done, but I'm guessing we'll have rain this afternoon.'

'Is that you being clever again or did you just look at the weather report,' asked Sarah with a smirk.

Feigning hurt surprise, John muttered, 'Huh, no-one takes me seriously,' But a sudden snort gave the game away, and he laughed. 'No! I just get a feeling.'

'Ok, so you'll need a hearty breakfast and so will the boys.'

As if in response to Sarah's words, Jamie appeared in the doorway and stood motionless long enough to read the atmosphere. Satisfied that all was well he weaved his way around the kitchen fetching cutlery and glasses and laid out the table. Traditionally Claire's task, Jamie had taken over this important role and Claire was more than happy for him to do so.

'What's for breakfast?' asked Joseph as he raced into the room.

'We're having something different for Halloween,' Sarah replied. 'I've made Colcannon to go with your eggs.'

'Cold what?' Can we eat it?' asked Joseph, stifling a snigger with a hand.

'Yes, cheeky,' laughed Sarah. 'It's potato mash with kale. Plenty of energy, and I'm adding the eggs for protein. Where's your sister?'

John turned to Sarah and with amusement asked, 'Sister?'

'Sister?' she repeated. 'What sister?'

'You asked Jo where his sister was.'

Sarah opened her mouth but shut it again. 'Oh,' she said after a moment's thought. 'Did I? Well, actually that's the way it seems.' She walked over to John and wrapped her arms around him. 'Doesn't it?' she asked him. 'The boys have been with us for almost three weeks but in some ways it's like forever. Bit of a Freudian slip, I suppose.' She turned towards Joseph. 'How do you feel about having a sister?'

'Cool. How long till breakfast?'

'Huh, typical man. The fewer words the better. It'll be another five minutes so Jamie, can you find Claire for me please?' Sarah turned to find the young boy had slipped unnoticed out of the room. But at that moment Claire walked in holding Jamie's hand as she often did. A frown furrowed her young brow and darkness dulled her eyes.

'Are you all right, sweetheart? You look pale,' Sarah asked and let go of John.

Claire looked deep into Sarah's eyes and for a moment

they stood silent, locked in an invisible and exclusive sphere – a deep metaphysical world where at that moment only two souls existed. Claire broke the silence with a voice soft and hoarse. 'A dream in the night. It woke me up.'

All eyes were on Claire, aware that something was wrong. Even Joseph stayed silent, understanding that this was a moment when his ceaseless chatter may be inappropriate. Sarah crossed the room and took Claire's other hand. Jamie did not loosen his clasp.

'A dream? Do you remember what about?'

Clare shook her head but stood on tiptoe and whispered into her mother's ear. 'Something's going to happen. I feel sick.'

Sarah knelt in front of her daughter and Jamie gave up his hold. Claire gave her other hand to Sarah and mother and daughter joined, delving deep into each other's souls.

Barely audible to the others, Sarah uttered a single word. 'Beryl.' For over a minute no movement or sound disturbed the peace within the kitchen. Even Mags lay still, curled up by the Rayburn as was her habit when she felt encroaching winter, with only her eyes flitting back and forth, watching the play.

Claire drew in a deep breath and held it for many seconds before letting go and relaxing. She nodded at Sarah. 'Yes mom. I understand. I need something to eat now.'

'Good girl.'

Sarah stood and turned to her husband. 'Answers. I know you want them, but let's get breakfast served up. We all have things to do.'

While Sarah finished off preparing the morning meal, John stacked plates in the oven to warm, and fried eggs. Sarah kept her voice low as the children chattered at the table.

'Claire had a dream, and it may be similar to yours.'

'I hope not.'

'No, not the detail. What I mean is it seems like she's had a premonition. Like you she feels that something's going to happen. All I've done is try to convince her to be prepared, keep safe, stay on the lookout. And more importantly, things will often happen and there's nothing we can do to stop them. Sometimes it's how we respond that matters more and all we can do is manage the fallout.' Sarah sighed. 'It took me a long time to accept that John, after Steve, but as Hamish always said – it is what it is. Claire needs to learn that, harsh though it may seem.'

Sarah turned to the table. 'Ok everyone,' she announced. 'Let's eat.'

They planned the morning's tasks over breakfast. Joseph wanted to help John with vegetable planting once more. The boy had shown such enthusiasm getting his hands dirty and loved being of use. Claire roped in Jamie to help carve out pumpkins to dress up the house during the evening. With no clients that day, Sarah was planning a beef and ale pie for dinner with blackberry and apple crumble to follow. They then planned to relax with an old favourite on the television, the classic Disney film Hocus Pocus.

John and Sarah let the children loose after lunchtime while they themselves continued with more mundane tasks. Claire still appeared a little tense but Sarah guessed some play time might ease her worry.

'Off you go,' she said. 'Enjoy yourselves but be mindful of what you're doing.'

Joseph ran through the hall and shot outside, booting

a football with precision between the hen house and the main house. 'C'mon!' he yelled. 'Race you up the hill.' With a relaxed laugh Claire chased after him with Jamie trotting at a more leisurely pace.

Sarah and John watched them until they were half way up the hill.

'You're right y'know,' John said.

'About what?'

'When you inadvertently said sister. Three weeks and it's like we've been a family forever. How does that happen so fast?'

Sarah nodded but stayed silent. The tension that disturbed Claire's spirit troubled her, but she said nothing to John.

'Anyway,' he continued. 'I've got some ordering to do. What about you?'

'Household chores. Need to carry on with the washing, change the beds. Exciting uh?'

'Well, if you leave the beds, I'll do those when I've finished.'

Sarah turned, kissed her husband. 'Yes, we need clean bed linen after last night.'

John returned the kiss. 'I can't help it if you have that effect on me. We could always dirty them again before I change them.'

Sarah slapped the back of his head. 'You said you had ordering to do.'

'God, you tease me and then leave me hanging.'

Sarah moved against her husband. 'Um … I don't think you're hanging at the moment. That thing is pointing in the wrong direction.'

As John predicted the rain finally arrived, close to half-past two. Light showers dampened the ground at first, but they were enough to convince John of the heavy rain heading their way. Sourced from the north Atlantic and rising over the mountains of the western isles, the moisture journeyed south west, condensed and dropped its life force onto the Ayrshire hills.

'Time they were in,' John said as he walked into the utility room, arms laden with bed linen.

'Yes. They'll still be up on the hill. Seems to be a favourite place. How about we put coats on, load up Robert and meet them?'

'Ok. Sound good.'

With the first load of washing loaded up, John dressed little Robert and sat him in his car seat while he donned wellingtons and a waterproof jacket. He turned and stood waiting by the front door, peering out at the gentle rain. Sarah was halfway through lacing a boot when the force that struck at their collective spiritual souls arrived with such potency that John gasped and Sarah toppled forward onto outstretched hands.

John uttered a single profanity and steadied himself against the doorframe. But Sarah gasped out Claire's name – the source of the disturbance.

The message they received surged along the indestructible spiritual conduit that bound them together, the hotline that never failed, never slept. It spoke of fear and horror – screamed for assistance, and that need was impossible to refuse.

'C'mon,' John gasped. At the same time Sarah said, 'Go, I'm right behind you.'

John launched himself out of the house and into an

urgent sprint, widening his stride as he passed Memorial cottage and raced up the hill. Sarah finished lacing her other boot and in a moment of practicality reached into the kitchen for her mobile. Only then did she remember Robert who sat staring at her from his car seat.

In an instant she reached out to Claire, probed her soul in a sudden and desperate search for affirmation. Was Claire hurt? Was she injured? Within the space of a heartbeat, Claire returned an answer, though not in words. The response simply conveyed that Claire's physical aura was unharmed, she was uninjured. However, the child's emotional and spiritual layers screamed in anguish. *The boys! Oh God. Jamie, Joseph.*

With John well ahead of her, and trusting him to do whatever he needed, Sarah forced herself to calm her rising panic. She lifted Robert and slotted him into the baby carrier huddled against her chest. With her phone in one hand, she pulled the door shut. By now John would have covered half the distance to the summit of the hill and with pounding heart Sarah followed as quickly as she could.

Twenty Seven

A strong gale buffeted the children as they neared the hilltop. Ahead, the lowering cloud obscured the uppermost arms of the electricity pylon while occasional spots of rain flew in from the west. Wrapped up and protected by waterproof coats, Claire, Joseph and Jamie cared little for the threat of the incoming weather. And anyway, their racing game had kept them warm.

'Ok, I win!' yelled Joseph as he clambered up onto the concrete pad that supported one of the pylon legs.

'Only because you started first,' gasped Claire with a laugh. 'I think Jamie could beat you in a fair race.'

'Never.' Joseph tried without success to affect indignation. 'Always too slow.'

While they stood under the extended limbs of the pylon catching their breath, Jamie trotted up to join them. The constant crackle of discharging electricity filled the air as moisture from the descending mist met the high voltage power lines high above them. In the distance, a lonely crow cawed once before deciding that amidst the roar of the gale, verbal communication was a waste of effort.

'Ok,' said Joseph. 'What's the game today? How about you try this?'

Jamie lifted the football and using his middle finger as support spun the ball with the other hand. Skilled in the trick, he held the spin for full on ten seconds before dropping the ball and bouncing it around like a basketball player.

'Here, have a go,' and he bounced the ball towards Claire, but a playful Jamie caught the ball mid bounce and ran a little way across the hill. Turning back towards the others, he dropped kicked the ball high into the air. As it descended, Claire and Joseph shouldered each other as they jostled for position, determined to catch the ball. With one last push, Claire nudged Joseph to one side and then leapt above her competitor and neatly caught the ball as it fell.

'Cool!' yelled an impressed Joseph. 'Let's do that again. Three kicks each while the others catch.'

'Ok,' said Claire. 'I win the first kick. Jamie? Do you want to take your other two kicks?' and she bounced the ball back across the hilltop. Jamie caught the ball with ease and once again drop kicked it across the top of the hill with practised accuracy. Once again Joseph and Claire fought with fierce but friendly competitive spirit for possession.

As the afternoon wore on they each took it in turn to kick the ball while the others challenged, pushed and shoved their way to catch and score points. While they played, grey mists sank lower and the spots of rain became more frequent and heavier. When a steady drizzle began, it was with reluctance that Claire suggested it was time to go.

'The rain's getting heavy. We'd better go before we get soaked.'

'No, not just yet. Jamie still has one kick left. I'm gonna beat you this time,' shouted Joseph over the noise of the wind. 'Come on, bro. Make it a really high kick this time.'

Claire had discovered almost as soon as the twins arrived at Manseburn that everything Joseph did or said to his brother contained a challenge. With ingrained intuition and an understanding of Jamie's choice to stay quiet, to hide himself, she guessed these challenges were Joseph's way of engaging his brother – of stretching his world. But at Joseph's words, a recent memory came surging back, the memory of the previous night's dream. A flood of nausea filled her soul.

Without knowing the reason, she knew in an instant she had to stop Jamie from taking the last kick – knew they needed to leave the game for another day. But she was too late.

Rising to his brother's challenge, Jamie stepped back a few extra paces, lifted the ball, and with his right foot stretched out as far as he could, connected with it in perfect timing. Jamie exceeded his brother's challenge as the ball rose in a steep arc, up and away, climbing higher and higher. But as the ball rose, a sudden gust of wind slammed against it, changing its course mid-flight. With the combined power of Jamie's kick and the additional sideways energy of the strong south-easterly, the ball flew straight into the rigid steelwork of the electricity pylon – and stuck.

Twenty Eight

As Sarah climbed the hill, the rain set into a steady drizzle soaking her hair, her legs and everything around her. Robert was silent, protected from the rain by his jacket and a hood. As she climbed higher and approached the hill summit, she spotted John kneeling with his back towards her. Claire was close by but on her knees, bent forward, her arms folded across her chest. Jamie stood back and to one side, rigid as a statue, unmoving.

Even from a distance, Claire's cry of anguish rang out above the roar of the wind.

'Daddy, do something. Help him, please. Please, Daddy. Joseph, get up. Stop messing around. Jo …' Her voice broke as she stumbled into gasps and tears.

Sarah slowed as she approached, fear of what she may find making her reluctant to learn the truth.

'John?' she gasped.

Only at the sound of her question did John turn, and

the torment that contorted his face filled Sarah with dread. Barely aware of taking the last few steps, she saw John shake his head from side to side, distress and disbelief evident on his features.

Twisted on a slab of concrete at the foot of the electricity pylon lay Joseph. Abhorrent in its uncaring nature, the rain diluted and spread an angry red stain across the hard surface, blood that escaped in slow waves from Joseph's head. From the sharp angle of his neck, it was clear the boy would not move again, though the head injury was reason enough to believe he was dead.

Sarah's breath came in shallow gasps, disbelief filling her heart, and for a moment she couldn't speak or move. Robert reached out and with tiny fingers caressed Sarah's face. At the same time, a gentle caress feathered her brow, and that was enough to bring her emotional spirit back to the moment.

Pushing aside her horror and grief, she stepped toward Claire, knelt in front of her to block the view. 'Claire, sweetheart. What happened? Tell me.'

'Mommy …'

'Ok. I know. Listen. I need you to tell me what happened. Get it out.' Sarah paused a moment. 'Sweetheart. Beryl is here, and your Nana.'

Claire lifted her eyes, gazed into the distance and sensed the truth in her mother's words. Though tears still flowed, as they should, she took control of her breath and spoke.

'It was an accident. We were kicking the ball, having a contest to see who could catch it. Jamie was winning until the rain started and I said we had to go. But Joseph told him to make one last kick … a high one. It went miles up, but the wind blew it and it got stuck on the pylon.' Claire's voice broke again, but through a fresh flow of tears she forced herself to continue. 'We told him not to, begged him, but Joseph started to climb up the metal, up the leg. He wouldn't listen, and he went very high. He kept going. He said he liked it up there. The higher the better. Mommy ... he tried to reach for the ball. It must have been wet.' Claire stopped, staring now with horrified recollection at her mother.

'Sweetheart.'

'He slipped. Mommy ... I heard ... I heard when he hit the ground. Mommy ...' and then Claire collapsed into Sarah's arms in a spasm of anguished and tortured grief.

With her eyes on John who had taken off his coat and draped it over Joseph, Sarah let Claire's paroxysm continue, holding her daughter within a mother's embrace until she quietened, and all the while the rain fell uncaring around them. Only when Claire lifted her head and whispered 'Jamie' did Sarah look for the boy, but he was nowhere to be seen.

Jamie had disappeared.

Twenty Nine

Sue poured fresh tea for Sarah, and after a questioning glance at John, filled his too.

'Ok,' she said business-like, even though raw emotion softened her eyes. 'There are things you need to understand.'

By now nightfall darkened everything outside Manseburn, apart from the harsh white light upon the hillside where the police conducted an examination around the place where Joseph fell. The gale had dissipated, leaving a steady rain to fall in a sombre descent. Apart from the spatter of raindrops, there was little sound outside. It was as if the sky itself hushed its voice, simply shedding tears for the tragic loss of a young child.

The emergency services had little left to do. An ambulance took Joseph to the mortuary at Ayr Hospital, and the police left the family alone with a Family Liaison Officer after taking statements from everyone. Jamie was still missing and whatever tracks he may have left lay hidden by the scrub or washed away by the heavy rain. There was no doubt that Joseph's death was accidental, but questions still needed to be asked. Sarah had dialled the emergency services as soon as she realised Jamie was missing. Then she called Sue asking her to come out to the farm. They needed her help. Upon hearing the news after she arrived, Sue collapsed into a chair and uttered a cry of grief. 'You silly, silly boy. How many times did I warn you about climbing. Oh, Joseph.'

But then Sue reigned in her emotions, and adopted a professional manner. The police were asking questions, and she took great pains to convince them of the Macintyres' competence, of their care and experience with children. But John understood the process and quietly mentioned the likelihood of an inquest. Of course, the immediate concern was for Jamie. No one noticed when he left the hillside and had no idea of the direction he'd taken. With the persistent rain forecast to fall all night, coupled with the low temperature, the police began a sweep of the area and called in a Helicopter to aid the search. There was little to see despite the powerful searchlight and infrared cameras. It was possible Jamie had travelled some distance by now or could be just huddled under the blanket of shrubs in the nearby forest. Their only hope was to keep looking.

Though John wanted to join in the search, the Police told him to stay at the house while their questioning continued. Once Sue arrived and the Family Liaison Officer had left, he was itching to go, but Claire had fallen silent and sat on the sofa with her eyes half closed refusing to speak. With a quick probe of her soul, Sarah knew she had withdrawn, retreating internally while she made sense of events. Sarah however dug deeper, reached into every layer of Claire's aura. With innate intuition, she sensed that despite the awful trauma Claire had witnessed, no scars appeared to be developing. Hurt and anguish disturbed Claire's emotional body. But within the high layers of her spiritual aura, an inherent and strong sense of acceptance existed – the belief that whatever had happened, happened, and could not be undone. Grief was ok, but she would survive by accepting and adapting.

Once they were alone, Sue put the kettle on and made a large pot of tea and carried it through to the living room. Sarah settled next to Claire as the child sat staring without seeing, while John stood gazing out of the window into the darkness, lost in his own grief.

Sue handed a cup to Sarah. 'Here, drink.'

Sarah obeyed, sipping at the rim of her cup.

'John? Drink. You need a hot drink inside you,' Sue insisted as she place a cup and saucer onto the window ledge next to where John stood. John blessed Sue with an automatic nod and did as he was told.

'Jamie is our first concern but the police are searching and will carry on as long as they can.' Seeing the tension in John's shoulders, she continued. 'I know you want to be out there with them, but right now it's your wife and bairns that need you. This isn't a case of helping to look for any missing child. You're all involved, you've all suffered. You're hurting and you need to stick together. If you have any idea where he may have gone, then just say.'

'No idea,' John muttered. 'The boys' only knew what's in the immediate vicinity. There's nowhere else apart from Straiton and the primary school, but why would he go there? No, he's hiding somewhere and if I understand anything about that child, he'll be blaming himself.' John spun around in one sudden swift movement – animated, eyes full of chagrin. 'But it's my fault, not his. I let them run off to play. I should have kept them down here in the yard or behind the house. If I'd had stricter rules, this wouldn't have happened.'

'John, we're both to blame … we both thought fostering was too easy,' Sarah said.

'No. I should have laid down the rules as soon as they arrived. Taught them about the dangers, made them stay close.'

'John stop!' Sarah rose from the sofa and walked across the room. She raised her voice to a hoarse whisper as she confronted John. 'We both should have had that conversation. Why should it be your fault? It's not about you.'

'I didn't say it was about me,' John hissed. 'But I let Joseph down. Should've watched him closer …'

Sue strutted over and in a stern voice interrupted. 'You can both stop that ridiculous behaviour immediately!' With a glare at Sarah and John, she continued. 'I won't let you blame yourselves or each other and you're not having this argument in front of Claire. Don't think I don't understand both of you, but it's no one's fault. I've lost count of how many wee ones I've place in foster homes or tried to place that have had problems. Sometimes just settling in, kids running away to begin with, or worse. With my list of foster carers, it's never their fault. Never has been. Do you understand? Never. They're trying their hardest to give a normal life to young ones who all too often never had one. Some of these kids are broken. Some are wayward and some follow their own rules. Joseph was one of the latter. A good child, just needed a place he felt gave him and his brother some safety. But he was also a devil for getting into dangerous places. The authorities picked them up on railway lines, walking along busy roads, and caught Joseph climbing places not meant for climbing. Though I hate to admit it, he was an accident waiting to happen.'

Sue paused a moment, long enough to allow a ragged breath to escape. In a more mellow voice, she continued. 'Listen. Joseph possessed no sense of danger. He saw a place he wanted to go, and he went for it. He liked heights, and no amount of warnings ever stopped him climbing. I will impress upon the authorities and the adoption agency the facts, and those facts will ensure no blame can be apportioned. So whatever rules you may or may not have set would have made no difference. I'm so sorry for you both.'

John found no words to say but collapsed into the nearest chair wiping a hand down his face.

'Thank you Sue,' he muttered. 'And of course you're right. You can keep children safe, but not always from themselves. But I feel like we've let you down, and Jamie. You came to us as a last resort. Asked us if we could help, put your faith and trust in us and now … well.'

Sue gazed down at the top of John's head. 'John, I'd place a child with you again tomorrow without hesitation. I would lay my integrity on the line because though we only met a few short weeks ago, I know you. I believe in you and what you do. What happened has not changed my faith and trust, and you've let no one down.'

'So what do we do now?' asked Sarah.

'Nothing. Not tonight. Let the authorities take over. You'll be of no use to anyone if you're worn out. Children often return of their own accord once they've calmed down or when they get hungry. Jamie won't stay away for long. I'm sure of it. So keep a light on. Keep your ears open, though I'm sure the dog will hear anything first, and keep a fire in. He'll be cold.'

Sue reached for her bag. 'I'd better get back to my own family. There's nothing else I can do either, but I'll make phone calls tomorrow. The Police may want to ask more questions.' For a moment Sue stood looking at the family she trusted, and pain filled her heart at their suffering. Too often she had seen it before, and for her the agony never eased. Tears filled her eyes. 'I really am so sorry for you all.'

John rose and walked over to where Claire sat unmoving. With eyes now closed, she appeared to have succumbed to a much needed sleep, so John carefully laid her down and draped a woollen throw over her legs. Sarah walked Sue to the door. 'Saying thank you seems wrong or not enough. I don't know which. But I'm grateful for your kindness.'

'There is no right or wrong Sarah, but call me if you need any more help tonight and I'll speak with you tomorrow anyway,' Sue said, and with a hug she headed out into the rain.

Sarah re-entered the living room and gazed at John. With mutual understanding of their needs, they joined, each opening their hearts and souls, seeking solace and a cure for their torments. For many minutes they stood as statues exploring the past, drawing upon the lessons their souls had learnt over millennia. The tragedy and loss, the joy and love – the finding. As each relinquished their hold on the other, they exhaled, letting loose a tension that robbed their physical strength.

'Ok,' Sarah said. 'Would you put Claire to bed? Or better still, leave her where she is. The blanket will keep her warm. I think we should stay in here tonight. I'll bring Robert's travel cot down. He can still fit in it. Claire can have a bath tomorrow if she sleeps all night. Would you put a couple of logs on the fire? Oh, and do you want something to eat?'

'Yes, I'll fetch more logs in too and actually yes please. I'm hungry all of a sudden.' Sarah nodded and turned to leave the room. 'Sarah?'

'Yes?'

'You were right. I was feeling sorry for myself, finding a reason to blame someone and who else but me. I'm sorry. And everything Sue said is right. Are you ok with that?'

Sarah turned back and stood in front of John. She reached down and teased a hair from Claire's mouth, placed a kiss on her forehead. 'She's out for the count, thank heavens. But yes. Yes I am, though I still hate myself. Hasn't there been enough loss in our family?'

John shuddered. 'Y'know we may have this gift but it doesn't mean we're immune to stuff that happens. We still suffer loss and pay for it. I guess we're able to understand how it affects us on our spiritual level, but we still have the emotion to contend with. So yes, I hate myself too and yes there's been enough loss. Too damn much.'

Sarah nodded and lowered her head. Moments later she raised tear filled and grief-stricken eyes towards her husband. 'John, I'm so glad I have you. I love you so much.'

With his own grief escaping, John kissed Sarah's brow. 'I love you too my princess. Damn it. I think I loved that kid.'

'I know you did.' And she reached up and pulled

John's head onto her shoulder, smoothing his hair with her fingertips.

'C'mon,' she said. 'Let's get this house ready for Jamie. And we've got leftovers I can warm up.'

The wait continued with no end. By midnight, the heavy but distant chop of the helicopter blades faded and the search called off until morning. The rain had become more than a steady drizzle limiting visibility for the aircrew.

After a late supper, Sarah settled Robert into his cot where he fell silent within moments. Careful not to make a sound, John built up the fire and while Claire lay motionless on one sofa, John and Sarah sat together on the other.

Sarah probed her daughter's soul once more but found the child spiritually settled, though distant. It seemed she had withdrawn still deeper, all but invisible to her mother. Unconcerned for Claire's retreat, Sarah understood that if she called, the child would awaken in an instant. But she knew Claire needed the time alone.

The night crept on with no sign of Jamie returning and as the clock ticked and half-past one approached, Sarah and John dozed off … at first into a fitful sleep but then settling into a deep exhausted slumber.

While John, Sarah and Robert slept, a disturbance entered Claire's beleaguered mind. A distant message crept into her thoughts and she awakened. She sat upright, feeling her way back to the present. Was it a spiritual message or did she sense something different or learn a new skill that opened an unexplored element of her gift? But then an image came to her, pure and distinct. The rain that shrouded the cottage where they all lay cocooned could not dull the dream, if dream it was, and the ache that pierced her heart following the death of Joseph held no power over the vision because love lay at its foundation.

As if he were standing in the room, Jamie appeared within her mind's eye. To Claire's powerful senses Jamie seemed to be shivering, a relentless quaking that shook him to the very core. The image spoke of a broken heart and a spirit dull and lifeless. And he was desperately cold. For a moment Claire wondered why this vision appeared, since Jamie had taken the conscious choice to hide himself. He had been as invisible to Claire as he had to Sarah and John.

Claire remembered the day her daddy's friend David died and John's aura collapsed in anguish. She couldn't sense her father, and it horrified her. How then could she sense Jamie with such clarity when Jamie had also retreated? But the answer came, and from an intuitive layer, her higher spiritual layer. She could see Jamie because her own gift had grown, ever more so after her brother was born and they began to share their strengths. But with the appearance of the apparition, she now knew what she needed to do, though she required help to achieve it.

Armed with this new understanding and mindful of the enormous task in hand, Claire stood and on tiptoes crossed the room to where Robert lay in his cot. Peering at her brother, she awoke his spiritual energy, energy that lay unused but potent since it was inherent in his being. Joined with Robert, she channelled her intent towards Jamie, a message aimed at guiding him to safety before he succumbed to the effects of the falling temperature. Her purpose was to trigger hope in his heart, show him he was loved and that there was a safe place to hide while he decided what to do. At the root of her intention lay a secret she had shared with him, and she hoped with every fibre of her being that his memory was strong.

Thirty

Within his dream, John stood inside the greenhouse hunched over the shelving while Joseph, keen and bright eyed, studied the plans John had sketched out for early crops the following spring. Potatoes here, Kale and Radish there, with lettuce as well. It was clear Joseph was eager to get his hands in a bag of seed compost but as John smiled and turned toward the boy his face faded, the colour in his cheeks leaching away to a translucent grey before disappearing.

John opened his eyes and stared at the glow inside the log burner as the ache in his heart returned. In a swift movement he sat upright, drawing a weary hand across his face. He glanced across at Sarah and listened. Propped up on large cushions she lay still, legs covered with a woollen blanket. John sensed she was awake and perceived a disturbance in her soul that mirrored his own. But then a sound reached his ears dragging him to full wakefulness. For a moment the noise made little sense until a glow around the edge of the curtains diverted his attention. Within an instant he shot to his feet, dragged a curtain aside and gazed with horror and disbelief across the front yard.

'John,' Sarah whispered. 'Why are the chickens making a noise?'

'Shit,' John spat. 'Sarah, the chickens … the henhouse. It's on fire!'

For a moment, Sarah couldn't quite make sense of John's words, but as her husband raced out of the room, she saw the red glow herself.

'John!' she yelled and yanked on her slippers.

Already inside the front porch, John dragged on his boots and ran out of the house. Without hesitation he twisted the outside tap and grabbed the hosepipe, but once more a jet of water sprayed him from a deliberate cut in the plastic sheath.

Blind in his anger to the effects of the freezing water, John turned off the tap and grabbed the hosepipe either side of the damage. With strength borne out of fierce rage he ripped the plastic piping apart, untwisted the tap connector and remade the joint. In less than a minute he was charging across the yard, spraying a powerful jet of water across the burning timbers. Hosing down the door, he flipped the latch and sprayed inside, soaking the flames that had ignited the dry straw. Amidst a shower of feathers and fluttering of wings, four of the eight chickens shot past him out onto the yard, but for the other four it was too late. John continued to douse the flames until they reduced and eventually failed. After ten minutes, only the roof, the rear and left hand side stone wall, and the heavy support timbers remained. John closed the flow of water and screamed into the darkness.

'Fucking GILLESPIE. I'll fucking kill you, you BASTARD! DO YOU HERE!' Only when he spun around looking for something to vent his rage upon did he notice Sarah and Claire standing close by, horror distorting their features.

'Daddy,' muttered Claire. 'Why is this happening? What have we done?'

'Nothing, ok?' he shouted. 'We've done nothing! It's not our fault. I don't want to hear any talk like that. It's that bastard Gillespie who's responsible!'

A firm hand on John's arm made him stop, a touch that carried a burning heat that engulfed and smothered his fury.

'Yes, you're right, John,' Sarah said with a calmness borne out of acceptance. 'It isn't our fault.' She moved around and stood between her husband and daughter. 'Claire, sweetheart. Can you make sure Robert's ok please?' Claire nodded and without a word walked into the house. 'I know why you're hurting,' Sarah continued. 'Believe me, we all are, but I need you to use your gift to stay in control. Claire is strong, we know, but she is that way partly because she knows *we* are strong. One thing that will break that strength is if she feels insecure because we've lost control. Steer you anger into a useful emotion. Anger will get you nowhere except to risk everything because you'll no longer think in a rational way. It's a long time since I learnt that lesson.'

John hung his head and Sarah could see shame in the action, and sense it in his heart.

'Damn it,' he muttered. 'I'm sorry. I need to apologise to Claire.'

'Maybe. She knows your sorry, but she needs your love

Broken

… needs to know your with her.'

John looked behind at the ruined hen house. There was a job to do in the morning – disposing of the hens caught in the blaze and making sure the building was safe. In the meantime, the remaining chickens he'd lock in the shed safe from marauding foxes.

'I woke out of a dream,' he said. 'Of Joseph. We were planning next year's spring crop. How can someone get under your skin so quickly? That poor kid.'

'The nature of the boy and the nature of you. It was meant to be that way, the same as we were meant for each other. Remember, there is no why, where or when. There just is, and the *is* at the moment concerns Jamie.'

John studied the face of his soul mate and saw many things. Accustomed to this measured response during difficult times, her words were full of wisdom. He perceived the light that shrouded her physical being, the white aura that spoke to him of intuition and understanding, that which he now understood to connect to a high level of consciousness and spirituality, though at this moment it wafted back and forth under duress. But though her spiritual strength was without question, the tears in her eyes gave away her current emotional state. Her grief mirrored his own, and he needed no special gift to see it. John took her hands.

'Yes,' he answered. 'Jamie? I just wish we could sense him. At least we would have some idea if he was safe.'

Sarah turned and led John back to the house. 'Come on. There's nothing more you can do here tonight. Let's check on the kids. Tomorrow you can figure things out.'

'You go on,' he sighed. 'I'll just scoot these chickens into the shed and I'll be right with you.'

'It'll be quicker with both of us.'

Two hours later, after a bold but ineffective attempt to doze off, John crept out of the living room, bottle of whisky in one hand, leaving Sarah and the children asleep. He slipped into the kitchen and poured a large dram before settling onto a chair. But before he had taken a sip, he rose to his feet, glass in hand and headed out into the hallway. Restless with the desire to do something, he made his way into the utility room at the rear of the cottage. After a quick nip of whisky, he dragged on a pair of waterproof trousers followed by his boots and topped them off with a thick sweater and a jacket. The rest of the drink he left until he returned.

With a shift of air in the upper atmosphere, a strong north-easterly gale drew tears from his eyes as he left the warmth of the cottage and he turned his back towards it to shield his face. At least the rain had stopped. A quick search through his pockets located a woollen hat which he dragged over his head. Equipped at last for a nocturnal excursion, he passed the rear of the cottage, then turning a few degrees west headed up the hillside to where tragedy had taken place earlier.

Despite the heavy cloud and lack of moonlight, he needed no torch to light his way. Out here he was confident in his direction and footing now that his eyes had become accustomed to the low level of residual light. While he climbed the hillside, he pondered Duncan's words, his warning concerning Gillespie's unpredictability. How was he meant to keep his family safe when even now, the man could be outside their property plotting or carrying out more acts of vandalism? He'd arranged for additional security after discussing plans with Sarah two weeks ago, but the alarm system was not yet installed. Floodlights had covered the grounds around the house front and back, but it was quite possible they were all disabled by now. To do so only required an illegal air rifle. Mags had always been an excellent guard dog, but with thick walls and a strong gale blowing, anyone could approach their home in stealth – unheard.

To calm his rising concern, John drew a deep breath, held it for a few moments, then exhaled through pursed lips. He paused and turned to stare back down the hill towards his home. Apart from the outside lamp that lit the rear door, the property lay in utter darkness, swallowed up by the wild landscape that stretched onwards across the Ayrshire hills. Without conscious thought, visions of the house in Ayr overwhelmed him, where Hamish spent his last years, where they had drunk many a dram and shared many stories. He heard his grandfather as he sat comfortably in his armchair, glass in hand.

'John, it is what it is. Remember that. You need to concentrate on the immediate future. Not a week, or a month, just now and tomorrow. The past is past so ignore it. Plan for the moment and what you need to do, and leave emotion out of it. Be practical son – it's the only way to keep your family safe.'

The image grabbed at John's throat and for a moment weakened him.

'But I don't know what to do,' he muttered. 'I need help.'

'C'mon John. This isn't you. You're tired yes, but take control. Can you see him? Have you tried?'

See him? Do you mean his spirit?

Then the penny dropped and humiliation clouded his features. Why did this not occur to him? Once before he'd sensed the 'wrongness' that surrounded Jimmy Gillespie, the day of the appointment with Rachel, before they understood who he was. A feeling had unsettled John, though he'd no idea why. He only knew he needed to stay near the house. Maybe the time had come to focus his gift and try to connect.

But therein lay a fundamental problem, he disliked this aspect of his gift, disliked what he thought of as an invasion of privacy both for himself and those he sensed. Apart from his immediate family and close friends, he blocked, as far as possible, spiritual energies, refusing to heed them. Only those with intense psychic fields would disturb his soul, those under duress or those responsible for creating it, those with evil intent such as Jimmy Gillespie. But now, with the wisdom of his grandfather ringing in his ears, he understood he needed to disregard these self-imposed rules. To prepare himself for what may come he needed to find Jimmy Gillespie.

Up there on the desolate hillside, he could clearly see his whole life's purpose and meaning spread out before him – everything he held dear and needed to protect. The farm hidden in darkness and closed down for the night – his family sleeping safe and warm. Maybe this vision would aid his search. With all this held in his mind's eye, John let go of his shield – that all powerful visualisation of Sarah's aura that he used as a protective cloak. But as he let go, and for reasons he failed to understand, a sudden barrage of spiritual energy overwhelmed him – some powerful, others less so. But within moments understanding came to him and he realised that by lowering his shield without specific purpose, he had opened his soul to any spiritual chatter within reach. It seemed, he thought, that unbeknown to him, the range of his gift had grown without conscious knowledge, even as he maintained his shield.

The potential power shocked John – the untapped nature of his abilities, and sudden nausea made him gag. But realising he needed to focus on a specific intention, he pulled into his thought the physical image of Gillespie and found it easy to do so such was the man's impact on John's wellbeing. He recalled the depth of the disturbance he'd experienced on the day Gillespie arrived at Manseburn and used that disturbance as a focal point. Holding the image and the sense of the man within his psychic memory, and using that memory to push aside the volume of other psychic energies, he spread tendrils of percipience out into the world. Within moments he received an answer to his efforts, and the effect shook his physical body as he stood alone upon the hillside. But he maintained control of his focus and pushed further, trying, without knowledge of how, to gauge where the man was. Whether John's own immature skills worked, or whether he borrowed additional strength from outside of himself he did not know, but the answer came, and he detected an element of physicality.

John knew from Sarah's retelling of Beryl's tale that their spiritual reach held no bounds – it was limited only by the individual's experience. Understanding his own limited range because of this lack of experience helped John realise that his perceived strength of Gillespie's psychic field meant he was not in the immediate vicinity of Manseburn. Also, Gillespie conveyed an inactive energy field and John guessed this meant he was asleep. *Practise makes perfect,* John thought with a moment's clarity, and so he closed down the vision and raised his shield. He had become practised at using a vision of Sarah to maintain a block upon the spiritual energy existing in every corner of his world. Surely it was acceptable that he could use the principle of practise makes perfect to focus an intention before opening his shield. With that idea in mind, he turned and continued his journey to the top of the hill. As he walked, he drew in once more the image of Gillespie and then lowered his guard.

There was a momentary delay before he detected once more his previous sense of Gillespie asleep – or as he assumed was asleep. Within that brief moment, he sensed as before the noise of psychic chatter, but it was less intense. Closing his defence, he repeated his efforts even as he walked, until satisfied he could switch backwards and forwards between sensing nothing and locating Gillespie with little or no initial disturbance.

Once more the power of this gift shocked John, but he tempered that shock with a new understanding – that it was within his power to accept, learn and control it, and it seemed within a short space of time. Sarah always said the gift grew quickly. How true was that statement?

Climbing out of his musings, John became aware of his surroundings. He had reached the brow of the hill and came to a halt a few feet away from a strip of police cordon tape. John had not been here since running up the hill in response to Claire's psychic scream for help, and the sight of it hit him as a physical blow. Wrapped around metal rods by the Police, the buffeting of the wind had ripped away one end of the tape and it flapped and danced in manic rhythm to the howling gale. John grabbed at the loose end and began gathering the tape into a bundle, unwrapping it from each of the four rods before thrusting it into a pocket. Then he peered at the place where he had found Joseph and lowered his head before sinking to his knees.

Tears stung his eyes once more, but this time the wind was not the cause and for a few minutes he allowed himself a quiet grief. Though he knew Joseph only a short while, the boy had built a home in John's heart and the loss tore at his soul. But then, driven by a need to lift himself out of sorrow, John lowered his shield once more and drew the smiling face of Joseph into his mind's eye. What appeared both surprised and comforted him.

Joseph stood before him clear and in focus and he wore a bright and cheeky grin. Behind and to one side stood a young woman who wore serenity on her face with the ease of someone long practised in its use. The purist of white light shrouded them both – a luminescence that carried a song of ceaseless love and tranquillity. A woman's voice spoke, though it seemed to John the voice came from within his own thoughts not from the young woman.

'I know you John, though we never met in person. Indeed, I touched your soul once – only once. You'll remember that, since I touched Sarah at the same time. The day you found the cave below our home. We are all of the same bloodline, broken, separated for many generations but re-joined and remade by you and Sarah. But what you see now should heal your heart, that this young life is reunited with his young mother. They understand your suffering and your grief, and that your love for this boy brought much joy even though the time was short. Joseph knew from the first time he met you, you would give he and his brother the love and hope that they have long searched for, and his gratitude goes beyond your current world. He knows you will find Jamie and make him whole once more – you just need to believe in yourself.

'Remember John, you are not to blame for Joseph's choices in life. His flame burnt bright, his song was strong, he was in control of his destiny as you are for yours. Now, Jamie is not far away – I know you will be able to find him. I can see him and you have the gifts to do so also.'

John spoke aloud into the darkness. 'Beryl? I need help. I don't know where to start. He's hidden from me.' But no answer came, just the howling of the wind as it gusted through the uncaring, harsh metalwork of the pylon.

John pondered the words. Had he actually heard them? Were they real or his own wishes voiced aloud? With sudden determination creasing his brow and driven by what he imagined as Beryl's compassion, John rose to his feet and turned to the west. Heedless of the strength of the gale that coursed along his neck and face, he recalled once more a vision from his psychic memory. This time, however, he focussed on Jamie. He pictured the boy's muted expression, the searching looks he gave, and the light in his eyes as they flitted back and forth. Within his mind's eye he held the image of Claire holding the young boy's hand, hoping that the strength of his daughter may lead him to connect with Jamie, but to no avail. He detected no spiritual activity, near or distant.

But contemplating once more the words spoken by Beryl, words of love and hope, he relaxed his limitations, understood and accepted still further the immeasurable powers of his gift. From an enormous distance, or so he felt, the most minute of psychic tendrils caressed the highest of John's auric layers, like wisps of smoke rising from an open fire that curled around and embraced the surrounding air. The touch conveyed no message, held no identification, but

Broken

John sensed a familiarity which, within his heart, reminded him of Jamie. With sudden hope blossoming, he understood he had sensed a layer of Jamie's soul that remained accessible, however disturbed the earthly spirit had become.

The boy was out there, but how near or far, John could not tell.

With an enormous yawn, triggered by the lack of sleep and the effort of his spiritual searching, John turned towards home feeling a measure of comfort. Certain he had sensed Jamie he took it to mean the boy was safe, if alone. Needing only to make it back to the cottage, John stumbled downhill. Entering the house using the way he had left, he downed the remains of the whisky and took off the outdoor clothes he had pulled on in a hurry. There was a warm fire and it was needed, and so creeping back into the living room, he slipped under the blanket he'd discarded earlier. Before he fell asleep, he ran through the last hour in his head. He accepted that his gifts had limitations compared to Sarah and Claire. He knew he was unable to pinpoint Gillespie as if the man were carrying a GPS tracker, but at least he'd learnt how to focus and read the psychic markers in an attempt to guess the man's mood. In a few hours, daytime would arrive, Gillespie would be awake and John could continue to his exploration.

But more importantly, he knew Jamie was out there – somewhere.

Thirty One

The Macintyres spent Sunday wandering in a world of disbelief, sadness and guilt. The house felt empty. Barely twenty four hours earlier, their home had been full of chatter and excitement, but a terrible accident had snatched that life away leaving them bereft and adrift, functioning on necessity alone.

The search for Jamie had re-commenced as soon as daylight and visibility allowed, but by three o'clock, and with no signs, footprints or any notion of which direction Jamie had taken, the authorities called off the search. The next steps involved a Television broadcast and an item on social media asking the public to help, to be on the lookout. The irony was not lost of John.

While John focused on clearing the carnage within the remains of the henhouse and pottering in the greenhouse, Sarah busied herself with the energetic cleaning of the treatment rooms before donning a jacket and strolling past the paddocks at the rear of the cottage with little Robert strapped on her back.

Claire stayed in her room until lunchtime, refusing breakfast. When Sarah gingerly opened her bedroom door late in the morning, she found the young girl lying on her back in the middle of the floor – eyes closed. Sarah guessed she was asleep. Mags crept past Sarah and curled up next to Claire, her chin resting on her paws. Sarah left them alone.

When she shared news of the tragedy with Rachel and Margaret, they were horrified and offered to help in any way they could. But Sarah thanked them and insisted there was no need. They'd decided to carry on as normally as possible. Sitting idle was not in her nature and sticking to routine was better than idling away the hours full of heartache.

Early Monday morning John ended a telephone call and sighed.

'Any use?' Sarah asked.

'Same message, really. The police can only record the incident and give us a number. Duncan will do that for us, we just need to sign a statement. I'll run down later. I've got work to do out on the back field.'

'And how are you feeling this morning?'

'I didn't say anything yesterday but I went out for an hour very early Sunday morning after the fire, but I guess you know that.' Sarah nodded and let John continue. 'I figured out how to connect with Gillespie.'

'Connect?'

'Yes, so I can find him and try to read his mood as a pre-warning. In fact …' John paused and turned his head to the kitchen window, gazing into the distance. 'I can sense him now, and his mood is just vile. It's like I'm breathing in a cloud of filthy smoke, choking.'

'Is that a good idea?'

'I can handle it. Remember, I was a copper once. I used to experience all sorts of foul people and see sights I'd never want to see again. Actually,' John fell silent for several seconds before muttering, 'I think he's not far away.'

'What? How can you tell?' Sarah moved closer to John.

'I can't be certain, but it feels like there's more immediacy to his nastiness, if that makes any sense at all. And …' John stopped, tilting his head as if listening.

'John?'

'Something's wrong. I can sense fear.' John stared at Sarah. 'Can you? Is your shield down?'

With widening eyes but trusting her husband, Sarah put aside her Circle of Friends, that talisman she had discovered as protection for her spirit. In an instant a violent shudder took control of her body and she dropped onto a chair for fear of falling.

'Margaret,' she whispered. 'Where is she?'

John checked the wall clock. 'She must be close, it's almost nine thirty.'

'I'm worried, can you go look for her?'

With a sharp nod, John hurried out of the kitchen. Hopping from one leg to the other, he dragged on his boots and ran out of the house followed by Sarah. Yanking open the car door, he was about to climb in to go in search of Margaret when they heard the roaring of a car engine and across the yard Margaret's Corsa shot through the gates. With a cloud of dust and gravel scattering in its wake, the car crossed the large driveway and skidded to a halt near the converted barn.

Margaret all but fell out of the car, but John

approached and stood close enough to catch her in a firm hold. Shock and fear distorted her features. 'Oh God. You wouldn't believe it.'

'Are you ok?' breathed Sarah, and Margaret nodded.

'Come on,' John said. 'Let's get indoors and you can tell us. Take a few seconds to catch your breath.'

Fifteen minutes later Margaret emptied a cup of tea. 'I couldn't be sure because the driver was wearing a hoody. And I didn't recognise the car.'

'So you can't be certain it was Gillespie,' John asked.

Margaret shook her head. 'I'm sorry.'

'There's no need for you to be sorry. We're the ones to be sorry for dragging you into this,' John replied.

Margaret shook her head again. 'It's not your fault. Whoever it is was crazy. Drove so close I couldn't even see the front of his car. He raced past me and braked so hard I had to slam on my own brakes. Then he crawled for ages. I didn't dare stop. But as we got close to the drive, he shot off. I didn't get his number.'

'Ok. It's ok. We're all pretty sure who it was,' said John. 'I'll call Duncan, so at least he's aware we now have intimidation with intent to add to possible charges … if we ever catch him in the act.'

Margaret rose to her feet. 'I'd better open up. We'll have clients arriving soon.'

'No, you take it easy,' said Sarah. 'I can manage that.'

'No. I'm not letting anyone scare me out of working here. I'm fine now, so I'll carry on as normal.' Margaret gathered up her coat and headed out of the kitchen door. But before she left the house, she looked back. 'I think we should warn Rachel though.'

Later in the morning, as Sarah's first client drove out of the gate, John arrived in the kitchen.

'Hi,' she said. 'How are you getting on out back?'

'More damage, I'm afraid.'

'What? What now?'

'The rabbit-proof fence has been cut in several places, just enough to cause hassle more than anything else. Worse is the second greenhouse. The new seedlings? Looks like weed killer or something, because they're scorched and wilted.'

For once, Sarah was at a loss for words and busied herself with filling the kettle. But as the silence lingered, she turned and spoke with conviction. 'We need to catch him John before he ruins everything.'

'Yes,' John replied with an air of solemn acceptance. For a few moments they stood waiting for the kettle to boil, but the strident ringing of the telephone disturbed their reverie. John answered it, recognising the number for Claire's school.

'Hello. John Macintyre,' he said. 'Is everything ok?'

'Hello Mr Macintyre. This is Mrs McBride, Claire's headmistress. Yes, everything's fine. We just wanted you to know that Claire refused to go outside today at break time.'

'Refused? Is she not well?'

'She seems ok. But she stayed inside looking through the glass window by the door. She seemed interested in something but wouldn't say what.'

'Can I talk to her?'

'Yes, of course. She's with me now. Maybe she'll tell you something she won't tell us.'

John heard the rustling of the handset, followed by his

daughter's voice.

'Dad?'

'Yes, princess. What's up.'

'I think Jimmy Gillespie was here.'

Six short words and delivered without emotion. But those six words reached in to John's heart and turned it to ice.

'John,' said Sarah, sensing his sudden change in mood. 'What is it? Talk to me.'

'Claire? I'm going to put you on loudspeaker so your mom can listen. Can you say that again?'

'Hi Mom. I think Jimmy Gillespie was here.'

'Oh God,' she whispered. 'How do you know, sweetie? Can you be certain?'

A moment of silence followed, during which they guessed Claire was searching her soul. 'Yes, I'm sure.'

'But,' John said. 'You've never met him.'

'*You* have though, daddy. I can feel him through you.'

'Ok,' Sarah continued. 'One of us will come and fetch you. We want you home.'

'No. I'm ok. I don't want to miss any classes. I'll stay indoors until after school. I promise. I'll never be on my own.'

John glanced at Sarah, who nodded. Claire was strong and sensible – leaving school early would not help the situation.

'Ok sweetheart,' Sarah agreed. 'Can we talk to Mrs McBride again please and we'll see you later? And Claire?'

'Yes, mommy.'

'Don't block. Keep yourself open.'

'I will.'

Then after a brief pause, 'Mr Macintyre?'

'Ok. We're happy that she's ok but can we ask a big favour please. For a while we'd like Claire to stay indoors during breaks and lunchtime. We think there's someone about that can't be trusted.'

'That's very worrying? Should we call the police? Are they a danger to the children?'

'If you spot someone acting suspicious, just follow your usual procedures. But he's not interested in anyone else. He's ... we think he's a disgruntled client,' John lied. 'Oh, and it would be very helpful if you could warn the rest of the staff. It won't be for much longer,' John added with sudden and unexpected conviction.

'Ok, and rest assured we'll keep Claire indoors. In fact, I'll bring her back home myself. She's a brave and sensitive child.'

'No, no. I'll come and collect her,' said John.

'Please, it's no bother. I live in Straiton anyway, but it'll give me a chance to talk to you properly, see what we're dealing with. Don't forget I have an entire school to consider.'

'Yes, of course. We understand,' replied Sarah and conveyed her thanks once more..

Thirty Two

'It won't be for much longer?' Sarah repeated John's words once he'd cleared the call. 'How do you know? It seems to me Gillespie won't stop until he's destroyed everything.'

John clicked on the kettle to bring it to a fresh boil. 'Dunno,' he muttered, as much to himself as to Sarah.

While speaking to Claire over the phone, he'd felt a more immediate connection to his daughter, as if their thoughts and decisions were one and the same. Each day from the moment of waking, John was aware of each member of his family, sensing them as keenly as his own physical body or his mood. Since his spiritual awakening this awareness had grown, and Sarah, Claire and Robert were ever present in his heart, separate entities but a part of the whole. But during the phone conversation, he perceived a change in himself that he couldn't quite understand. In some indistinct manner, Claire had strengthened her connection with her father, had reached into his psyche and intensified it.

As his daughter, and with the gifts she possessed, gifts that were a product of her parents, Claire understood John and all his strengths and weaknesses. She had seen first-hand his fear when Sarah lay in hospital, tortured in a dream world not of her own making. At the same time, she'd noted the inherent strength in his nature, the power he possessed to comfort and protect. She had seen his anger, a weakness that threatened his well-being and his ability to rationalise and make controlled choices. But love was John's greatest strength, and Claire had seen how her father shared this emotion with two young boys in need of help. From John's outburst following the henhouse fire, Claire realised her father needed help, his psychic well-being was under duress and his individual strengths and weaknesses were erratic and uncontrolled and it frightened her. How would John protect them all if on a basic level he couldn't think straight?

And so she gave more of herself to him.

During the previous night she sensed his waking, knew he'd wandered into the kitchen then leave the house. She also perceived his attempts and eventual connection with Jimmy Gillespie. Knowledge of this connection allowed her to sense the man's presence outside school, even though she had never seen him. Gillespie had left a marker stored within John's psychic memory and she detected it herself. As John sat making and remaking the link, Claire leant her skills in a way of which John was unaware. She offered a little of her measured view of life, inherited from her mother, to calm John's spirit. With a skill unknown to her parents, Claire maintained this offering in such a way that when John discovered his ruined seed crop and the damaged fence, his reaction was also measured – his anger non-existent. And then during the phone call from school, Claire removed the veil from John's senses and allowed him to see the link that connected him to the past, present and future which allowed him to believe on a spiritual level their problems would soon be over.

'Actually,' John said once the kettle had boiled. 'Talking to Claire is like talking to an ancient teacher. Sounds crazy, but I wonder who is the parent sometimes, who has the knowledge.'

'I know what you mean, but what makes you say that now?'

'I told you about my dream and how it felt like a premonition? I think Claire has done something to me.'

'In what way?'

'Well, you've had premonitions and we all have intuitions of some sort but they happen in a random way. You can't predict when they will happen or what would influence or trigger them. I feel as if Claire has given me the gift of doing just that, if I want to … at will?'

'So is that why you think this'll all be over soon?'

John nodded. 'Yes, but I didn't specifically think about it. It's a conviction that came to me.'

Sarah poured hot water into their mugs. 'Well, I hope you're right. This is certainly one prediction we need to come true.'

Ten minutes later the phone rang again.

'John?' Duncan said. 'Good news and bad news.'

'Hang on Dunc, I'll put you on speaker.'

'No bother.'

'Hi Duncan,' said Sarah. 'What have you got for us?'

'Hi Sarah. I called in a favour with the labs. Strictly

backhanded but the test on the cigarette butt you gave me John? We got a DNA sample and sure enough, it identifies Jimmy Gillespie. At least you now know for certain he was there. The problem is of course this doesn't link him to any crime. It may be a reason to pull him in for questioning, but remember I said he's adept at providing alibis.'

'Huh ... I guess so. And the bad news?' asked John.

'He's disappeared. Gone to ground somewhere. Been keeping an eye open, but he's not at home. His car's not there, at least the one he has registered. A couple of my people are discreetly making enquiries, but no one's talking.'

'Thanks, Duncan. It's really kind of you to help us,' said Sarah.

'It's no bother, but I must stress again, he's unpredictable, dangerous, so be damn careful.'

'We will. Thanks again Dunc,' John said and ended the call.

'So what's next?' Sarah asked John.

'Work. We still have a business to run. You have a client arriving soon and I have planning to get on with. At the moment let's carry on as normal. We can talk again later once Claire's home.'

'Ok,' sighed Sarah.

Claire arrived home just after two thirty, earlier than expected but unfazed by her experience. Mrs McBride was clear and direct with her concerns.

'I may sound over cautious and unfeeling but if this man poses a risk at school, I have to suggest that Claire stays away until the situation is resolved. If you say this man is only interested in your family, then he's not likely to turn up if Claire isn't in class.'

Broken

Claire had been in her room changing out of school uniform but heard the suggestion as she came back downstairs. She walked into the kitchen and stood silent, waiting for her parents to reply.

'This is another way he manages to disrupt our lives,' John murmured. 'Damn the man.'

Claire piped up. 'Miss, can I do my lessons at home for a bit?'

'That was in my mind too,' Mrs McBride replied. 'We do this sometimes for a child that can't make it in for a number of reasons, so we have everything prepared according to the year and stage the child is at.'

Sarah accepted the logic of the suggestion and since Claire appeared happy with the situation, agreed. 'Ok, that'll work. It is what it is, and there is something else to consider. With Claire at home, we'll be together to keep an eye on each other. No need to worry about her at school.'

'Yes, good point,' replied John and turned back to Mrs McBride. 'Ok. It is annoying but it makes sense and means you won't have to worry about extra security at school. Starting tomorrow, Claire can stay at home. How will she pick up her work?'

'I can email you in the morning. I'll double check with her teachers and get everything to you before nine.'

By the time the headmistress drove out of the yard, Sarah's last client arrived and John headed back to the top field making the most of what daylight remained. Claire took over babysitting duties and sat in the living room with Robert, television on trying to distract herself and read through a picture book.

Some one hundred and fifty yards behind the house,

John measured out a plot of ground using his lengthy stride as a marker. In his hand he held a large battered notepad opened onto a sheet with a rough rectangle sketched out divided into smaller rectangles. Within each small area, he'd written the name of a vegetable. John was planning early spring crops. He needed to keep busy. Wracked with guilt and grief, a little normality, he thought, might take his mind away from himself. But it wasn't working. Joseph's death was too recent and though the young boy had barely settled in, John could sense him everywhere. Joseph had left his spiritual mark on all their lives. But, as much as he ached with the tragic loss of Joseph, John worried for Jamie's safety. From the moment Sue brought the twins to meet them, John recognised an untapped need within his own soul, the same need that drove Sarah into her chosen line of work, the necessity to be of service to others in need.

When John learned of the root of Jamie's reluctance to speak, the horror of his trauma, he'd decided without hesitation he was happy to foster. As Sue drove away with the twins after that first visit, he had fallen silent and probed both boys with his inexperienced skills. Though his gifts were under developed, the lack of aura emanating from Jamie mystified him. In some hidden part of his burgeoning spiritual awareness, he understood that this lack of aura was unhealthy – it was damaging to the growth of the child – he needed help. John's spontaneous decision to foster surprised him, and that in itself only strengthened his commitment. But where was the boy? November was no time for a child to be out on the hills of Ayrshire. With winter knocking on the door, they were all desperate to find him.

As if in response to that desperation, John came to a

halt, automatically noted the number of steps he had counted and drove a wooden marker into the ground at his feet. Repeating an action he'd taken several times in the past thirty six hours, he scanned the hilltops, hoping to see Jamie walking towards him – but to no avail. There was, however, always hope.

John brought his sight back to the task in hand and began pacing once more. But before he had taken more than a few strides, his eyes unfocussed and he had the sudden sensation of falling backwards as if his balance had failed. Falling wasn't quite right though – pulled felt closer to the mark. In reality he stood upright and still in mid-stride, but something dragged at his soul, unsteadying his physical body, something elemental and overwhelming.

A few weeks ago, when he sensed Sarah's soul under duress after receiving the unexpected solicitor's letter, he had opened his soul to her in a spiritual manner, lending a soothing intention. Though he responded to the threat to her well-being with little forethought, the result was immediate since Sarah calmed in an instant, as soon as she received his message. This, however, was the opposite. Instead of receiving the committed and loving intent of a calming spirit, this intent focussed on borrowing John's strengths, for an unknown purpose and without his consent.

With the same immediacy with which the message entered his soul, his natural and protective instinct resisted, but only for an instant because the message carried a recognisable signature. The urgent request travelled along the unbreakable conduit that linked his soul to Sarah's and mingled with it were other energies he recognised – those of Claire and even little Robert. Sarah was calling for help with a desperate urgency that begged an immediate response. Without further resistance, he gave himself to her.

Thirty Three

Claire had the television tuned into cartoons while her parents went about their business, but neither she nor Robert paid much attention. They had switched from reading to playing an endless game of build and destroy. While Claire attempted to build a variety of intricate and vertical shapes with Lego bricks, Robert took great delight in knocking them down again. And hence the game repeated with much giggling.

Aware of their mother's last client leaving, the two children sensed in different ways Sarah's spiritual shift as she wandered over to Memorial cottage and sat on the bench against the wall. They continued their game for many minutes until in the midst of reaching out to demolish Claire's latest construction, Robert stopped and sat back, his smile fading and eyes shifting up towards his sister. Claire gazed back as she too perceived that something was about to happen.

Claire and Robert possessed immense gifts, as did their parents. But being a product of Sarah and John gave them a strength more than the combination of the two. As yet untapped, and though Robert's spiritual gifts were inherent in his making, he was more than capable of sensing spiritual messages from his family and those close by on an emotional level. Though Robert's auric layers were in place, his emotional growth had barely begun, and so he was unable to translate many messages into a mature or coherent understanding. However, his gifts were there to be used – or shared.

Claire, who had been through the same awakening and progression as her parents, but with a far greater reach of emotional understanding compared to Robert, recognised the signs of an imminent event and laid open her auric shield. With a spiritual nod to Robert, he did the same, and with patience and acceptance they waited for the moment to arrive.

Thirty Four

An hour after the conversation with Mrs McBride, Sarah bade a farewell to her last client of the day. 'Does that make sense?' she asked.

'I think so. So, all I need to do is focus on me, on what *I* need instead of putting everyone else first?' It was more of a question than a conviction.

Jennifer Osbourne was a regular visitor to Manseburn, and each time she came seeking a resolution to her personal complexities. Sarah was happy to give her an hour's treatment and send her on her way with advice and support. However, it seemed Jenny was one of life's victims. She would speak the words after listening to Sarah, agree with the suggestions, but as soon as she left and headed home, the advice would fade and be forgotten.

'Yes,' Sarah replied. 'I know it's not my place to tell you how to live your life, I can only relate what I sense within my mind's eye when I look into you, what comes to me. But remember … though you're a mother, a wife and a daughter, you're also a woman in your own right. It's not as if you have small children anymore who need you every moment of the day. You have the right to time out, to take some of the day and spend it on yourself. Even if it's just fifteen minutes out of the house walking, try to remember that it will make you a happier person. Fifteen minutes of *me* time not spent worrying about others.'

'I'll try, I will, I promise and thanks again. I'll see you next month.'

Sarah walked Jenny across the yard to her car and waved a farewell as she drove out through the gateway before disappearing from sight.

For a few moments Sarah remained as she was staring through the gate and beyond, probing Jenny's weak energy as the older woman turned out onto the road toward Straiton. She sensed urgency, as if Jenny was in a rush to get back home. Sarah gathered her energies and for once leant herself to a client. *Slow Jenny, slow. Take your time and think about what we've discussed. Do it and mean it.* After a few seconds, Sarah detected a vague relaxation and took hope. She closed her shield and turned away.

Free for the rest of the afternoon, she headed towards Memorial cottage and lowered herself onto the rough wooden bench John had erected along the front wall near the doorway. The late afternoon sunshine was hazy and though mild, a cool breeze blew in from across the hills to the East. Sarah shivered and flipped up the collar of her thick cardigan.

Free from the diversion of work, her mind focussed onto Jimmy Gillespie and his vandalism. She had hoped, once their solicitor refuted the claim, life would have returned to normal, except she understood normal was transitional, never more so following Joseph's accident. These unlinked events culminated in a disturbance to the tranquillity of Manseburn, a curse placed on her family's peaceful life. But then she recognised such thoughts as selfish and childish.

Do not trouble, my angel. It is only a test … one of many that life thrusts upon us. Be comforted that all will be well.

'Beryl?' Sarah whispered. 'Is that you? I wish I could see your face.'

Even as she whispered the words, a once familiar caress fluttered across her brow. A smile touched her lips, and she drew a deep breath, shaking her head to unlatch the unrest.

She switched her thoughts to someone more needy of concern – Jamie. Where was the young boy hiding? Was he safe? How was he feeding himself? There had been no sign of him since he'd disappeared from the hilltop. November was here and autumn would change quickly to winter. Sarah worried how the boy could survive. If only she could find him and tell him he wasn't to blame for anything in his short life, and if possible, that he had a home if he chose and a readymade and willing family.

A gust of wind rounded the corner of the barn and Sarah lifted her gaze, squinting into a cloud of dust. Beyond the house, and visible in the narrow gap between it and the barn, she saw John pacing out on the upper fields. He had a notepad in one hand and a pencil in the other, and Sarah guessed more planting occupied his mind.

Casting her sight towards the house, she reached inside and sensed Claire and Robert huddling close together, playing or reading.

But as she sat against the wall of Memorial cottage, she detected a disturbance in John's soul and something she didn't recognise emanating from her children. The energies coming from John she knew to be concern for Jamie's wellbeing, since the disturbance mirrored her own. But the aura surrounding Claire and Robert appeared to her to possess a shared intent – an energy she knew to be from two sources but coalesced into one. For a moment she puzzled over why and how her children appeared to join with each other, what had driven them to make such a connection. In a sudden leap of faith, she guessed they were preparing for something and almost in the same instant a thought from within voiced itself. 'We're here, mom. We're ready.'

As puzzlement crowded her thoughts, a slight movement disturbed her peripheral vision, a tiny dark shape in a place where no shape should exist. Turning her head to the left, she peered beyond the gap between Memorial cottage and the house. Up on the hillside, some four hundred yards distant, a shadowy figure appeared immobile, staring in her direction. The figure stood beside the place where a playful and adventurous Joseph had fallen to his death. The distance was too great to show any clarity, but it was obvious to Sarah who the figure was.

Jamie.

With sudden urgency, Sarah shot to her feet, and without conscious effort or forethought, laid aside her auric shield, opening her percipience wider than ever. At the same time, she drew strength from within her soul and reached out to her family. Not understanding what she was about to do, or the possible consequences, she combined the love she had for John, Claire and Robert, and even those no longer alive, and borrowed their strengths. She called on each person's spiritual energy – those inherent elemental forces that shaped them, linked them, and made them as they were. Within an instant, Sarah coalesced these energies into a single thought, a powerful and focused wish, and fired it with immeasurable speed straight at Jamie.

Jamie, you are not to blame. We love you. Please come back to us.

The result was immediate and terrifying.

Thirty Five

For almost six years, Jamie Walker had not spoken.

In the beginning, Joseph often told him he was stupid, even at the age of five, but his blunt approach held no malice. The link between the brothers was so resilient even death could not break it, and though as boys they would not have used the word, love encompassed all they meant to each other. After six months of refusing to speak, and despite professional support and a diagnosis, Joseph gave up trying to get his brother to communicate, gave up calling him names and began expressing Jamie's thoughts on his behalf.

The problem was, Jamie blamed himself for everything. He believed it was his fault their father left them. Then the accident that killed their mother, and now the death of his spiritual other half, his brother.

The interminable two hours he'd lain trapped under his mother's broken body horrified Jamie – unable to move, unable to escape or call for help. Not that help would have changed the fate of Heather Walker. Lying prone and gasping for breath, Jamie knew the accident was his fault. How many times had he been chastised for leaving toys lying on the floor? How many times had his mother scolded him for being careless and leaving things on the stairs? It mattered little that Heather should have been using the handrail while carrying him down from his bedroom – in Jamie's mind there was no one else to blame. Joseph was with a neighbour's boy. There was only he himself and Heather in the house, and he had broken the rules. Now their mother was dead.

With nothing to divert him, no words of wisdom to reach him, Jamie continued to convince himself that everything was his fault, including Joseph's accident. Though Jamie verbalised no wish to play on the hilltop, Joseph voiced his thoughts for him and off they went. If Joseph hadn't understood his mind, they wouldn't have gone. If Jamie himself hadn't kicked the ball high in the air and got it stuck, Joseph wouldn't have climbed up to get it back – he wouldn't have fallen.

So, in guilt and fear Jamie ran away and hid himself. Refusing to speak wasn't enough. It was better if he wasn't among people where more accidents could happen. He'd stay away until he figured out what to do without Joseph to guide him. But with the weather turning chill and wet, he may not have even survived that first night had Claire not intervened. Though the young boy still had a spiritual connection to his brother, there was no such tangible connection to Claire other than his trust and love. But that was enough. With the aid of Robert and feeling her one sided connection to Jamie, Claire awakened that night and sent forth a message she hoped Jamie would receive. And Jamie did, but perceived it only as a triggered memory. It was enough, however, to take him from the exposed hillside, through trackless woodland to a place of sanctuary.

But during the darkest hours of the night before he appeared on the hillside where Sarah spotted his shadowy figure, Joseph came to him in a dream.

Told you years ago you were stupid. Told you, but you never listened. You got to go back cos they need you. All these years where we went from place to place, all that fostering with nowhere the right one. We were just looking for the right people. This time we found them. Well, I won't be there and that's ok. I never needed help, but you did. It's time to go back, and remember, stupid, and here Joseph laughed, *none of its your fault. Time to find a home.*

Jamie had woken with wide staring eyes but saw nothing in the darkness of his refuge. Listening to his brother as he had always done, Jamie knew what he had to attempt, though in his guilt he feared the consequences. Tomorrow he'd make his way back to the farm, see Claire, whom he trusted and loved, and face the music.

Thirty Six

Once the force of her spiritual intent dissipated, Sarah Macintyre was horrified at what she had done. Though she understood that love and an urgent desire to help Jamie drove her actions, she felt she had invaded the soul of everyone she held dear.

Without conscious thought she forced her own psychic strength upon others, dug deep inside their essential being and borrowed their own personal energies. This combined force strengthened her spiritual reach and allowed her to violate Jamie's right to block himself, his choice to remain hidden. With her inner sight, she saw the effect of her attack immediately. In the same instant she focussed her wish, she sensed the invisible cloak with which Jamie shrouded himself shatter and vanish. A murky red aura flared around the young boy, spreading for several feet, a colour that spoke to Sarah of internal struggle and a fight for survival. There was of course no physical effect on

Jamie. This manifestation was visible purely within Sarah's inner eye and no doubt sensed by her family. However, apart from the awful realisation of her actions, the sight of Jamie's spiritual appearance caused an intense nausea to flood through her soul, sapping her physical strength, and she stumbled to her knees. But in the wake of the sickness, Sarah realised she could now sense Jamie – see his tortured spirit. The energy she used hadn't changed Jamie at all but had, she understood, broken through her own limitations. His choices remained intact, his soul unharmed. But Sarah herself had learned a new lesson – her gifts still had abilities of which she was unaware.

Up on the hill top, realising he'd been seen but by more earthly means, Jamie's courage failed him and he turned. Within moments, he disappeared over a rise in the land and vanished.

Staring after him, Sarah became aware John had ceased his work and was now running toward her, while Claire emerged from the house in a more sedate manner carrying her young brother in her arms. John and Claire met half way across the yard where John took Robert from his daughter.

'What was that?' he asked Sarah. 'What did you do?'

Sarah tried to rise to her feet, but another wave of nausea forced her back to her knees. She spoke to the ground. 'I'm not sure,' she coughed. 'It just happened. What did you feel?'

Claire spoke first, sensing the discomfort in her mother's manner. 'It's ok mom. I know what you were doing. You were only borrowing a bit of us. Did it work?'

'Did what work?' asked John. 'I'm confused. I sensed you calling for me, but in a way I never felt before. More like a yell. Am I missing something?'

Ignoring John's question, Sarah spoke to Claire.

'Did *you* understand what I was trying to do, sweetheart?'

'Yes, of course. Jamie's blocked himself. He has no colour. You tried to break through.' Claire paused and stared at her mother as if she already knew the answer to her previous question. However, she asked again. 'Did it work?'

'Yes, it did. I, or I should say we, broke through. I can sense him now but I don't know where he's gone. I was blind to him before, even from two feet away.'

'So you needed our help?' asked John.

Sarah turned to John and saw discomfort written across his face. Her actions had clearly had a negative influence on him also, though Claire appeared untouched.

'Well, I didn't realise I could do that until I did.' She paused and sighed before rising from her knees and lowering herself back onto the wooden bench. 'I'm sorry. I've been so worried about Jamie. Frightened for him all alone out there living God knows where. I was sitting wondering where he might be when I saw him in the corner of my eye. He was up on the hilltop.'

'The hilltop,' said John and he took a few steps across the yard gazing ahead. 'Where? Did you see where he went?'

'No, I didn't. I fell onto my knees and next time I looked he'd gone again. I'm sorry. I didn't stop to think about the whole thing. Well, actually, I didn't have time to think what I was going to do. It's like my need to help him overrode any control. I feel like I've made a very personal violation of you all.'

Seeing the shame on his wife's face, and understanding her inherent need for self-control, John sat down next to her. For several moments he said nothing, but then swallowed and cleared his throat. Softly he spoke as if his concentration focussed elsewhere.

'I can sense him too now. A weak energy that's familiar, reminds me of Joseph. But so distant or just weak. My God, the boy must be suffering so much heartache. But listen,' and now he returned to his immediate surroundings. 'I'm sure Claire will agree with me there's no harm done. In fact, at least we now know Jamie's near. I don't feel any ill effects, any hurt or anything long lasting. Nauseous, but I'm sure we're used to that. As soon as you stopped calling I sensed nothing else, just needed to find you.'

Claire agreed with a nod. 'Mom, dad's right. Think of it the same as if you needed a hand to pick up something heavy. That's all.'

Sarah gazed at her daughter and a smile touched her eyes. She had wondered how Claire might handle her growing gift and what effect it may have as she approached her teenage years. So far, there was no foundation to her worries. Far from it, as her daughter's acceptance was absolute. It occurred to her that as the daughter of two people with extraordinary spiritual capabilities, Claire's strengths may be multiplied. Little Robert could be the same, regardless of she, Sarah's, acceptance and John's caution. But for both she and John, the skill was inherent, an essential element of who they were and therefore would be passed to their children. And of late John appeared more willing to explore his gifts as if circumstance had overridden his reluctance. Yes, Sarah pondered, their children's gifts would be strong.

'Thank you, angel,' she said to Claire. 'That means such a lot. I can see Jamie now and sense his mood. He's safe for the moment though troubled. But as long as he hides, there's nothing we can do. I can't locate him any more than the air sea rescue team.' She rose to her feet and brushed the dirt from her knees. 'Well, the lights fading so I think it's time to go in and light the fire. At least now I'm less worried for his safety. He's obviously found a sheltered place to hide. Now, I need a cup of tea and a piece of cake. Who's with me?'

Thirty Seven

John was used to creeping downstairs in the middle of the night, making no sound as he left the bedroom. Since his dream had begun several weeks ago, an hour spent on the sofa with a cup of tea during the wee hours had become commonplace. But in the days since he'd confessed to Sarah about his dream, he had slept soundly, only rousing to use the bathroom and even that was infrequent.

Tonight, however, was different.

Since the events of the previous Monday, Sarah, John and Claire had stumbled into a modified routine with the help of Rachel and Margaret. They tried to carry on with life as normally as possible. Clients still had appointments, work in the fields needed to continue, and Claire conducted her school work at home meaning no early mornings for her, and she helped a little more with Robert. And as often as they could they all scanned the hilltops for a another sighting of Jamie.

Broken

But on that Saturday night not long past twelve o'clock, John became restless, checking the bedside clock every ten minutes. Something disturbed his sleep and after an hour of distraction he slipped from under the quilt and left the room.

A faint glow found its way up onto the landing from a light somewhere downstairs, and once in the hallway it was obvious the kitchen was its source.

'What are you doing up, sweetie?' he whispered to Claire as he entered the room. 'Are you alright?'

Claire sat at the table with a small glass of milk and a half eaten cookie – one of Sarah's homemade almond biscuits. 'Yes, daddy,' using an old endearment. 'But I woke up and couldn't get back to sleep.'

'You too, uh?' John lowered himself onto a chair next to his daughter. 'Are there any more of those biscuits?' Claire slid the tin across the table.

'Milk?' she asked.

'Yes please. Why not?'

Claire rose, grabbed a small glass and filled it with milk.

'Dad,' she said, placing the glass in front of John before settling back on her own chair. 'Why has all this happened, this horrible man? And why did Joseph have to die?'

'I wish I could give you a reason, angel. Why does anything happen we don't plan for? One of the hardest lessons to learn in life is to accept that many things happen we wish hadn't. Or some situations or people are the way they are and we have to accept them and move on. To dwell on these things, to think about them all the time, is not good for us. Things have happened, or people are made in a certain way, and there's nothing we can do to change them.

Let's see, who was that boy you punched?'

'Fraser Anderson.'

'That's him. Well, you didn't want him to be horrible to you or the twins, but he was. There are some children who enjoy making fun of others or like being a bully, but there's little you can do to change them. It's difficult for anyone to change the way another person is. Usually people only change when they choose to for themselves. As an adult, I feel sorry for him. Why is he like that? Maybe he's unhappy at home. As a child, *you* are stuck in the middle of it, and it's different and harder for you because young people like that won't listen to reason until they're ready, if at all.'

'Do you feel sorry for Jimmy Gillespie?'

'No,' replied John without hesitation. 'He's different. Fraser is still a boy trying to find his way in the world. He's still learning how to treat people, about what's right and wrong – what's acceptable. Jimmy Gillespie is an adult, long past being a child and would have learnt those lessons years ago. He *knows* what's right and wrong but he chooses to be the way he is, to be cruel and nasty ... to live beyond the law. Trying to reason with him is a waste of time because he's just out to get what he wants for himself and doesn't care about anyone else. The needs of others would not even occur to him.'

'Do you think I should have punched Fraser?' Claire asked.

'Sweetheart, you know violence is wrong but sometimes you're given difficult choices and all you can do is what you feel right at the time, or perhaps not right but what you think is the only action you can take.'

'Will you punch Jimmy Gillespie if you find him?'

John couldn't help but smile.

'I'm not going to lie to you. Yes, I feel like punching him for what he's done but the Police will catch up with him soon enough.'

For a few moments, Claire fell silent, but then turned once more to her father. 'I suppose what your saying is what Papa Hamish used to say.'

'What's that, angel.'

'It is what it is.'

John smiled once more. 'Yes, I am and yes he did … many times. Good words.'

Claire nodded and her focus appeared to have drifted out of the room. A skittering of rain scratched at the kitchen window and John shuddered as he stared back at his daughter – a shudder more spiritual than physical.

'Daddy,' Claire whispered as her sight drifted back. 'I'm scared, like I was when mommy was poorly.'

Claire's sudden fear became infectious and John had to resist the temptation to peer over his shoulder. He answered his daughter in soft tones. 'Yes, I know. It scared me too when your mom was in hospital, scared we were going to lose her like we lost Papa and David.'

'Except we didn't lose them,' Claire said with conviction. 'We know exactly where they are,' and while wide and unwavering eyes shone bright and clear at her father, the young child lifted an arm and placed a pointed finger on John's chest – over his heart.

With a sudden ache, John bit onto his lip and gazed at the light that shone deep within Claire's eyes and the sudden glow that shrouded her head and shoulders. For a moment he felt he was gazing into vast pools of knowledge and awareness, bottomless, without boundary. There seemed to be a consciousness lying inside, all powerful and benevolent, to revere and love without fear. His thoughts drifted, and an understanding came to him that the spiritual world he had become aware of was but a tiny part of the whole. With immense possibilities, his gift and knowledge had barely scratched its surface, and for an instant the notion overwhelmed him. But then his thoughts shifted back, and he saw before him a young girl who needed reassurance and comfort. A young girl that, though possessing of gifts as yet beyond his understanding, still required the emotional support of an adult. John had utmost faith in his ability to fill that role.

'No need, sweetheart. Your mom and I will keep you safe.'

'No,' Claire muttered. 'I'm scared for you.'

'For me? Why?'

'Daddy. Something's going to happen.'

Claire's words hung in the air as they sat still, until behind them the kitchen door creaked and Sarah whispered.

'Are you two coming into the living room? I've been listening to you mumbling for ages.'

John turned in surprise. 'Oh hello. I thought you were still in bed. How long have you been up?'

'Huh,' Sarah teased. 'So you didn't realise I wasn't in bed when you got up then? About half an hour before you. I've got Robert in with me.'

Claire rose to her feet, tightening the belt of her dressing gown as John turned back to her, a question forming on his lips. 'Sweetheart,' he said. 'What do you mean? What's going to happen?'

But she was already leaving the kitchen, either refusing to answer or not knowing how. She followed her mother across the hallway.

'John,' Sarah spoke over her shoulder. 'Why did you get up? Was it the dream?'

John half closed the living room door behind him. Soft light lit the room from a single table lamp and candles Sarah had set across the hearth. 'Not really,' John answered. 'I've not had it since I spoke to you about it. But I couldn't get off to sleep. How about you?'

In answer to John's question, Sarah turned to Claire who had settled on the end of the sofa next to Robert who lay quiet but awake in his old travel cot.

'Did you have a dream, sweetheart?' she asked.

'Yes, but it was the same as yours mommy. I can tell.'

Sarah nodded. 'More like a premonition?'

Claire returned the nod.

'John,' Sarah said. 'We've all had a premonition – your dream is your version. I'm not sure about Claire, but for me I just feel on edge, as if I'm waiting for something to happen. Without detail.' Sarah looked to Claire for confirmation. The young girl nodded again.

'Ok,' muttered John and glanced at the wall clock. Twelve thirty it read. 'A premonition then, but of …'

A sudden rush of adrenaline coursed through John's body and stopped him in mid-sentence as the light from the table lamp ceased. Spinning around., he shot a glance towards the door, but he could see nothing but utter darkness. No light reached across the hall from the kitchen lights he'd left turned on, which meant the power had failed or someone had cut the electricity supply. In his heart though, he was convinced he knew which was true. Without hesitation he stepped towards the door, putting himself between the hallway and his family. Claire rose to her feet and without thinking mirrored her father's protective stance and stood between the window and the cot where her brother lay. The hair on John's arms stood up as unbidden into his mind came a question. Why had Sarah lit candles – she didn't usually do so if she came downstairs in the middle of the night? *Premonition. Something's going to happen.*

Turning to face the room, he stood tall and firm as he scanned the faces of those he held dear. 'Ok,' he whispered. 'This is it. This is what we're going to do.'

Thirty Eight

Young Jamie was no stranger to grief. He had walked hand in hand with such pain for most of his young life, though he never succumbed to displays of emotion. The trauma of his mother's death while his brother played not twenty feet away, shut down his spirit and locked away his heart. Throughout stays at a succession of care homes or with foster parents, he maintained his silence, fearing to trust anyone or maybe fearing himself more. His elective mutism and apparent lack of internal motivation – his willingness to trail along, was safe – he couldn't hurt himself again or anyone else if he remained closed. But those who tried their hardest to break through only became frustrated or distressed, and in one case angry. Little did he understand that his choice held a power over those who communicated with confidence and ease, who could not or would not understand his choice, and felt threatened by it. And so ever more he and his brother moved onwards.

But since arriving at Manseburn and joining the Macintyre family, his self-constructed wall softened – became malleable, and despite the belief that his brother's death was due in part to himself, that process continued as he stayed hidden. During the long hours of solitude, and despite his failed attempt during the previous day at rejoining the family when Sarah had, in desperation, broken her own blindness making Jamie's soul visible, Jamie realised that grief was not a pain known only to himself. While Joseph lay twisted and broken on a bleak hillside, his carers exhibited their own grief, Claire especially whose anguish infected Jamie to his very core. No-one ever displayed such pain on his and Joseph's behalf. It was as if no-one else tried to or wanted to understand them. But the family who agreed to care for them had done so with utter selflessness, sheer compassion, implicit acceptance. In short, Jamie began to trust them, and hope flared in his soul.

But now, in the semi darkness, within his black refuge lit only by a single candle, he rose to his feet. Something disturbed his reverie – some unnamed and vague uneasiness. With racing heart he turned full circle feeling suddenly exposed, though he knew he was alone. But from somewhere deep inside, he heard his brother's voice whispering words of encouragement and strength.

'Up ya wee bugger. It's time to get up. It's time to climb. The higher the better. You see different when you get high up. Looking down on things. It's different, remember. I know I took the piss all those times about you being an eejit, but you're stronger than me ... always was, to stay quiet all these years. You can do this ... for them ... for yourself. Up ... get up and away now.'

Without hesitation, Jamie grabbed the oil lamp he'd found when he'd arrived at his hiding place. Using the candle, he lit the wick and within moments the walls of his shelter receded as the orange flame flared and banished the darkness. With no more encouragement needed than the words of his brother, he closed the glass bowl on the lamp and with such purpose he'd never before experienced, strode forward and began to climb.

Thirty Nine

'Everyone outside – now,' John hissed as he scanned the living room by the torch light from his phone.

Sarah shook her head. 'I'm not leaving you in here on your own.'

John locked his gaze on Sarah. 'Look, I don't want you staying indoors. It's too easy to get trapped. There's only the front and back door and they're on the same hallway. If you're stuck somewhere, you might not be able to reach either door. We know he's capable of starting a fire. Safer to be outside where you can hide in the darkness – or run.'

'But ...' Sarah began.

'But nothing. Sarah, I never insist on getting my way, but this time I am. Please. Get your coats on and get the kids outside. I'll watch where you go, and keep my eyes open. I guess he'll not be far.'

For once, and seeing that John would stand no argument, Sarah relented. 'Ok. But please be careful. I can sense him, but I've no idea where he is. It's like I can't focus, as if he's shifting around, unless …' Sarah paused, mulling over an idea. 'Unless it's me. I'm scared and it could be that's preventing me from seeing properly.' Sarah turned to Claire. 'Sweetheart, can you help me get ready?'

'Everything *is* ready,' the young girl replied, pointing across the room. Only then did Sarah notice their padded waterproofs and Robert's thick blanket draped across the back of an armchair. Sets of boots sat in a neat row nearby. 'I got everything together when I came downstairs.'

Fear and shock prickled the back of Sarah's neck and a shudder coursed through her body. How much had her daughter known about this moment? Sarah herself had experienced prophecies, as had John, but how much stronger and more frequent were these moments for Claire? What had she seen and did she understand how much danger lay ahead? Though they still had no definitive proof, it was clear Jimmy Gillespie was outside and would go to extreme lengths to destroy their livelihood and maybe even their very existence.

Aware that John was growing more tense, she nodded at her daughter and reached for Robert's padded coat. 'C'mon then. Let's do as your dad says. Let's wrap up warm and get out of here.'

In less than two minutes they were ready and John led them into the hall. He turned off the torchlight on his phone and with utmost care opened the front door and stepped into the boot porch. Waiting a moment until his eyes grew accustomed to the gloom, he then opened the porch door. With the house in darkness, the only light came from outside despite the low cloud and steady rain. They stood inside the porch for a moment listening and gazing across to Memorial cottage and the remains of the henhouse. With eyes now adjusted, they could see the gap between the cottage and henhouse clearly, and the dense tree foliage that loomed over the old croft swaying in the breeze.

Claire turned to her mother and pointed towards the gap. 'I think we should head over there,' she gasped. 'We can hide behind the cottage and if we need to, we can go down the hill. There's a path near the gate that goes down into the trees. Me and Jamie explored.'

John opened his mouth to speak, but everyone recoiled in sudden shock as a heavy object slammed against the back door. The crunch of shattering glass sounded like an explosion in the stillness of their home, but recovering, John pushed at his wife. 'Now,' he hissed in her ear. 'He's round the back. Time to go.'

With Robert wrapped up and held secure in her arms, Sarah dashed out of the cottage but Claire slipped ahead, making for the gap and refuge behind the old croft. John stared after them, with lips compressed together and a deep furrow above his eyes. *Who the hell is the adult here?* With a rapid glance over his shoulder along the hall to the rear door, John confirmed the door was still in one piece. Against the dim light from outside he saw that a myriad of cracks covered the toughened glass, but it held firm. Turning back, he could just make out his family's progress as they passed between the cottage and the henhouse before disappearing around the rear of the solid stone walls. In a moment of unease, he feared the separation, but knowing Gillespie was behind the cottage tempered his fear, believing that he would not have seen Sarah and Claire fleeing their home.

To keep Gillespie away from the others, John acted as

decoy, staying as he was within the darkness of the porch where he could survey Memorial cottage and keep one eye on the hallway. As Sarah hinted, John became aware of what he thought of as a spiritual darkness that sapped at his wellbeing, and he associated Jimmy Gillespie with the sensation. However, since Gillespie's energy was so unsettled, it wafted back and forth in intensity, John could not pinpoint even a rough location, though he lacked that skill. So far, his gift only responded to a simple measure of strength. If he perceived a potent energy, he figured that meant close proximity and the opposite for weak energy. At this moment, that lack of clarity filled him with frustration. So, unmoving he waited, switching his visual attention between the hallway and the front yard.

While he stood motionless, but for the turning of his head, a different spiritual touch coursed through his heart and he recognised the fragrance of his daughter. The young girl's caress spoke to him of care and caution, and the tension in his muscles eased. But a sudden spiritual cry reached deep into his soul and he recognised the invasion as the same sensation he'd felt during the previous day when Sarah pulled together the combined energies of her loved ones. In the same instant he received the warning message, a sound reached his ears, even above the constant hiss of rain. Hearing the soft crunch of gravel compressed under a heavy boot, he whipped his head towards the front of the house and strode outside into the rain, fists balled and senses on full alert.

But he had no time to react as from his left a dark shadow loomed, a shadow that leapt towards him, hands outstretched. Held within one hand, a slim object slashed downwards striking him hard in the chest and a piercing pain flared. An instant later and with the full weight of a body behind it, the other hand slammed into John, and caught off balance he fell backwards against the solid granite of the cottage. As John hit the wall, the impact knocked the air out of his lungs. Still falling, his head whipped back and collided with the stonework and his legs gave way.

'Ha,' hissed Gillespie. 'Fucking easy, ya bastard. Couldn't stop me even with your lights and sensors and stuff. This is my fucking house, always was, but nothing'll be left by the time I'm done. Still, you'll be nice and warm while it burns. And talking of warm, I'll keep that woman of yours warm too. Bet she's never had a real man.' As he taunted John with his cruel words, Gillespie leaned in close, so close that John felt his breath and almost tasted the whisky.

John tried to speak but through his pain only managed to suck in air.

'What?' Gillespie mocked. ' Uncomfortable? Let me help.' And gripping the handle of the thin blade protruding from John's upper chest, he leaned in, pushing the blade deeper. John moaned through gritted teeth, and satisfied at the reaction, Gillespie stood, turned around and walked with purpose towards Memorial cottage.

Forty

After John pushed her out of the cottage, Sarah hurried across the yard with Robert perched on one hip, Claire a few steps ahead. As they passed between the henhouse and Memorial cottage, she took a last glance towards the house. Visible only as a deeper shadow within the darkness of the porch, John stood immobile as he watched their progress. Though he was almost hidden to earthly senses, Sarah perceived his aura without difficulty, a shroud that now shone a brilliant white, and she took comfort in knowing that his spirit was untroubled despite the physical threat. But at last, reaching the rear corner of the cottage, she turned away with a heavy heart and stepped out of sight.

Claire had halted a few feet from the edge of the hillside and as Sarah stepped close, she turned towards her mother.

'The path's not far away, near the gate, but I don't want to leave dad,' she whispered.

'Neither do I, but be careful of the edge,' Sarah warned.

The space behind Memorial cottage was only a few feet wide, and a row of heavy stones marked the edge of the hill. Many yards from where they stood, and to the left of the main gate, an unmarked path began and wound its way in twists and turns down the hillside. But this close to the cottage the slope was steep, studded by thick trunks of Scots Pine, Birch and Rowan, and dotted with heavy rocks protruding from the ground. A few feet above their heads and bereft of their leaves, several branches spread towards the cottage and the henhouse. Though hidden in the darkness, Sarah knew that the slope here fell sheer for more than twenty feet before turning into a gentler gradient which still, however, continued to fall sharply away. Though she had not discovered the precise route from the farm, she knew the entrance to their secret cave lay somewhere below where they now stood. She recalled the bare back of a huge rock face through which water had eroded the stone over millennia creating the cave and their sanctuary. From the property, the hillside fell in a series of steep or sheer falls interspersed with gentle grades. If they could use the winding path and make their way to the bottom of the hill, gaining access to the cave in the darkness would be easy since she sensed its location. But even with two small children to protect she refused to leave John, especially with a madman nearby.

Unable now to see her husband with her eyes, she focussed her thought on him and perceived his spirit, strong and alert. Claire joined her, and as their energies combined, Sarah felt other sources of spiritual strength – that of her young son cradled in her arms, and the distant and tenuous song of a source she did not recognise. For a moment she puzzled over who or what it may be. But then more urgent needs crowded her soul. Using Claire and Robert to broaden the reach of her senses, Sarah took their united strength to calm her emotions and steady her fears, and as her heartbeat slowed she tried to locate Jimmy Gillespie. Within moments she knew where he was since the darkness that surrounded him created a shadow and dimmed the reach of John's auric sphere. This meant he was near her husband. Overwhelmed with horror, she drew once more on the combined strength of her children, and merging that strength with her own fired a warning message towards John.

But it was too late.

Barely had she delivered her intent, when a sudden and immense disturbance reached into her soul and she collapsed onto her knees.

'Daddy,' Claire gasped, and she too sunk to the hard ground.

Sarah grabbed Claire's arm with one hand and bowed her head in fear, tears starting in her eyes. For several seconds she stayed as she was, probing John's beleaguered soul and felt her children searching too, even little Robert whose understanding came not from his emotion but from something far deeper. But then a soft caress fluttered across her brow dispelling the horror, and she lurched to her feet.

'Claire,' she said, heedless of the sound of her voice. 'Take Robert and stay behind me. Do you understand?'

'Yes mommy,' and she reached for her brother even as the child held out his hands.

While Sarah passed her son to Claire, a new dreadfulness reached into her heart and it was clear from the disturbance in Claire's spirit and indeed Robert's that they sensed it too. An appalling resolve emanated from the man whom they saw as protector and partner, an intent that spoke of finality. A thought and feeling struck at their hearts – an ultimate action that horrified them, and one they could not bear.

Once more and without conscious thought, Sarah, Claire and Robert united their energies. And as they became one, their combined essence grew into a large spinning wheel of pure brilliance that screamed at John's soul not to do what he intended. But in a heartbeat, and understanding that John would not heed their wishes, Sarah withdrew from the wheel of light and scanned the ground. She quickly found what she wanted – a stout branch, small enough to hold but thick enough to wield with little effort. Placing one end against the stone wall of the cottage, she leaned her weight against it and it held firm, proof that it would not splinter under impact.

Anger had now overtaken her fear. How dare this man threaten her family? How dare he attack them, trying to destroy their home and livelihood? But as with everything Sarah did in life, even her anger she controlled. Only once had the red mist fallen, blinding her to reason and sense, and that had been when she was young. She had sworn back then she would never let such a thing happen again, that every action she took would be taken with care and consideration. Now, out here in the darkness, with her husband injured and under threat of spiritual danger, and her children, small and under her protection, she grasped the branch with both hands and peered out from behind the cottage.

Forty One

At times the climb had been steep, and Jamie had to clamber on all fours over rough-hewn steps carved out of the solid granite. The surface was damp with an occasional trickle of water, and the young boy had to tread with care so as not to stumble and fall within the confined space. If he hurt himself here, no one would find him – except maybe one soul with whom he had a subconscious connection.

During his ascent he heard in his head his brother once more, laughing at him but encouraging him as he had always done.

'C'mon, slowcoach,' the voice said. *'Get your ass in gear. Mind your step, but hurry. They need you and you need them. And be quiet ... be secret, like when we used to sneak downstairs to the kitchen in the middle of the night. Quiet as church mice mom used to say we were. Quick and quiet.'*

While Joseph's words warmed his heart, Jamie came to a halt as he reached the end of the hidden path. His route now lay above, a vertical climb up what appeared to be a wooden ladder and though he had no proof yet, Jamie had a sudden conviction where it may lead. He glanced up and in the amber glow from his lamp discovered that the ladder was little more than twice his height. With urgency still driving him onwards, he heaved himself onto the first rung and without a sound moved upward one step at a time.

As he neared the top, cool air wafted across his face and a solid wooden ceiling lay above him. But then he spotted two large hinges and guessed part of the ceiling could be a trapdoor. Still sure of where his climb would end, Jamie retreated to the bottom of the ladder, and with care opened the lamp and blew out the flame. Lost now within utter darkness and with a renewed sense of urgency he crept back up, feeling above with every step for the wooden surface. When his knuckles rapped against the timbers, he placed the flat of his hand and with infinite care pushed upwards. Though heavy, the door opened a few inches with ease and he stepped up another rung until he could peer through the gap. Compared to the pitch black of the cave, the scene that appeared before him was clear and he waited a few seconds to survey his surroundings.

As he expected, his climb had led him to the underside of the henhouse, though the state of the wooden structure came as a surprise. The last time he stood inside the building, it was whole and in one piece. Where he expected to meet the gaze of a puzzled chicken, and wrinkle his nose at the ammonia stench of droppings, now all he detected was the acrid scent of charred wood. The front of the henhouse was open to the elements, the side that looked towards the house, but the timbers on his right that stood facing Memorial cottage appeared intact. Ever so gently he opened the trapdoor wide, climbing as he did so, and leaned it back against the rear wall. With a quick glance towards the house, he saw John rising to his feet, fighting his way upright as if the action was a struggle that caused him pain. Jamie froze in horror as he watched John reach a hand up towards his chest and withdraw from his shoulder what appeared to be a knife. For a moment panic flooded the young boy's heart and thoughts of escape filled his head. But an image of Claire's smiling face overwhelmed his terror, and a faint sound reached his ears. Concerned and curious he looked to his right. Through a gap between the timbers he spotted movement, and he rose up out of the hole until he stood fully within what was left of the henhouse. He peered through the crack.

No more than three feet from where he stood, he saw a dark shadow creeping forward past the cottage, heading towards the rear and the edge of the hillside. With sudden clarity, Jamie understood from seeing John's injury that whoever this man was, he must be responsible. Another thought occurred to him. Where was Claire and Sarah and little Robert? And where was this man going – why was he creeping on tip toe?

Sudden rage flooded Jamie's soul, an emotion of which he had little experience and he balled his fists. John and Sarah had taken himself and Joseph in, and cared for them, he and his brother, the first grown-ups who had made them feel welcome and safe. How dare anyone hurt or threaten them, how dare they come onto this land. But what could he do – a small boy against an adult? But as John approached, and the man came to a halt, the voice of Joseph spoke once more.

'C'mon bro. You were always a chicken ... never did anything

risky or exciting. Time to copy me ... get some height. It's the only way. You see different when you get high up. Looking down on things. It's different.'

Height, Jamie thought. *Yes it's only a few more feet. I've climbed a ladder in the dark so I can do this. I can do it for Claire.*

Certain now of what action to take, Jamie Walker turned and stepped around the gaping hole in the henhouse floor. With pounding heart, he reached above his head, grasped one of the charred timbers and began to pull his lightweight frame up onto the roof.

Forty Two

Peering around the corner of the croft, and despite the inky darkness, Sarah saw John slumped against the stone wall of the house, his aura wafting back and forth – now purple, now tinged with a deep red. Calling once more on the combined perceptions of herself, Claire and Robert, she probed John's psyche, looking for a change in his heart, but still she sensed his ultimate goal – to destroy Jimmy Gillespie.

Even from the distance of her hiding place, she saw Jimmy lean over John, and a wave of nausea flooded her stomach as John's agony coursed through her own soul once more. Then John's assailant turned on his heels and began to walk towards Sarah, stepping lightly across the gravelled yard. Sarah slid back behind the cottage and out of sight, glancing back at her children. With one hand she signed for Claire to stay where she was, hiding in the shadows. Then she waited, gripping the log with determination until a faint sound reached her ears, the crunch of small stones. Drawing in a deep breath, she held it for long seconds until her pounding heart slowed, allowing her to focus. Within moments she sensed that John was now close by, she guessed on his feet and approaching Memorial cottage. His soul screamed in pain, but his focus was fixed. But then the sounds of a scuffle became clear and gripping the log still tighter, Sarah peered back around the corner.

What she saw filled her with dread.

John now lay on his back, an angry red stain spreading across his chest. His face reflected the pain he was in, but still his intention held firm. Jimmy Gillespie was spitting words of evil and in his hand he gripped a thin blade. Gillespie raised his arm, pointing the blade towards John as he took a step forward. With widening eyes, Sarah realised that the time for action had arrived, and with unwavering purpose she strode out from behind the cottage. Raising the log above her head, she closed in on her target, one aim in mind – to disable Jimmy Gillespie. But as Sarah stepped forward, a movement in the darkness caught her eye – a moving shape that appeared to rise up and soar from the henhouse roof. A vibrant orange aura blazed forth from the shape, an energetic colour that triggered a memory for Sarah. In the same instant, a sound she had never heard before filled her ears, a sound that tore at her heart.

Forty Three

Darkness surrounded John Macintyre, and the gloom overwhelmed his soul.

Even the silence smothered him, as tangible as a heavy weight pressing on his senses, robbing him of any desire for action.

It seemed good to lie here warm and peaceful within the embracing darkness, and he sensed a deeper darkness approaching – an endless sleep. But then within the dark he became aware of three tiny points of brilliant white light, three centres of need.

The points of light spoke to him, though not with words. Soundless they were, but the urgency he sensed emanating from them demanded his attention. The call they sent forth awakened his spiritual energy and with that awakening, more earthly senses roused themselves. A stabbing pain blossomed in his head and chest, a pain that was both physical and emotional.

Memories flooded back, recalling words of madness and anger, and with the memory his own anger flared, a black cloud of fury that overwhelmed his other senses, dulling the pain. The words he remembered were full of conviction and finality – the end of all that he cherished – the end of all things.

Moments later his vision returned and across the open ground between where he lay and the charred henhouse, John Macintyre sensed a dark shadow receding. To his spiritual awareness the shadow carried an aura of evil, an aura that symbolised fear, but one he must confront.

Driven by rage, John lifted his sturdy six-foot frame from the ground and rose to his full height. Heedless of the pain, he wrapped his fingers around the handle of the thin blade buried within his upper chest. Gritting his teeth against the agony that flared from his ruptured flesh, he withdrew the blade and raised his arm above his head with the razor-sharp edge pointing towards the shadow.

Ahead of him, other shadows appeared, threatening to engulf him as he moved forward one silent step at a time. But he ignored them. Even the coloured shade that rose above the charred timbers of the henhouse. Taking them to be a manifestation of his struggling consciousness, he moved onwards.

John's conviction overwhelmed him. No law of man or reason or plea would turn aside Jimmy Gillespie. He was bent on destruction and there was only one way to stop him. He needed to die. It was the right thing to do, to protect and save his family.

As John reached the corner of the henhouse, he lifted his arm higher and still he crept forward in silence. Gillespie had come to a halt midway between the cottage and the ruins of the henhouse and he appeared to be listening, his head angled first one way then the other, but after a few seconds he continued. Still John crept forward. But as he closed in, the three pinpoints of light suddenly merged and blossomed forth into a large spinning wheel that screamed at his very soul not to do what he intended to do – but it was too late. Sure of the need for his act and his sacrifice, a sacrifice based on protecting all that he held dear, he readied himself for the final step. But he never had time to make his move.

Now level with the henhouse, a sudden wave of nausea shook John's balance, and he stumbled. In an instant Jimmy Gillespie spun around, grabbed John's wrist and twisted it, at the same time punching him in the chest. With his stability gone, John's footing failed and he flew backwards landing with a grunt on the gravel yard.

'You don't realise do ya, ya pussy. You're finished and so will everyone else be once I'm done, and no one'll track me down. Too fucking smart for that, ya bastard. Nothing here to point the finger at me.' And with that Jimmy Gillespie raised the blade once more, but then he faltered as something caught his eye.

'What the fuck?'

Above him and to the left, a dark shape appeared to rise out of the roof of the building he had set fire to only two days ago. For a moment he puzzled over it until the shape took on meaning.

'Ya gotta be kidding, pal,' he spat. 'You and who's army?'

The answer became apparent, but he had little time to react. Closing fast from behind, Sarah Macintyre swung the log she wielded with all the strength she possessed, and with all the conviction of a soul in danger. The log smashed into Jimmy Gillespie's shoulder, splintering the bones that supported his arm. The scream he let forth was horrifying, and he lurched sideways towards the cottage. But in the same instant the shadow that had stood immobile, balanced on top of the burnt timbers of the henhouse swung into motion.

Calling on the strength of his brother, and along with his own need to help those who had given their support, love and compassion, Jamie Walker launched himself from the roof. With supreme accuracy and in a headlong dive, he reached up and wrapped his hands around a low-lying branch, using it as a pivot to rotate himself back to the horizontal, feet first. Though he was slight of build, he used the height of the scorched roof, the words of his brother and every ounce of his strength to increase his speed.

Now rising, and with knees locked, he rammed his feet straight into the chest of his target and with a scream yelled, 'LEAVE MY FAMILY ALONE!'

The impact forced the air from Jimmy Gillespie's lungs, and he grunted and hurtled backwards, catching his heels on the marker stones at the edge of the slope. With no time to react, he flew over the brink and disappeared from sight.

While dark shadows raced toward him surrounding him on every side, John Macintyre heard the crackling of small branches and the crunching of small stones as Jimmy Gillespie's uncontrolled descent continued. But moments before John succumbed to his injuries and slid into unconsciousness, a sickening crack reached his ears and he heard no more.

Epilogue

John Macintyre wandered lost and alone within the darkness. Vague though the sensation was, he acknowledged that his body moved, though he was not in command of its movement. This he accepted with little concern, as with innate understanding he understood any threat to his physical form had now passed. He felt elevated, aloft, and with sight not of this world gazed upon a scene littered with colours of varying hue. Some blazed with the fire of purest white – others flared a deeper red or orange. To one side, bright pinpoints of red lit the scene with intermittent flashes of impossible blue. Removed from the others and noticeable by its immobility, a weak and pale light-green flickered and wavered, and on an elemental level John recognised a soul in need of spiritual healing. Without emotion, driven by intrinsic compassion, he extended his reach to the physical form at the centre of this soul and offered a part of himself. Within moments, the faltering green settled, becoming stable, and it moved closer to the others.

For a moment, or maybe for an age, John's spirit cast its perception away from the scene that played out below and settled upon the distant horizon. Gone were the clouds, the rain and darkness, and with far reaching sight he perceived an untainted radiance comprising every imaginable colour, unblemished, clear and sharp. Nothing else remained to his sight but this place of no limitation, where the past, present and future co-existed, and human memory was accessible without restriction. Up here, nothing mattered. No peril, no threats, no petty concerns. Only peace and tranquillity lay ahead, interspersed with an impossible harmony, a multitudinous chorus—the song of the infinite.

But as he gazed ahead, listening to the music as it became ever more present, a shadow disturbed his vision, a shadow that began at his feet and stretched away towards the horizon. His senses perceived a bright light that came from behind, and despite the smiling faces that had appeared before him shifting in and out of focus, he looked away.

Three pinpoints of brilliant white light caught his attention as they began to revolve and coalesce. The merging of the lights drew his perceptions away from the everlasting towards the darkness where love, heartache and the emotions and vulnerabilities of earthly reality held sway. A voice floated through the ether, a voice choked with anguish and fear, but one that spoke with strength and determination.

'No,' the voice commanded, or maybe there was more than one voice. 'I won't let you take him. You can't have him yet. It's not time. Leave him.'

For a moment John felt his soul torn between the vision so easily within his reach and a spiritual need to care for the distressed. But within his torment he sensed yet another voice, one that was familiar though he had heard it only once. Its focus was aimed at the anguished speaker.

'Sarah, my child. Do not concern yourself. John has found peace since he has sensed it, and listened to the song of eternity. But it is true that it is not yet time. He has much to do, much love and compassion to share. Be at peace and take his hand. You too, Claire. Hold him and wait.'

As the voice fell quiet and the harmonies slipped away, John recognised the revolving lights using the perceptions of his spiritual and physical bodies, and a more earthly ache coursed through his heart. With that ache returned pain, sharp and agonising, and a moan escaped his lips. For John Macintyre, the ethereal vision faded and with it every level of consciousness, and for a while time itself held its breath.

Sarah shifted within the chair that lay next to her husband's hospital bed and gazed across at John, searching for a sign. Curled up on another chair on the other side of the bed sat Claire who now roamed within her own inner world, closed to the realities around her, searching maybe for her own answers and for her father.

John's injury was severe, resulting in heavy loss of blood. But luck had been on his side. The thin blade that pierced his upper chest missed a major blood vessel. A few inches to the right and John would not have survived. Despite his arrogance and conviction, Jimmy Gillespie's aim was poor. While Claire called for an ambulance, Sarah compressed the wound limiting further blood loss. Once at the hospital, John was given emergency surgery and sedated.

For two days Sarah and Claire stayed close keeping vigil, refusing to leave except for refreshment and other urgent needs. John's sedation, Sarah guessed, was more than just a result of the medical team. She knew her husband and sensed him retreat into his own world as soon as he understood his family was safe from harm. Indeed, a part of her wondered at the time if she, Claire and even Robert had sent him, or allowed him to escape into his fugue state, knowing he required the sanctuary. And there he remained. Sarah hadn't tried to explain to his carers that whatever sedation they gave him would make no difference. John would awaken when he was ready.

But on the third day, Sarah sensed John's return even before he opened his eyes. Claire must have sensed it also as she stirred and sat upright.

'Mom?' she whispered, to which Sarah nodded with a tender smile.

John moved his head towards his daughter and with caution lifted an eyelid. 'Hello sweetie,' he croaked and attempted to clear his throat.

'Welcome back, daddy. Do you want a drink?'

'I doubt if they'd let me have a wee dram here, but a sip of water would be good thank you.'

Claire topped up a glass with tepid water and placed a straw into it before offering it up to John. Sarah reached over and placed a supporting hand behind his head.

'How are you feeling sweetheart,' she asked?

John reached out for Sarah's hand. 'Actually, quite comfortable. Stiff and sore – bloody starving.'

'No pain?'

'Nope. Just an ache in my chest, but I guess that's

expected. Y'know what?'

'What?'

'I'm ready to go home. How long have I been here?'

'Well, its Thursday so a while. You've been away, but we knew you were safe.'

'Where's Robert?'

'I didn't want to keep him here. I'm sure he'd be quiet, but I thought some routine would be better. Rachel has him, so of course he's being spoilt rotten.'

'And Jamie? I did hear him speak, didn't I?'

Sarah chewed on her lip, and moist eyes gave away the sudden emotion she felt. 'Yes, he did, though it was more like a shout. John, that boy saved us. If it wasn't for him, I can't imagine how things would have turned out.'

'Best not to think about it, but where is he? I hope he's not gone missing again.'

'He's with Sue at the moment, safe and sound and quite chatty?'

'Can he come home again when we leave?' asked Claire. 'Please?'

'I hope so and I see no reason why not,' replied Sarah?

John yawned, closed his eyes and settled his head back onto the pillow. 'Nor me,' he muttered. 'We owe him everything.'

Sarah shared a glance with Claire, who gave a nod. 'It's time to leave you to sleep … natural sleep this time. I'll try to find out when they'll let you home and then I'll take Claire back and we'll get cleaned up and some rest. Ok?'

A barely perceptible nod was all she needed.

Two days later just before lunchtime, a car crunched through the gates of Manseburn and pulled up in front of the house. Near the kitchen window and sheltered from a soft drizzle, John sat on a chair with a heavy blanket wrapped around his shoulders and a mug of coffee in one hand. In another chair, Pete Danescourt sipped at his own mug. 'I recognise this man. An old friend of yours, I believe?'

DCI Duncan McBride climbed out of the car and hurried under the cover.

'Yes indeed,' replied John. 'How do you know him?'

'He visited you in hospital a couple of times when I was there and Sarah introduced us.' Peter stood and stretched out a hand.

Duncan took it as he stepped under the terrace roof. 'Hello again. How's the invalid, Doc? Behaving or becoming intolerably impatient?'

'I'd say somewhere in between,' Peter said.

'Huh, why am I not surprised? He could never sit still for long. Had to be doing something. Now me, on the other hand, give me half an hour and I can happily sit with a dram and gaze into space.'

'I am here, y'know,' huffed John.

'Moody as well,' laughed Duncan.

'So, to what do we owe the pleasure,' asked John. ' Do you want a hot drink, or something more warming? It's a chill day.'

'No, I'll not stay long thanks. Just loose ends,' answered Duncan. 'Thought you'd like to hear them from the horse's mouth.'

'Sounds good.'

'Well, it's all good news. We have to follow protocol, but there's no plan to contact the CPS concerning the death of Jimmy Gillespie. It's what we call a perfect claim of self-defence. Basically, and quoting the text, a perfect claim of self-defence is accepted as the need for deadly force to protect life and involves no wrongdoing by the defendant. Its clear Gillespie was the aggressor with the intent to cause damage to property and life. And anyway, from everyone's description of events, it would be difficult to say who landed the fatal blow. Forensics state it was blunt force trauma to the head caused by impact with a large chuck of granite sticking out of the ground, so let's lay the cause there shall we. His smashed shoulder could have occurred during his fall. As for further evidence, as you already know, the discarded cigarette held Gillespie's DNA, and we also found tiny traces of his blood near to where the fence was cut … your rabbit-proof fence. Must have nicked a finger. As for the blade, the idiot must have handled it before pulling gloves on.'

Duncan paused and sighed.

'John, I'm sorry we couldn't have caught up with him before any of this happened. I said he was slippery, and he's got away with so much in the past, but I guess he miscalculated the Macintyre determination. You guys freak me out. I mean, how did that young lad turn up just at the right time? And where had he been hiding?' Duncan checked his watch. 'Don't answer that. Maybe I don't need to know. Anyway, better go … people to see. Just focus on getting well and getting back to normal. At least there's one less predator to worry about.'

'Duncan! I thought I heard your voice.' Sarah slipped out onto the terrace. 'Has John offered you a drink?'

'Hi Sarah. Yes, but I'm on a flying visit. Need to go, but I'll catch up soon.'

'Thanks for dropping by Dunc,' said John. 'We'll have

you over for dinner.'

Duncan stepped back out into the rain and with a wave of his hand climbed into his car and left.

Later in the afternoon the gentle drizzle turned heavy until a steady rain hissed around Manseburn and the Macintyre family retreated in doors.

Claire was excused from attending school but was busy with schoolwork set by her teachers. Sarah spent a few hours rescheduling appointments, apologising to her regulars, though local news was all the explanation required.

Peter and Rachel had dropped by for a few hours in the morning but headed off mid-afternoon to pick up Sophie and settle in for what promised to be a bleak autumn evening.

'Why not come back for dinner?' Sarah suggested, but they declined her invitation.

'Wouldn't dream of it,' Rachel had replied. 'You guys need family time without worrying about feeding us or listening to screaming girls. No. We'll see you soon but get some peace and quiet.'

Sarah and Rachel had taken the chance to catch up while the boys sat out on the terrace contemplating the weather.

It was Rachel who climbed inside Sarah's internal preoccupation and drew her thoughts out with a blunt question. 'How do you feel about having a death so nearby?'

Sarah lifted her eyebrows and smiled at her friend. 'Ooo, listen to you. Straight to the point.'

'I learnt from the best.'

Sarah said nothing for a moment, just listened to the faint murmurings of John and Peter while she gathered her thoughts. 'Well it's not the first violent death that's taken place here. There was Rose over two hundred years ago when all this started. And more recently, Joseph.' Sarah took a moment to sigh. 'Did I ever tell you what we found out about Nana Rose?' Rachel shook her head. 'To put it simply, we found old papers, very old like a diary. The name Amber appeared on many of the pages who we guess was Rose's daughter ... at least we know that Rose had a daughter called Amber, so makes sense they were the same person. Amongst her writings we found out Rose was murdered. It took place in Memorial cottage. A tragic tale that spawned a lifelong search between Amber, my ancestor, and Hamish, the line through which John was descended.'

'Does it change the way you feel about Manseburn?'

Sarah shook her head without hesitation. 'No. I have thought about this, but Manseburn is more than just a home to us. It's a part of our history, of what made us ... where we came from. For John and I, and the kids, this place has so much energy and spirit, it's like a link to what makes us fundamentally who we are, rooting us in an ancient past, and no tragedy or anything else can change that. Joseph's death will take a while to find a place, but as for Gillespie, his loss is meaningless and has no bearing on anything.'

'Huh, well I don't care he's dead,' muttered Rachel. 'Hate to say it but he deserved it and I know how unchristian that sounds.'

Sarah sniffed and smiled. 'Don't worry about it. For me, I only care that my family is safe and we can all resume from where we left off, helping those that need help.'

'I'd drink to that if it were later in the day.'

'Why not now,' laughed Sarah? 'But send me a selfie of you and Pete with a glass of something once the kids are in bed.'

'I promise,' and Rachel laughed back.

After Rachel and Peter left and the rain closed in, Sarah stepped out onto the terrace to check on John and call Jamie indoors. John sat still with a gentle curl on his lips, a peaceful smile as he gazed over at the remains of the hen house.

'Still awake then?' Sarah questioned.

'Figure I slept long enough in hospital, so yes, I'm still awake.'

'Yes, those hours were endless. Now I know a little of what you went through.' Sarah walked to the end of the terrace and shouted across to the back of the house. 'Jamie! Time to come in!'

John continued. 'I've been trying to work out what to do about the henhouse but I'm afraid the chickens will have to wait a bit for a new home. Some of the old timbers will be fine so it'll look much the same.'

'I don't think you'll need to do it on your own.'

'No, I think you're right,' John agreed just as Jamie trotted round the corner. 'Hi Jamie. What have you been up to.'

The young boy shook the rain from his hair and smiled. 'Replanting in the greenhouse cos everything was shrivelled.'

'Replanting?' John's surprise was unmistakable. 'But how and what?'

'It was easy enough,' Jamie replied. 'Joseph used to tell me what he did when he was in there. I emptied the old pots and put the same kind of seeds back in … they all had wooden labels with the names on so I didn't have to guess.'

'Cool,' smiled John. 'Watered just a little?'

Jamie nodded and smiled again.

'Did you sing to them?'

Jamie looked puzzled.

'Ignore him, sweetheart,' Sarah laughed. 'He's winding you up. If he sang to his plants, they'd *all* shrivel up.'

'Mom?' Claire's voice from inside the house. 'Are we having dinner out there or are you coming inside?'

John looked up with a satirical smirk and remarked to no-one in particular. 'Was that sarcasm by any chance?'

Claire stepped out onto the terrace. 'Robert's getting hungry.'

'Yes, and I guess that goes for all of us,' Sarah said. 'John? Are you ready to close the shutters and batten down the hatches as my dad used to say?'

'If you mean can I close the curtains with one arm yes, I can manage that.' John rose to his feet and grabbed his blanket with his good hand. 'But first,' he said. 'I've been puzzling about the henhouse and Jamie. I think it's time someone explained this to me because the only recollection I have, and that's vague, is one of Jamie throwing himself off the roof.'

But even as John asked the question a different recollection appeared to him – equally vague. As he'd approached Jimmy Gillespie from behind with the thin and blood-soaked blade held high, a spinning wheel of light had appeared in his mind's eye. Within an instant he had recognised it since it was in essence an integral part of him. The message it conveyed was one of concern for his spiritual well-being, knowing his intent to destroy Gillespie, though he was too enraged to pay heed to the message. But behind and to each side of the spinning wheel tenuous shadows rose, appearing in long vaporous lines. They originated from both the henhouse and the edge of the hillside and came to rest either side of the spectral, argent wheel of light. The shadows spoke of home, of belonging, of ancestors, and an immense gulf of time presented itself to John's sight where history and limitless possibility walked hand in hand. And all the while an intense and vibrant orange aura flashed across the roof of the henhouse.

As he stood on the terrace under cover from the falling rain holding a cooling blanket in one hand, an idea occurred to John Macintyre. When he'd crept towards Gillespie, amidst his searing pain, John remembered becoming distracted by these visions. As if destiny played its hand at that very instant, John had stumbled and Gillespie realised he was under threat. Throwing John to the floor he had laid himself wide open to attack from behind – Sarah wielding a heavy branch and Jamie armed with nothing more than his rage, pent up grief and fear for the family who had taken him in and made him safe. John was saved from making an attack while Gillespie's demise was due to clear self-defence, two souls protecting an injured party. Pure semantics, John guessed, since the courts would have ruled self-defence either way, but he wondered about the shadows and their purpose.

'John?' Sarah prodded.

'Jamie throwing himself from the henhouse roof,' he repeated. 'How did you get there Jamie,' he asked? 'Without being seen.'

'It was me,' answered Claire.

'Claire? But how?'

For once Claire looked sheepish. She was unused to keeping anything from her parents. 'A few weeks ago when me and Jamie were clearing out the henhouse I had a premonition.'

'A premonition?' prompted John.

'I didn't know what about, but I knew something was going to happen and Jamie was a part of it. I thought he was in danger. So I took him—I showed him how to find the cave.'

'*The* cave?'

Claire nodded. 'I'm sorry Daddy because I know it's our family secret, but he needed to go there when he ran away. I helped him.'

Sarah glanced across at John and smiled. 'Well, I guess you saved his life sweetheart. All that cold and rain, he would have suffered out on the hill.'

John still had a question for Jamie. 'Thank heavens you were safe, though I still don't understand how you got up on the roof of the henhouse just at the right time?'

Jamie shrugged his shoulders, but again it was Claire that answered. 'There's a tunnel.'

'A tunnel?' asked John.

Claire nodded once more. 'Jamie found it while he was in the cave. I sneaked food to him and one day he showed it to me. I didn't know where it went though. But on that night when that bad man was here, I saw Joseph in my head. I heard him speak to Jamie, and he told him to hurry.'

John shook his head in disbelief. 'Oh, for a normal life. So you had a premonition and took Jamie to the cave where he sat and waited to appear at just the right time to save us all.'

'John,' muttered Sarah. 'There may be other worldly guidance behind what happened, but for us this *is* normal life. And if you cast your mind back, do you remember the evening we spent in the cave? How much energy we felt there before any of this began.'

John nodded. 'Yes, I remember.'

'Well, maybe if Jamie hadn't been in the cave, with all that spiritual and ancient energy, Joseph would not have found him, his own spirit unable to reach him. Can you imagine?'

For a minute, John considered his earlier memories and Claire's explanations and then smiled at everyone. 'Y'know. I guess trying to work all of this out is wholly unnecessary.'

'Unnecessary?' asked Sarah.

'Yes, because in the words of your father and my grandfather, 'it is what it is'.'

'Robert's getting hungry,' muttered Claire again, but the rumble in her own stomach gave the game away.

'Yes, and so am I,' answered Sarah before heading indoors.

Jamie and Claire followed, but just for a moment before John entered the porch he turned back to gaze at the henhouse and Memorial cottage. He ignored the police crime scene tape, now part of a history that had no effect on the future. Instead, tenuous within the deepening gloom, he saw once more the vaporous shades that wafted back and forth in and around the ancient stonework. Each had their own colour and song, and with a warmth coursing through his heart, he recognised their benevolence, and raising his good hand in a slow and loving wave, turned and closed the door.

The End

Broken

ABOUT THE AUTHOR

R V Biggs lives with his wife Julie in a small ex-mining community near Wolverhampton in the West Midlands, England. He and his wife have four grown-up children and a growing number of grandchildren.

Robert spent 35 years working for a large international Communications company, but now works for Birmingham Children's Hospital helping to support the mental health of young people.

This novel is book three of the Sarah Macintyre series.

The author would be most grateful for comments and star ratings via the website where you purchased this novel.